PENGUIN CRIME FICTION

SARATOGA SNAPPER

Stephen Dobyns's novels include *Dancer with One Leg*, *Cold Dog Soup*, and three other Charlie Bradshaw mysteries — *Saratoga Longshot*, *Saratoga Swimmer*, and *Saratoga Headhunter* — available from Penguin. His sixth volume of poetry, *Cemetery Nights*, was published by Viking Penguin Inc. in early 1987. Mr. Dobyns teaches literature and creative writing at Syracuse University, near which he currently resides.

SARATOGA
SNAPPER

Stephen Dobyns

PENGUIN BOOKS

PENGUIN BOOKS
Viking Penguin Inc., 40 West 23rd Street,
New York, New York 10010, U.S.A.
Penguin Books Ltd, Harmondsworth,
Middlesex, England
Penguin Books Australia Ltd, Ringwood,
Victoria, Australia
Penguin Books Canada Limited, 2801 John Street,
Markham, Ontario, Canada L3R 1B4
Penguin Books (N.Z.) Ltd, 182–190 Wairau Road,
Auckland 10, New Zealand

First published in the United States of America by
Viking Penguin Inc. 1986
Published in Penguin Books 1987

Excerpts from *Where the Money Was* by Willie Sutton and
Edward Linn. Copyright © Royal Production Corporation,
1976. Reprinted with permission.

Excerpt from interview with Walker Evans from *Yale Alumni
Magazine*, February 1974 issue. Copyright by Yale Alumni
Publications, Inc. Reprinted with permission.

LIBRARY OF CONGRESS CATALOGING IN PUBLICATION DATA
Dobyns, Stephen, 1941 –
Saratoga snapper.
(Penguin crime fiction)
I. Title.
[PS3554.O2S268   1987]   813′.54   86-30467
ISBN 0 14 00.8812 1

Printed in the United States of America by
Offset Paperback Mfrs., Inc., Dallas, Pennsylvania
Set in Times Roman

For Margot Balboni and
Michael Peavey

INTERVIEWER: Do you think it's possible for the camera to lie?

WALKER EVANS: It certainly is. It almost always does.

INTERVIEWER: Is it all right for the camera to lie?

WALKER EVANS: No, I don't think it's all right for anything or anybody to lie. But it's beyond control. I just feel that honesty exists relatively in people here and there.

Yale Alumni Magazine
February 1974

Saratoga Snapper

1

In New York State, Route 9 is Broadway. It doesn't matter if it's Manhattan, Saratoga Springs or any of the burgs between. And for Victor Plotz, who had once lived on lower Broadway in Manhattan and now lived on upper Broadway in Saratoga Springs, it sometimes seemed he'd only moved a little farther uptown.

Victor liked that. He thought of himself as a city creature, at home wherever his sneakers touched concrete. Not that Saratoga was much of a city as far as size was concerned, but at least it had Broadway and it was far more sensible than living out at the lake like his friend Charlie Bradshaw. Here at least he could buy a fresh bagel and read the *Post*. Out at the lake one was limited to the company of fishes—fine in a pan or broiled with a little lemon but of no help in keeping away the lonelies. There were no women at the lake, in the ordinary course of things, and too few jokes.

A need for bagels, the New York *Post* and a couple of rolls of film had caused Victor to leave his apartment in the Algonquin shortly after eight o'clock on this particular sunny Monday morning in early June. The air was decidedly better than anything New York City had to offer. It had a soft quality as if strained through the stamens of millions of flowers. Victor stood on the sidewalk and breathed deeply. He was a rather rumpled figure in his late fifties with frizzy gray hair that rose about three inches from his head as if he had just stuck a bobby pin in an electrical outlet. His face seemed to have been quickly slapped together from bread dough, and his nose had a rough and aggressive quality, more like an elbow than a nose. He wore khaki pants and a gray sweat shirt and over his left shoulder he carried a camera: a Konica AE1.

It was as a professional photographer that he now saw himself—a profession begun just in the past three days, Friday night to be exact. In his role as a private detective, of course, he had been taking pictures for several years, but those were what he called bad luck pictures, quick takes of people who didn't want to be photographed, shot through the back window of a car parked at what someone had mistakenly imagined to be a private spot or through a motel doorway or over a wall—unhappy pictures which brought little cheer even to the person who had paid to have them taken.

These new pictures were more festive and had nothing to do with the detective agency. He had begun on Friday night to work as a strolling photographer in the Bentley, which was the hotel owned by Charlie Bradshaw's mother. The Bentley had been open a week, opening on June 1 as a matter of fact, and the single reason that Mabel Bradshaw had named the hotel the Bentley was that she hadn't had the nerve to call it the Rolls-Royce.

Victor had actually been working at the hotel for the past six months—painting, plastering, putting up wallpaper. It was a big four-story hotel right downtown—a firetrap according to some, an example of Victorian splendor according to others. Charlie had also been working at the hotel and was now acting as night manager, just to give his mother a hand until the hotel got going smoothly or until he found a better job. Victor was also in charge of security and had a little office with a brass plate on the door that said "Hotel Detective," but so far there had been no detecting which needed to be done, so he also helped out with room service and had just started taking these pictures in the lounge and cocktail bar and restaurant—happy pictures of happy people who wanted the occasion remembered, and Victor, for a few bucks, was glad to oblige—snap, snap, he was your good-natured Saratoga snapper. Then when the people got home they could take out the pictures and see that despite the bills and heavy losses at the track, despite the overeating and overdrinking and too little sleep, they had really had a great time after all.

As he turned left down Broadway toward Bruegger's Bagel Bakery, Victor felt a little wobbly on his pins, a result, he well knew, of his own overeating and overdrinking the previous night at a bar called the Backstretch, where he had been entertaining a Mrs. Heinz with low jokes and high-priced drinks, while taking snaps of her various profiles and double chins for posterity. Despite the attention, Mrs. Heinz had gone home by herself in a cab. Victor had felt somewhat dispirited and stayed at the bar far later than was wise if he wanted to make a bright start in the morning. Technically, he had been waiting for Charlie, even though he'd known there was little chance of Charlie appearing. For several years Charlie had been dating a waitress at the Backstretch but now they had recently split up, or rather she had dumped him for someone else, and Charlie never came into the bar unless it was to look mournful and make Doris feel bad.

Also, Charlie wouldn't have left the hotel, since he took his job seriously even though he disliked it and particularly disliked his daytime counterpart: a dry stick of a man named Raoul whom Mabel Bradshaw had brought up from Atlantic City, one of those fellows who is only happy walking on tiptoe and speaking in a whisper, as if he didn't want to insult the world by calling attention to himself. Of course Victor wasn't fooled, or Charlie either for that matter, because they had both heard complaints from the maids about Raoul's pinchy fingers.

Raoul felt that Charlie had no class and didn't properly appreciate that Saratoga was a summer town where much money could be made. On the other hand, Charlie, Victor knew, would not have been heartbroken if Raoul had tumbled into a vat of boiling milk. But Charlie had agreed to help his mother get the hotel started. Not that his mother did much work except give directions. Instead, she seemed to see the hotel as her private home, while the employees were her servants and the guests her own guests and particular friends. She didn't see the hotel so much as a business but as the setting for her own particular jewel—as if it was the ring and she the diamond. So most of the time she was to be found glittering in the lobby, welcoming guests and asking if their travels had been difficult, while Raoul glared at Charlie and shook his head and Charlie looked depressed.

Victor bought a *Post* from the machine on the curb, then waited to cross the street to go up to the bakery. Staring around him with the paper tucked under his arm, he seemed to be admiring the lush trees in full leaf and the red brick Victorian buildings. Actually, he was thinking whether he would have cream cheese on his bagel, raspberry jam, or both.

As a result, he wasn't paying sufficient attention when he stepped out onto Broadway. When he had gone about eight feet, he noticed a rapid movement to his left. Turning, Victor saw a dark maroon car rushing down upon him. He jumped back and the car veered toward him; he leapt forward again and again the car turned to bear down upon him. It occurred to Victor almost without fear that he was being purposefully run down. The driver was slouched behind the steering wheel, and all Victor could see clearly was a gray fedora hat. There was no other traffic at that moment, nor were there people nearby on the sidewalk. Someone's trying to kill me, thought Victor. At the last possible moment, he leapt into the air. He was not a good jumper but at least it kept him from being crushed.

The car struck his legs and he bounced on the hood, then was thrown up over the roof and down the other side, but all very fast and violent, a painful tumble that landed him half-conscious on the pavement. The newspaper went flying into the street. Hearing the screech of brakes, he looked to see the car slide to a halt. Then, instead of someone jumping out and running to see how badly he was hurt, the car accelerated backward and Victor knew that the driver meant to flatten him under his wheels.

Victor lay a few feet from a car parked at the curb. Despite the pain he rolled toward it as the maroon car swerved toward him. Practically at the last moment, he got himself wedged under the side of the parked car as speeding black tires whooshed by a few inches from his head. Then the maroon car stopped again, swerved forward into the street, stopped again, and Victor heard the door swing open. Looking up, he saw his nice new camera lying on the pavement almost beneath the maroon car. Then a hand reached down and plucked the camera from the street, and the car roared off. Victor thought of saying, Hey, that's my camera, but his thoughts felt fuzzy and there seemed a lot of blackness. He hurt in about fifty places and didn't want to move. The matter of the camera could be dealt with later, and so, slowly, he lowered his head to the pavement and let the darkness fill him in the way water fills a ditch. The license plate, he thought, I should look at the license plate. But it was too hard to open his eyes—better to rest, he decided, better to let the darkness do its job.

A phone call from the hospital woke Charlie at ten o'clock. He had gotten back from the hotel at six-thirty a.m., then stayed awake for another hour reading a book about bank robberies. As a result, his eyes felt gummy and unwilling to focus. When he heard that Victor had been run down by a car, however, he became completely alert.

"How bad is it?" he asked the nurse. "How did it happen?" Victor had a broken leg, a broken arm and shoulder, several broken ribs, some internal injuries and a possible concussion. As for how it happened, the nurse couldn't tell him, although apparently he had been run down while crossing Broadway. Six weeks before racing season and already pedestrians were being brutalized.

Charlie hung up and quickly got dressed. Normally, he would have worn jeans, but now, as night manager of a big hotel, he had been told he had an image to project— or was it protect? In any case, he put on a white shirt and a reddish tie with small blue whales and a rather wrinkled blue seersucker sport coat. Then he hurried out to his car, pushing his fingers through his sparse gray hair and tugging at his tie to make sure it was straight. On his feet were a pair of ancient brown loafers, the backs of which were so crushed that he had to walk in a kind of shuffle to keep them from falling off.

Charlie had lived out at the lake for several years, ever since resigning from the police department as a sergeant in the Community and Youth Relations Bureau, what any normal police department would have called a juvenile division. He liked the water. He liked looking at it when he was worried. He liked the sound of it lapping the small pier behind his house when he felt lonely. He liked how the air tasted having crossed all that wet acreage. He liked being seven or so miles from town where people didn't drop in too often or stay too long. It seemed that Saratoga had always been full of people who wanted him to do things and then felt dissatisfied with how they were done, and so, when he had a little money, it seemed wiser to put some distance between himself and his . . . were they tormentors? No, that was part of the trouble, they all meant well.

The car was a 1974 red Renault station wagon and definitely creaky. Even so, Charlie gunned the motor, passing several slower cars as he rushed toward Saratoga. Hearing about Victor had pushed everything else from his head. Not that any of his current thoughts would be missed. Although he was normally a fairly cheerful individual, the past six months of preparing the hotel for the summer season had so frustrated him and sapped his energy that he hardly had time to follow the box scores in the paper. Added to this was the dismal fact that the woman with whom he imagined himself in love had decided she would be happier with a high school science teacher.

In ninth grade exactly thirty-four years ago, Charlie had gotten a D in general science, which had been the last bit of science he had ever studied, apart from looking at the stars and trying to learn the names of the more obvious constellations. When Doris told him how she felt about Roger Phelps, one of Charlie's gloomy reactions was that here was that D in general science come back to haunt him after all these years.

The trouble was that Doris didn't even dislike Charlie. She just liked Roger Phelps more. He played squash and had a sort of ruddy vigor. If he could just forget her, Charlie told himself, he could continue with his life and maybe meet other women—women who liked him and didn't mind if he wasn't too tall and was a little overweight and getting bald. The awful truth was that despite his age he was still liable to the paralyzing crushes which had plagued his high school years. These were never appropriate. Nor had he much interest in "sensible" women. Even recently one of his respectable cousins had introduced him to a perfectly nice Sunday school teacher. But although Charlie thought her pleasant, what he really fantasized about were boom-boom girls, or women who did dances with feathers, or even cheerleaders, and though Doris Bailes was no cheerleader she was certainly pretty and the touch of her skin left Charlie breathless.

Reaching the hospital, Charlie parked on Van Rensselaer, then ran across to the front entrance. He didn't see why Victor should have been hit by a car, especially at a time when there was little traffic. He kept hoping it might be some other Victor and not his friend at all. At the desk, he gave the nurse's aide one of his cards identifying him as Charles F. Bradshaw of the Bradshaw Detective Agency and learned that Victor was on the third floor. Not wanting to wait for the elevator, Charlie took the stairs. The hospital had an antiseptic smell that seemed to bring to mind every injury he had ever had.

Victor's door was open, and crowded into his double room were a family of eight Hungarians, two policemen and a nurse. It took Charlie a moment to realize the Hungarians were visiting someone on the other side of the curtain and the policemen were there because of Victor. Charlie knew them both, although they had been hired since he left the department and represented the cool and efficient ex-military men whom Chief Peterson tended to favor: emotionless young men who had traveled to Saratoga from other places, mostly the south, and saw Saratoga as a town where a lot of money was being made and people were needed to protect it. The detective, Ernest Tidings, was as thin and sharp-featured as a race dog. The sergeant, Ron Novack, lifted weights at the Y, and some years before Charlie had noticed that Novack never stood still but was constantly flexing. He must have had a nineteen-inch neck. Both men wore dark suits and looked at Charlie with disappointment.

Charlie hardly paused but pushed past to where Victor was lying. Victor's left leg was up in traction, his left shoulder and much of his left arm were in a huge cast, and there was a white bandage wrapped around his head. But what was most frightening to Charlie was how pale he was, how old he looked. He had never thought of Victor as being any age, and now he looked not only old but frail and ill-used. On the other hand, Victor also looked angry, and Charlie judged that to be a good sign.

"Charlie, for cryin' out loud," said Victor, "will you tell these guys there must have been more to me being run down than the simple swiping of a camera?" A plump middle-aged nurse stood on the other side of the bed adjusting the IV in Victor's right arm. When Victor spoke, he tried to wave the arm and the nurse tried to hold it still. She kept making exasperated little sighs.

"But you told us that somebody in the car stole the camera," said Novack patiently. He stood at the foot of the bed with his hands in his back pockets. Tidings stood a little to his right. The Hungarians kept looking at them, then disappearing behind the curtain to whisper in a language that sounded more like chewing than talking.

"Yes, but there musta been some other reason for the fella to smack me in the first place. I mean, what's a camera worth? It's not enough to kill a guy for, no matter how hungry he is. Shit, if he was that hungry, he could of sold the car."

"You mean someone hit you on purpose?" asked Charlie, not entirely following.

Victor rolled his eyes. "That's what I been trying to tell you."

"Do you hurt?" asked Charlie, looking at his friend's injuries. Victor's eyes were glazed and the bandage around his head came down to his eyebrows like a football helmet. But it was really the expression of fragility, a sort of dazed look, that bothered Charlie the most.

"Nah, they got me full of chemicals. Slap my face and I don't feel a thing. Apart from these two guys, I haven't felt this good in weeks." The nurse finished adjusting the IV and filled Victor's glass with water.

"It seems your friend was a victim of a hit-and-run," said Tidings. "There're two other witnesses but no one got a license number. The part that's difficult to understand is that Plotz said the driver backed up to roll over him, then reached out, grabbed his camera and took off."

"Do the witnesses corroborate that too?" Charlie wasn't sure if it was as complicated as it sounded or if he was just suffering from a lack of sleep.

"They say the car backed up and that something was definitely going on, but for the theft of the camera we only have Plotz's word. Not that we doubt him, but it seems hard to credit unless it was in order to steal the camera that he was run down in the first place." Both Tidings and Novack looked somewhat severely at Victor as if he was the culprit and not the victim. The nurse also wore a disapproving expression, but whether she disapproved of Victor or the policemen, Charlie couldn't tell. She had blond hair with gray roots that tumbled out from underneath her little white cap.

"Jesus, Charlie, tell these guys. I mean, why should I make anything up?"

"What kind of car was it?" asked Charlie.

"A maroon Oldsmobile or Buick," said Novack. He was a tall, squarely built man who gave the impression of wanting to knock something down like a door or brick wall. "We've put out an all-points, but we didn't even know about the car until an hour later, so it could be anywhere."

"What we're trying to ascertain," said Tidings, "is whether this was a chance event or if the person had a motive. We understand that Mr. Plotz works for you?"

The trouble with Tidings and Novack, thought Charlie, was that, like many of Peterson's new policemen, they had both wanted to be FBI men but either flunked out of the John Jay College of Criminal Justice or hadn't gotten in or hadn't had the money, but the result was there was an element of parody about them, as if they spent several hours a day washing, slept on boards at night, and practiced looking immobile before mirrors as a major form of recreation.

"Well, we have the detective agency, as you know," said Charlie, "but for the past few months we've been working for my mother. She owns the Bentley Hotel downtown. If someone ran Victor down on purpose, it would seem the person must have had a motive. Did you get a description?"

"He was all hunkered down behind the wheel of the car," said Victor. "Could even be a broad for all I know."

Victor lay staring at the ceiling, as if it hurt to focus first on one person, then another.

"Is there anything in your personal life," asked Novack, flexing his arms, "which could have angered someone to the extent that he or she might have wanted to do you an injury?"

"Come again?"

"He wants to know why someone would want to hurt you," said Charlie.

Victor was gently touching his bandaged head as one might try to touch a soap bubble. "I got people who like me, people who don't like me and a lot of others in between, but there's no one I can think of who'd want to run me down."

"What was in the camera?" asked Charlie.

"Nothing. I mean, I was just on my way to buy film."

"What kind of pictures have you been taking?"

"Nice pictures. The last role was mostly full of a Mrs. Heinz. Otherwise, I've been taking pictures at the hotel—honeymooners, people celebrating birthdays, anniversaries, retirement parties, happy vacationers who've got tickets to the ballet. Nice people. At least no one you could figure would want to run me down."

"Where's the film?" asked Charlie.

"I'm not sure. Last night got a little hazy. Probably someplace in my apartment, although there's some back at the hotel as well. I been a busy snapper."

"If we had the film," said Tidings, "maybe that would tell us something. You sure you're still not doing those divorce pictures?"

"Nah, haven't done any of that for a coupla months." Victor was beginning to sound tired, and there was a far-away quality to his voice.

The nurse finished making some marks on a sheet of

paper attached to a clipboard and hung the board on the back of the bed. "You have to let Mr. Plotz get some rest. He's been badly hurt."

"You tell 'em, sweetie," said Victor. The nurse sighed again and left the room, pushing past Novack and Tidings, who didn't seem to notice.

"Maybe it was someone you photographed a couple of months ago," said Novack, "someone who's trying to get even." He had linked his hands under his chest and appeared to be trying to pull them apart.

"None of them were that bad," said Victor. "I mean, to kill a person, you got to be really pissed."

"Not necessarily," said Novack. "It could have been an impulse. He saw you. He recognized you as someone who had snapped him with some girl or boy or whatever. He saw your camera and decided to run you down. I guess you have to feel lucky you're not dead."

Victor looked skeptically at the policeman. "And you're going to put this joker in jail?"

"We have to find him first," said Novack.

"That's what worries me."

"Are you suggesting that we won't find him?"

"Look, Ron," said Charlie, "Victor's been through a lot and probably feels lousy, no matter what he says. Why don't you just let him rest?"

Tidings stood by the doorway. "Let's get moving. Maybe they got a lead on the guy already."

"The trouble with a case like this," said Novack, following Tidings out of the room, "is there're probably half a million guys who'd like to smack Mr. Plotz with an automobile."

With the policemen gone, the Hungarian family, which had been whispering around the bed of their relative, all began to talk in loud voices.

"The trouble with cops," said Victor, "is they're too touchy."

Charlie continued to stand by Victor's shoulder. "Are you sure you're not in pain?" He wished he could do something to make it better and felt useless and ineffectual.

"Nah, I'm just tired, that's all."

"And you're positive you haven't been taking any of those compromising pictures?"

"Nothing. I swear I been a saint for months. Look what it gets me."

"It would seem," said Charlie, "that someone ran you down because of the camera, which means you were either taking compromising pictures, or they thought you were taking compromising pictures, or you were indeed taking compromising pictures without really knowing it."

"You got a complicated way of putting things," said Victor. "All I know is that I was crossing Broadway and someone smacked me. Here I got to worry about getting murdered and all you want to do is practice your syntax."

Charlie sat down on the edge of the bed and glanced at the Hungarian family—small furry people who smiled and nodded at Charlie whenever they saw he was looking.

"You're lucky and your friends are lucky but I'd like to know more about the kind of stuff you've been shooting."

"Jesus, Charlie, can't you hear? Weddings, honeymoons, parties, all the good times at the hotel which your old lady hopes will make her rich. There doesn't seem to be a killer in the bunch."

"How long are they going to keep you in the hospital?"

"Coupla weeks, I don't know. They say the leg's tricky and the shoulder's a mess. It looks like a pretty dull time. Maybe you can get me some stuff from home, and feed the cat too." Victor had a one-eyed cat named Moshe that Charlie had never liked. Mostly he disliked it because he was allergic to cats, but Moshe seemed to understand about Charlie's allergy and take a perverse pleasure in making him sneeze.

"Sure," said Charlie. "What do you need?"

But before Victor could answer, still another policeman hurried into the room. This one, however, was someone Charlie had hired himself: Emmett Van Brunt, a large red-haired man given to wearing mismatching plaids. Although Emmett was one of the old style of policemen, born and raised within fifteen miles of Saratoga, he hung around with the newcomers, with the result that he was particularly intolerant of Charlie as if to show that no trace of the old loyalty remained.

"For Pete's sake, Charlie," said Van Brunt, "we been looking for you all over town. How come you're never anywhere when we want you?"

Charlie could think of no polite answer, so he remained silent. Van Brunt had a freckled face, and even his big tombstone teeth had a reddish color. Charlie thought of how Emmett's Dutch ancestors had moved into the area over three hundred years before and how Emmett was the sum total of all their digging and planting.

"Peterson wants you," continued Van Brunt. "There's been a murder at the hotel. It seems it happened during the night, right on your shift. I got to take you back there if you don't mind. I guess I got to even if you do mind." Emmett smiled, a cheerless facial contortion indicating that he wished Charlie would protest or try to escape— some activity that Emmett would take keen pleasure in putting a stop to.

2

The body was crammed into a laundry hamper on the third floor. It was a young girl and she was naked. Charlie recognized her. She was one of the young maids that his mother had hired three weeks earlier. Her name was Annie Weston and she came from Glens Falls. She had been about sixteen and this was her first job. Charlie had thought she possessed one of the prettiest smiles he'd ever seen. Annie lay on her back at the bottom of the hamper with her feet straight up. Her eyes were open and she appeared to be staring at Chief Peterson, who was slowly raising himself up and down on his tiptoes, trying to look unconcerned and official. Around them on the walls were Currier and Ives prints of thunderstorms and disasters.

"Another maid found her a little after nine," said Peterson. "There were a lot of sheets and stuff on top of her. She was pretty cold, and the manager said you'd been on duty. He asked if I could keep it out of the papers. Can you believe it?"

Peterson was a large man in a blue three-piece suit. For over ten years he had been Charlie's boss. They had never gotten along, mostly, Charlie thought, because Charlie had once said he hadn't like the Army, while Peterson, who had long been an officer in the Military Police, was convinced that the Army, and specifically the Military Police, was the only spot of sanity in a mad world. They also tended to chafe because Peterson was a great believer in public relations, while Charlie thought of himself as no more than a small-town cop.

Charlie continued to stare at the dead girl. She was very pretty, with a fragile, porcelain look about her. Strands of long blond hair lay across her face, which wore a somewhat startled expression as if she had just met someone unexpected. Around them in the hall a few other policemen, the local coroner and several technicians from the lab crew were talking quietly as they pursued their various duties. They kept bumping the pictures, making them crooked. Charlie kept straightening them again.

"I don't know what her schedule was," said Charlie, "but I'm sure she wasn't working last night. At least I didn't see her. She and the other maids have a couple of rooms on the top floor in the back. You know the cause of death?"

"Not yet. We'll do an autopsy later."

"She looks pretty peaceful," said Charlie. "Are you sure she was murdered?"

"For Christ's sake, Charlie, she's probably got a knife hole a foot long in her back. You think she died here naturally, naked in a hamper, all covered with old sheets? Use your head."

Charlie said nothing. He couldn't imagine why anyone would want to murder such a nice girl, although he knew that was a foolish thought. Glancing at Peterson raising and lowering himself on the balls of his feet, he guessed the police chief was already considering what strategy to take with the newspapers and TV stations. It seemed odd that the assault on Victor and this girl's death should occur so close together. Charlie wondered if it was only coincidence.

Half an hour later Charlie was climbing the stairs to Victor's apartment in the Algonquin. He meant to pick up a few shaving things for Victor, and a couple of books and the new *Penthouse,* and to feed Moshe, but also he was glad for the chance to rest his mind from all the questions—why had Victor been run down, why had a girl been murdered. As yet he hadn't seen his mother, who liked to sleep late and generally appeared around noon, leaving the business to Raoul, whom Charlie had managed to avoid except for a silent encounter in the lobby as Charlie was hurrying out the revolving door. Raoul seemed to think that since the death had occurred on Charlie's shift, then he was at fault. Consequently, he had given Charlie a look of long-suffering and regret, as if Charlie had filled the hotel with policemen just to irritate him.

In the hallway, Charlie took out his key to Victor's apartment, but as he touched the door he found it already open. From the other side came a frustrated and dissatisfied meowing. Immediately Charlie's eyes began to water. Opening the door no more than eight inches, Charlie squeezed through the crack to keep Moshe from getting out. Then he stopped thinking about the cat. The living room looked as if someone had picked it up and shaken it, leaving everything upside down. The furniture was turned over, books and papers were scattered everywhere. No wonder the cat was angry. The place was a wreck.

Charlie stood by the door as Moshe wound back and forth between his ankles. Someone had clearly broken in after Victor had been run down and ransacked the apartment. Drawers were opened and their contents scattered on the floor, cushions were thrown around, closets had been emptied and the clothes were in heaps. Charlie walked slowly through the three rooms. Knives and forks had been dumped on the kitchen linoleum. Plates were broken. Always as he walked, Moshe wound between his ankles. Glancing in the bathroom mirror, Charlie saw the astonishment on his own round face—a kind of open-mouthed expression. All the pills and lotions and razor blades which had been in the medicine cabinet were now in the tub. Charlie collected the shaving stuff and a tooth-brush and returned to the kitchen, where he put some cat chow in a bowl for Moshe. Even the refrigerator had been searched, and six broken eggs dotted the kitchen floor.

Charlie went back into the living room and sat down on the couch. From the bathroom, he could hear Moshe scratching furiously in his cat box. At first Charlie thought that the searcher, whoever it was, had been angry, but maybe he or she was just in a hurry, as well as being frantic. But what had the person been looking for?

Whatever it was, it was small. Small enough to hide in a butter dish or medicine cabinet or in a coat pocket. Something, Charlie thought, like a key or a coin or a roll of film. Charlie collected Victor's magazines, his Walkman and half a dozen tapes of disco hits. He put everything in a ragged plaid suitcase and left the apartment before Moshe could return to being affectionate. The apartment bothered him. It seemed crazy. The frantic quality of the search seemed so desperate that he felt a certain anxiety at ever meeting the person who had done it.

Down on the sidewalk, Charlie decided not to go directly to the hospital but to check the office that he and Victor shared on Phila Street. Ostensibly, it was Charlie's office, since he was the head of the Charles F. Bradshaw Detective Agency, but for some reason that Charlie could never fathom, Victor managed to attract most of the clients, despite Charlie's reputation for honesty and his high success rate. It wasn't that Victor took all the sleazy cases—Charlie had put a stop to that—but that Victor was somehow easier to confide in. He seemed more like a detective, while Charlie, or so Charlie had heard it said, was like a priest or high school principal. So although Victor was supposedly working for Charlie, it often turned out the other way around, with Charlie tracking down runaway schoolgirls or husbands off on a fling in Albany.

Charlie swung the Renault into a U-turn and drove back along Broadway toward his office. As he passed the boutique run by his ex-wife and her sister, he glanced toward it to see if he would have to duck. Even after seven years, she glared at him, still angry that the request for a divorce had come from Charlie rather than herself, since she felt he had every reason to be content. After all, he was the one without manly ambition, the one who spent his free hours pottering through old histories about outlaws, murderers and bank robbers when he could have been doing something useful like learning about computers.

Charlie turned left onto Phila and parked. Climbing the stairs to his office, he unlocked the door and entered the small anteroom, which was separated from the office by a wall of frosted glass. Charlie paused and looked around. In front of him were a coat rack, several armchairs covered with cracked green vinyl and a low coffee table. The magazines, which had been in a neat pile, were now scattered and the cushions of the chairs had been disturbed.

Cautiously, Charlie opened the door to the office. When he saw it was empty, he released a little puff of air. The office was furnished with a wooden desk, four straight chairs, a green metal safe, a bookcase and several pictures—one of Jesse James, another of Gina Lollobrigida

flinging up her skirt and looking surpr*ed. He began looking around, and after a minute or so he decided that not
only had the office been searched, it had been searched
by someone other than the person who had searched Victor's apartment—nothing was overturned or thrown on
the floor. Charlie stayed about five minutes, long enough
to make sure the office had been truly searched and wasn't
just messy. But the desk drawers were disturbed, as were
the drawers of the file cabinet. And the safe door was
open. He couldn't remember if it had been locked. In any
case, there was nothing inside. Usually he kept his .38 in
the safe, but since working at the hotel he'd left it at home.
The safe must have been unlocked, thought Charlie. Who'd
crack an empty safe or know how to?

Charlie decided to go back to the Bentley to see if
Victor's small office had been searched as well. Perhaps
it had been searched by some third person, although that
seemed a frivolous idea. It was nearly one o'clock and he
was getting hungry. But he also wanted to learn more
about Annie Weston, whose body had been found in the
hamper. And he would have to talk to his mother and
Raoul, or rather he would listen as they explored themes
of inadequacy, immaturity and general ineptness—anti-
qualities which Raoul spent much time attaching to Charlie's person, although it seemed to Charlie that his real
faults were that he wasn't fastidious enough, thin enough
and sleeked-back enough for Raoul's taste. Raoul ate like
a pig, and remained skinny as a whippet. Charlie ate like
a bird, and despite endless swimming and long walks, he
stayed fifteen pounds above average and thirty above what
Raoul most admired—that death-camp leanness where
you disappear when you turn sideways.

As he walked up Phila Street toward the hotel, Charlie
began to think of the dead girl. Blond and pale-looking,

she had seemed very shy, although once she asked Charlie if she could bring him some coffee and a hot roll, and another time she had modestly pointed out that a seam had come undone at the back of his sport coat and part of the lining was hanging down. She offered to mend it but Charlie was embarrassed and did it himself. Still, he had been grateful. If Raoul had noticed the lining hanging down over Charlie's buttocks, he would have brought out the entire staff to bear witness and express dismay. So Charlie had liked the girl, and always said hello, and wondered what she was doing there, since she was quite young and shy and clearly had not worked in a hotel before and had to be told how to make the beds so they were perfect and had to put up with a lot of correcting from Raoul.

The Bentley was on Broadway near the corner of Phila. It had six great white pillars and a long porch with a row of white wicker rockers just like in the old days. Fifty years earlier, it had been rather cozy and modest, but then, after the Grand Union, the United States and several other huge hotels were torn down to make room for supermarkets and hamburger stands, the Bentley emerged as the largest example of potential Victorian splendor available for renovation. And renovate it Mabel Bradshaw had done, with the help of an architect from New York City and her own inimitable taste for the ostentatious. Already they were swamped with reservations, and the only thing to put a damper on the profits might be some sort of scandal, like an unsolved murder, some death to remind the vacationers how fragile was the illusion of good times.

Neither Raoul nor Mabel Bradshaw was in the lobby, which was decorated with soft chairs covered with purple velvet, fake Tiffany lamps, a crystal chandelier and red-and-black wallpaper resembling a bloody war in the bacteria world blown up to mammoth proportions. Suzanne stood behind the desk—a beautiful but androgynous young woman with closely cropped blond hair, half a dozen earrings and a tattoo of the state of Texas at the top of her left breast. She was Raoul's assistant and maintained a cool disdain for Charlie, who in turn was amazed by her beauty, although he didn't like her much. Often she dressed like a Vienna choirboy, which made Charlie's sexual attraction more complicated than he would have wished. As a result, he never stared into her eyes but focused around the area of her chin.

"Is my mother around?" asked Charlie, pausing at the desk.

Suzanne looked up from a pile of letters as if she didn't quite recognize him. "She's at the lawyer's, along with Raoul."

"Is there any trouble?"

"Don't you call a murder trouble? Raoul thought it best to find out about our responsibility in case there's a lawsuit. Apparently there's some question if the girl should have been hired, since she was only sixteen." Suzanne wore a tight blue knit dress unbuttoned at the top so that Charlie could just see the Panhandle area of her Texas tattoo. He thought of all the outlaws and desperadoes who had galloped across that very area. It depressed him that she thought he was inconsequential.

"Are there any messages for me?"

"Your friend Victor wants his toothbrush and magazines, and a Doris Bailes called and wants you to call back. She wouldn't say what it was about."

Charlie felt a little surge of pressure in his stomach. "She didn't say anything?"

"Just that you should call her."

Charlie continued down the hall toward Victor's office

at the rear of the hotel—more of a pantry than an office. Doris Bailes had said she didn't want to talk to him again, and the fact she had called filled Charlie with hope. Maybe she had seen through her science teacher with his endless noise about squash scores and running statistics. Charlie was tempted to call her immediately but decided to wait. It wouldn't be good to let her know how desperate he felt.

The office door, with the brass plate saying Hotel Detective, stood open. The room was about eight feet by eight feet and furnished with an old wooden desk, three barstools and a cot where Charlie sometimes took naps around four a.m. when all the world seemed dead. The stools had been moved slightly, and several desk drawers were ajar. The room had been searched, but neatly. The preexisting mess had only been rearranged. Something small had been searched for—the pockets of a coat had been pulled out, papers and old Styrofoam cups had been shifted around on the desk. Charlie thought of Victor's description of someone reaching out of the maroon car and picking the camera off the pavement. If the camera had been empty, then that might have been enough to send someone off—or two people off—to look for the film. But why should anyone want photos of honeymooners and silver anniversary celebrators laughing and rollicking? Sitting down at the desk, Charlie fiddled with the cord on the black office phone, then decided to call Chief Peterson.

Charlie was put on hold and had to listen to three minutes of "Moon River" before Peterson came on the line. It occurred to him to ask the police chief why he imagined that people needing police assistance would be calmed by listening to music, but recently he had been getting along relatively well with Peterson and didn't want to offend him without fair cause.

"Did you discover what killed Annie Weston?" asked Charlie.

"They should be doing the autopsy right now. There were no marks on the body. Possibly she'd been poisoned or even strangled. There're all sorts of ways to kill a young girl. We've been trying to contact her parents, but they must be at work." Peterson's gravelly voice exuded certainty and confidence. It was only in the flesh that he appeared to have doubts.

"What about the car that ran down Victor?"

"No sign of it. Maybe his being run down had nothing to do with the girl or even his picture-taking. I can think of lots of people who don't like him. Perhaps he made one enemy too many."

"That's a thought," said Charlie. He could hear Peterson's slow and heavy breathing coming through the earpiece. It occurred to him it was at the same tempo as the music he'd just been listening to. He decided the police chief needed to be stirred up a little. "By the way, the main reason I'm calling is I thought you'd like to know that someone broke into Victor's apartment and tore it to pieces looking for something. Then someone else searched both the detective agency office and his office at the hotel. You might want to send a lab crew to all three places. I can let you in."

The breathing on the other end of the line stopped for a bit, then sped up. "You're saying two different people were involved in the searches?"

"It would seem that way. The apartment was ripped to shreds, while the two offices were done more delicately. They seemed to be looking for something pretty small."

"You mean like money?"

"I was thinking of something like a roll of film. You going to send someone over? I know you don't particularly

like Victor, but, well, attempted murder is pretty serious."
The speed of the breathing increased a fraction, and Charlie wondered if he'd said too much.

"I know attempted murder is serious, Charlie, and I like to think I'd investigate a crime even if the victim were my worst enemy. I'm sorry you think I've been slighting your friend."

"Not at all, chief," lied Charlie, "I just wanted to let you know about those break-ins. Do you mind if I call back later this afternoon to find out about the autopsy?"

"That'd be fine, Charlie."

After Peterson said he'd send someone over to look at Victor's apartment and the two offices and after Charlie agreed to be there, Charlie hung up and considered how in the past year the local newspapers and TV stations had made much of his detecting successes and kept plaguing Peterson with unfair questions, asking, when he seemed stumped, whether he was going to call in Bradshaw on this one or if he had asked Bradshaw's advice, and Peterson would sit as still as possible and let a few seconds go by and then say that of course he and Charlie were close friends and always in touch.

Charlie picked up the phone and dialed the front desk. When Suzanne answered, he asked, "Did the police question the other maids and other members of the staff?"

"They talked to the people on the night staff, but the maids were busy, so Chief Peterson said he'd send someone back this afternoon."

Charlie glanced at his watch. It was just one-thirty. "How many girls worked with Annie?"

"Three altogether."

"Are they here now?"

"Of course."

"Tell them I want to see them. I'm in Victor's office."

"I'm afraid they're working right now."

"That's all right, send them in anyway."

"I don't think Raoul would want—"

"Look, Suzanne, either you send them or I go get them. As for Raoul . . . " Charlie paused, thinking of all he wanted to say but then deciding against it. "Just send them in, okay?"

3

The three maids were in their late teens and blondish with pale complexions, although splashes of pink would appear on the cheeks of whomever Charlie addressed directly. They were large to the point of being ungainly, and Charlie thought they would have been happy as farm girls but as maids they seemed sullen. Charlie had been talking to them for about five minutes, but all he had learned was that Annie Weston was extremely shy and rarely spoke. Three of the maids, including Annie, slept in small rooms at the top of the building. A fourth commuted from Ballston Spa.

"Secretive," said a girl named Eunice. "I got a cousin who went to school in Glens Falls and I asked Annie if she knew her and Annie wouldn't say one way or the other."

The three girls stood in front of the desk in Victor's tiny office. All wore the old-fashioned blue uniforms and blue caps meant to emphasize the Bentley's Victorian theme. Eunice stood in the middle, assuming the role of spokesperson. She had a large red boil in the exact center of her forehead, as if she were growing a third eye. Charlie thought it must be painful and probably accounted for her ill humor. The other two, Trudy and Millie, were cousins but looked enough alike to be twins. They kept glancing around the room without turning their heads, which made their large blue eyes seem loose in their sockets.

"What about boyfriends?" asked Charlie. "Did she ever go out with anyone?"

"We're not allowed to have boyfriends here," said Eunice, "leastways not while we're working. Raoul doesn't like it."

"But Annie was very pretty," said Charlie. "There must have been young men who were interested in her?"

"Annie stayed mostly by herself," said Eunice. "If she had any boyfriends, she didn't let on about it."

Trudy and Millie looked uncomfortable and their eyes shifted down to the floor.

"Are you telling me that none of the men around the hotel, no workmen or waiters or busboys, none of them even talked to her?"

"Not that we saw," said Eunice.

"Tell me, Trudy," asked Charlie, "what about Raoul? Did he ever bother Annie the way I've seen him bother you?" A week earlier Charlie had seen Raoul pat this girl's buttocks. "Did he ever touch her or try to get her in some corner?"

The result of the question was that Trudy burst into tears. Charlie felt embarrassed and sat looking down at the blotter, where someone, presumably Victor, had drawn pornographic stick figures. Charlie moved a small notepad to cover them up. The other two girls offered Trudy bits of crumpled tissue and patted her shoulders while looking disapprovingly at Charlie. After a moment, the tears subsided to occasional sobs.

"We never," said Eunice, "saw Raoul making approaches to Annie or anyone else. He's been nothing but decent to the whole lot of us."

Charlie slowly got up and walked around the desk so he faced the girls from about two feet away. All three moved back and seemed to be staring at Charlie's loafers. He remained silent until they looked up at him again.

"You see," said Charlie, "there's a serious problem. Annie may have been murdered, and if so, she was presumably murdered by someone who knew her and who knew the hotel. Who that person was won't remain a secret for long. Now, I'm trying to be as nice as possible. Soon the police will come and ask these same questions. If it turns out that Annie had a boyfriend and you're protecting him and if it turns out he was involved with her death, well, you may be in a lot of trouble."

"Would we lose our jobs?" asked Trudy. Eunice turned to shush her.

"Fired?" said Charlie, as seriously as possible. "That'd be the least of it. You'd go to jail."

This time Trudy and Millie burst into tears together, while Eunice looked depressed and touched a finger to the boil on her forehead. Charlie regretted making them cry and wondered if he was being sadistic.

"Since you're quite young," he continued, "they probably wouldn't keep you in jail for long, maybe just a year or two. But murder's a serious charge, so there's no telling what a judge might do."

"He didn't kill her," said Millie in a rush. "He loved her. He wouldn't hurt a single hair on her head."

"Who wouldn't?" Charlie asked gently.

"Don't tell!" said Eunice.

"Joe Riklin," said Trudy.

There was a pause as Charlie walked back around the desk and made a small show of writing the name on the notepad. "And why shouldn't she tell?" he asked Eunice.

But Eunice was done talking and stared steadfastly down at the floor.

"She's just protecting him," said Millie. "We all decided to. They loved each other, just like in the movies. He would come up to her room at night. They would spend the whole night just holding hands and talking."

"So what's wrong with that?" asked Charlie. "Why does he need protecting?"

"He's nice," said Trudy. She was twisting the crumpled bits of tissue, turning them into a kind of sodden confetti that fell to the floor and speckled her black shoes. "But I guess he's been in jail and he's got a bad temper."

"Did he threaten you?"

"Of course not," said Eunice. "We were his friends. He doesn't even really have a temper. He just gets mad sometimes." She glanced at her companions as if she wanted to shake them.

"What's he been in jail for?" asked Charlie.

"He stole a car once," said Trudy.

"And breaking and entering," said Eunice. "But he didn't steal anything, he was just looking around."

"And fighting," said Millie. "He's been in some fights."

"So how old is this fellow?" asked Charlie. He couldn't quite place who they were talking about but thought it might be a young red-haired man who worked in the kitchen.

"Eighteen," said Millie.

"And what do you like about him?"

"He's been nice to us," said Trudy, looking into Charlie's eyes for what seemed the first time. "I don't mean he made passes at us, he was too stuck on Annie for that. But he'd bring us treats from the kitchen or give us rides on his motor scooter or just talk. And then he was gentle with Annie, trying to help her when she got behind in her work and taking her out to movies. They were really happy together and he even gave her earrings with red stones that looked almost like rubies."

"Was he with her last night?" asked Charlie.

The girls looked at each other again, then nodded.

"And you haven't seen him today?"

"He might have called in sick," said Eunice.

The other two girls looked doubtfully at Eunice. They knew he wasn't sick, no such luck.

After Charlie told the girls to go back to work, he walked out to the lobby to speak with Suzanne. Charlie's mother and Raoul were still with the lawyer.

"Did Joe Riklin come in today?" Charlie stood by the front desk, which was about twenty feet long and made of dark wood.

"No, and the kitchen's a mess. We had a big lunch crowd and the waitresses had to bus their own tables."

"Did he call in?"

"No again. I checked with his rooming house but they said he wasn't around." Suzanne looked impatiently at Charlie. "I'm very busy. Is there any point to these questions?"

Charlie considered a hundred answers but found none acceptable. The trouble with beauty, he thought, was it made you want to be liked by the beautiful person, which threw you off balance when he or she turned out unpleasant. "Give me Riklin's address," he asked, then waited as Suzanne looked through a card file and wrote the address on a slip of paper. As she bent over, Charlie could see the whole of her Texas tattoo with the tip of the state pointing down toward her nipple.

Instead of being able to look for Riklin right away, Charlie had to meet Ron Novack at Victor's apartment to show him that someone had indeed broken in. Novack was waiting out on the sidewalk and made it clear he didn't like to wait, no matter how nice a day it was. Charlie guessed he was one of those people who didn't care if there was rain, snow or blue sky. Leading the way up to Victor's apartment, Charlie then stood by the door while Novack looked around. It amazed Charlie that there were women—fashion models, for instance—whose waist sizes were the same thickness as Novack's neck. The cat, Moshe, ignored the policeman and gave all his attention to Charlie, making him sneeze about thirty times. Novack agreed that somebody had made a mess of the place. He carried a green hand grip and squeezed it ten times with one hand, then ten with the other. From the apartment, they drove over to the detective office. It looked fine to Novack.

"What do you mean, searched?" he asked. "Where's the evidence? Was the door open? Unless you can prove forcible entry, you don't have a case." The hand grip made a slight squeaking noise as Novack spoke, making his voice seem rusty. Charlie decided not to show him the office at the hotel, which Novack would put down as another example of Charlie's paranoia. Had the two offices really been searched? wondered Charlie. But he knew they had been.

After leaving Novack, Charlie drove back to the hospital. Ostensibly he had to give Victor his magazines, toothbrush and shaving stuff but mostly he wanted to find out if he knew this ex-convict busboy whom the three maids thought so nice. Because Charlie worked nights, he had only seen the young man a couple of times—thin, tall, freckled, red hair. They had never spoken, Charlie was sure of that.

Charlie found Victor asleep and snoring loudly with his mouth open while several new Hungarians kept glancing at him with a mixture of awe and respect, impressed that someone so damaged could make a noise like a power-boat. Charlie again thought how fragile Victor looked, how pale. On the shoulder of Victor's cast someone had drawn a heart with red lipstick. Inside were Victor's initials, a plus sign and the initials A.G. He touched his friend's arm and Victor opened his eyes.

"Could the person who ran you down be Joe Riklin?" asked Charlie.

Victor looked at him blearily, then rubbed at his eyes with his good hand. "You mean the busboy? Why the hell should he run me down?"

"His girlfriend was found dead in the hotel this morning and I thought there might be some connection." Charlie told Victor how Annie Weston had been discovered in the laundry hamper and that Riklin hadn't shown up for work.

"She was the pretty one, right? I never even went near her. Those angel types make me nervous. You think Riklin bumped her off?"

"I don't know. It's not even certain she was murdered."

"What does Peterson say?"

"I haven't told him about Riklin yet."

Victor made a clicking noise with his tongue. "Hey, Charlie, that's withholding evidence. How long have you known about this guy?"

"I just found out about him." Even as he said it, Charlie knew that wasn't good enough. But something made him hesitant to turn Riklin over to the police. Maybe it was the maids calling him nice. It made Charlie want to learn more.

"But why should Riklin want my camera?"

"Did you take pictures of him and the girl?"

"Hell, I took pictures of *everybody*. That's the only way to get good—hit all the facial types. I guess it could of been Riklin. Like I say, I could see nothing but a gray fedora. But it seems pretty farfetched. By the way, you bring my skin mags? I need something organic for when the pain starts up."

"Sure, it's all right here." Charlie put the plaid suitcase on the night stand and unzipped it. "You ever have any dealings with Riklin? I was told he was an ex-con."

"I didn't know anything about that ex-con stuff or I might have paid more attention. About a week ago I found him in one of the guest's rooms. The door was open and he was the only one around. There was an open purse on the bed but nothing to say he'd touched it. He'd brought up a tray of drinks from the bar and I guess the tenant had stepped out for a minute. I told him he wasn't supposed to enter a room unless someone let him in. He got a little huffy."

"What'd you do?" asked Charlie.

"Nothing. I just repeated what I'd said and if he had a complaint, he could take it up with Raoul. I also told him if he was found in a room by himself again, he'd be out of a job. I wasn't being hard on him. I just didn't want there to be any confusion."

"Then what happened?"

"He just left. Couldn't tell if he was angry or what. I mean, maybe he was completely innocent but I thought I had to say something. Since then I haven't seen him except, you know, in the distance. Jesus, you really think he might have run me down?"

"I don't know. He's supposed to have a temper, but that's pretty extreme." Charlie sat down on a blue upholstered chair. Several vases of yellow flowers were placed around the room, and Charlie wondered who had sent them. "By the way, someone broke into your apartment and tore it apart looking for something. Then someone else more neatly searched the detective office and your office at the hotel." He went on to describe to Victor what he had found while Victor scrunched up his forehead and by turns looked depressed, then irritated.

"Is Moshe okay?"

"Just hungry. I fed him. Whoever did it was looking for something pretty small. Considering that the camera was taken, I thought it might be a roll of film. You sure you haven't been taking any more compromising pictures?"

"Charlie, I swear I haven't done that for months. All I been snapping was a whole bunch of this Mrs. Heinz and then honeymooners and stuff like that."

"And the camera was empty this morning?"

"You got it."

"What about the stuff you shot yesterday?"

"That I'm not sure. Mrs. Heinz took a lot of entertaining and maybe I drank more than was smart. I must of had the roll in my pocket, then put it someplace in the apartment."

"Well, if the person got the film, then I guess we'll never know. What exactly had you been shooting?"

"There were thirty-six shots and maybe twenty of Mrs. Heinz. The other sixteen I shot last night at the hotel—a few of this, a few of that, but mostly these honeymooners from Utica. I'd put the roll into the camera around six. The one I took out I left on my desk. It had snaps from Friday and Saturday night. Honeymooners again, nice tasteful pictures. People would buy me drinks and I'd immortalize their happy faces. It's what's called a symbiosis, like pilot fish and sharks."

"There's no roll of film on your desk now. Could Riklin have taken it?"

"Sure—I mean, he's always around and the office is never locked. But the big question, Sherlock, is why bother?"

"I guess that's what I'd like to find out," said Charlie. "I mean, if he's the one who ran you down, I want to know it. By the way, were those pictures color or black and white?"

"For Pete's sake, Charlie, don't you know anything? Ansel Adams, Walker Evans, all the biggies use black and white. That's what art's all about—contrast."

From the hospital Charlie drove to police headquarters to talk to Peterson. He realized that almost without being aware of it he had become engaged in an investigation which, technically, was police business. On the other hand, whenever Charlie thought of someone running down Victor, then trying to back over him, his skin started to itch.

Peterson was in his office with Emmett Van Brunt when Charlie arrived. Both men looked up somewhat guiltily as if Charlie had caught them telling secrets or eating between meals.

"Your secretary was busy," said Charlie. "I happened to find out who Annie Weston was with last night—one of the busboys. He didn't show up for work today, so maybe you want to go after him."

He had expected Peterson to be immediately attentive, even to be angry with Charlie for keeping the information to himself. Instead, Peterson began shifting some papers around on his desk as if Charlie was distracting him from more important work. "Who was it?" he asked.

"A kid by the name of Joe Riklin. He and the girl were pretty heavily involved. You know him?"

Peterson shook his head. "Doesn't ring any bells. What about you, Emmett?"

Van Brunt stood by the window looking down at the street, trying to pretend that Charlie wasn't in the office. "Should we talk about this with Bradshaw here?"

Peterson heaved his shoulders up about two inches, then let them drop. "What's it matter?"

"Riklin was arrested for car theft a couple of times when he was fourteen and spent about a year at Warwick. Since getting out he was caught breaking and entering but got off with a trespassing charge. He's also been arrested for fighting and for illegal possession of alcohol." Emmett wore glasses with heavy black frames. As he spoke they kept slipping down his nose and he shoved them back with his thumb.

"Is he from Saratoga?" asked Charlie. He couldn't see why they were responding so indifferently to someone who was obviously a prime suspect.

"His parents moved away when he was twelve," said Van Brunt, talking to Peterson and not looking at Charlie. "They left him with an aunt. Not that she has much time for him. She's a waitress at the Spa City Diner."

"What's he like?" asked Charlie.

Again Van Brunt spoke directly to Peterson. "A little wild but not bad. He's had no one to look out for him."

"Could he have murdered the girl?" asked Charlie.

"There wasn't any murder," said Peterson. "The coroner just called. It was something in her brain, a kind of hemorrhage. Her blood vessels were too thin, or the veins, I don't know, he's sending me a full report. Some kind of birth defect. The point is it makes the death accidental. The coroner said he was surprised she'd lasted so long."

"Aneurysm," said Van Brunt. "He called it a berry aneurysm."

"Yeah," said Peterson. "All of which means that it

wasn't murder, which suits me fine. No reporters, no TV, no unpleasant questions."

"But who put her in the laundry hamper?" asked Charlie.

"That's still a problem," said Peterson, "but maybe it was this Riklin character. I'll have someone pick him up."

"And who ran down Victor?" Charlie found himself getting mad again just thinking about it.

"Yeah, that too. Novack's working on it. For that matter, we don't even know who the girl is anymore. We contacted her parents in Glens Falls and they said their daughter's fine. I even talked to her on the phone. No telling who the dead girl is, but it's not Annie Weston. I sent Tidings up to see them just to make one hundred percent sure. Look, Charlie, I know you're upset about your friend, but why don't you just leave it to us?"

"Have you sent out descriptions of the girl? Has anyone reported her missing?"

Peterson sat back on the edge of his desk. "Sure, sure, we done all that. It's just going to take some time. But you can tell your mother the Bentley's reputation is safe and sound. She's had some lawyer calling and asking a lot of questions. At this point the only criminal charge is for dumping the body in the hamper. Not much of a charge, though."

"But if Riklin did it," said Charlie, "and the girl died when she was with him, he probably thinks he caused her death. He might even have run down Victor. I mean, he's probably desperate. I just don't see how the camera fits in or why the film would be important."

Peterson yawned, then began fiddling with a chain of paper clips. "Relax, Charlie, it's all going to work itself out. I got men assigned and today or tomorrow they'll pick up Riklin and that will be that."

"It was my friend who got run down," said Charlie.

"Don't tell me my job. This is a busy town and there's more happening than just this case of hit-and-run. Trust me, sooner or later we'll put the guy behind bars."

When he returned to the hotel, Charlie learned that Doris Bailes had called two more times and wanted to see Charlie right away. Charlie's heart made a little leap, a sort of cartwheel. Raoul and Charlie's mother were in Raoul's office still trying to decide, according to Suzanne, how to deal with the murder. They feared cancellations, a summer of empty rooms. Instead of seeing them and explaining there had been no murder, Charlie hurried out the door and drove to the Backstretch.

When he had last talked to Doris the previous week, she had told him there was no hope—her heart was set on the science teacher. It seemed impossible to expect that she had changed her mind and decided Charlie was Mr. It after all, but what other explanation could there be? Deep down Charlie knew there might be dozens of other explanations, but he cared not to entertain them. He imagined her apology. He saw himself feigning irritation, possibly even anger, but then accepting it. They would embrace. They'd kiss right there in the bar with everybody watching.

When Charlie entered the Backstretch, he saw Doris standing by one of the rear tables. She was a dark-haired, almost stocky woman of about forty with a round symmetrical face and a smile that did electrical things to Charlie's stomach lining. He had felt so much grief because of her during the past several weeks that he approached her cautiously. He hated having a broken heart. It made his whole life awful. The bar was about a quarter full, and

Charlie nodded to several people he knew—a mailman, a local realtor, a reformed bunco artist.

Doris was wearing a dark skirt and white blouse. Her short hair framed her face like a bowl. "I heard about Victor this morning," she said. "One of the ambulance drivers was in here for lunch. He said how Victor's camera was stolen by whoever ran him down. Is that right?" Doris's voice was concerned but perfectly even and showed nothing that Charlie could interpret as warmth intended for him alone. All the hope which he had brought with him began to float away like bits of fog. He wanted to touch her cheek but knew he had no right.

"The camera was stolen," said Charlie. "I think the person was after the film."

"Victor was in here last night. He had quite a lot to drink." Doris reached into her pocket, took out something and handed it to Charlie. It was a roll of film. "He left this on the bar. I thought it might be important."

4

Later that Monday afternoon Charlie drove up to Glens Falls to talk to the parents of Annie Weston. Ernest Tidings had already spoken to the Westons earlier and even to their daughter Annie, a girl about sixteen who didn't have much to say for herself. Tidings had described the dead girl, but no one recognized her. They couldn't imagine how the dead girl had got their daughter's ID. Then the daughter had said she had lost her wallet some months earlier. But why didn't you tell us? the father had asked. The girl said she was afraid they'd get angry. It was Tidings's view that the girl knew more than she was saying. That was Charlie's view as well, which was why he was driving up to Glens Falls. He wanted to talk to her himself.

Before leaving Saratoga, however, Charlie had taken the film to Henry Perkins, a photographer who had a studio just off Broadway. A contact sheet would be ready when Charlie returned. Charlie had known Perkins for over forty years and wanted to tell him to be careful: Victor had almost been killed for this film and various places had been searched. But Perkins was already a jittery man with a tendency to drink more than was good for him, and Charlie was afraid of making him nervous.

Charlie hadn't said anything to Doris after taking the film. He had been so positive that she wanted to be with him again that he only nodded rather vacantly. Most likely she thought he was angry. It seemed ridiculous to love someone who liked him all right but was generally indifferent. He thought of the few times they had slept together, and as he drove toward Glens Falls he could almost see the curve of her naked body stretched across the Northway between the semi trucks and cars rushing toward Montreal. If it had to come to an end, then he was glad it was over, but he wished he could cut her out of his mind like taking out an appendix or a mole off the back of his hand. As it was, he felt like a victim, not much different from Victor after having been knocked down by a car, and, basically, that made Charlie feel foolish.

He thought again of Victor lying in his hospital bed. Had Riklin run him down? Who had searched the offices and Victor's apartment? Charlie felt if he could throw himself into answering these questions with energy and determination, then he might forget Doris for a while. Very briefly he asked himself what right he had to investigate anything. After all, he was no longer a policeman. But Victor was his best friend. Certainly it was his duty to discover who had tried to kill him.

The Westons lived right downtown in Glens Falls, only two blocks from the Crandall Library, which was maybe the best public library north of Albany. Charlie often went there to get books on American history, especially the history of the old west. The Westons' house was a small white house in the Greek Revival manner with two peaks in front and a long porch with four Doric columns. A fat man about forty answered the door. He had a small bandage on his cheek, and Charlie guessed he had cut himself shaving. Charlie handed him his card saying he was a private detective and a second card saying he was night manager of the Bentley in Saratoga. From inside the house, Charlie could hear the rattle of dishes and smelled meat cooking. The man looked from one card to the other, then looked back at Charlie.

"That's that old place they fixed up, isn't it? I was meaning to take my wife there for a drink. She likes to go out."

Charlie nodded in such a way as to indicate that he often liked to go out himself. "I realize that Detective Tidings has already spoken to you," he said, "but I thought of some additional questions. I hope that's okay."

"No problem at all," said Mr. Weston, stepping aside so Charlie could enter. "Come in and have a glass of ice-tea."

Charlie passed through the doorway, then Mr. Weston preceded him down the hall. He was so fat that he first bumped one wall, then the other. "Mildred, Annie," he called, "there's a detective here with more questions." Charlie noticed he was wearing one brown slipper and one blue. On the walls were photographs of trotters in winner's circles. The driver in each was a thinner and younger version of Mr. Weston. Charlie thought the pictures had been taken at the Saratoga Raceway.

Several minutes later, Weston, his wife and his daughter Annie were gathered with Charlie in a small living room while Charlie sipped a tepid glass of iced tea. In twenty bowls scattered around the room were arrangements of silk flowers. It turned out that Mrs. Weston made them, and Charlie had already said they were very nice. She was an efficient-looking dark-haired woman a few years younger than her husband and probably one-third his size.

"I was wondering," said Charlie, "if your daughter belongs to any club or YWCA or Girl Scout organization where she might have left her wallet. Maybe she even left it at school. We need to start looking for this dead girl someplace."

Annie's parents looked at her with a kind of benevolent curiosity. "I'm sure it wasn't at school," said the daughter, "and I belong to the Y but I don't think it was there either." Annie was a thin dark-haired girl with braces and green eyes who seemed nervous. Charlie smiled and tried to appear friendly.

"What about church, dear?" asked Mrs. Weston. "Perhaps you left your bag someplace during choir practice."

"No, I know it wasn't there. I probably just dropped it on the street."

"Could the girl have gone to your school, was she in one of your classes?" asked Charlie, still trying to maintain his smile even though his lips ached. He was certain the girl knew something. He described the dead girl, then watched Annie shake her head.

"She doesn't sound familiar," she said. "I'm sure it's no one I know."

Charlie continued to suggest possible places and to go over the actual loss of the wallet, but the girl seemed vague and forgetful, unable to help.

After ten more minutes, Charlie stood up and walked to the fireplace. On the mantel was a picture of Mr. Weston in a Marine uniform. He wondered why Weston had let himself get so fat. Maybe he had been in love and had his heart broken. Maybe Charlie would get fat now that Doris had rejected him. Charlie turned around and tried to look very concerned. "Would you mind if I spoke to your daughter for two or three minutes by herself?" he asked. "Sometimes it's easier that way."

Weston glanced at Charlie, then at his daughter. He seemed to realize something was wrong and that the girl knew more than she was saying. Charlie tried to look particularly kindly—the sort of fellow you could trust your daughter to. The girl clearly wanted her parents to stay but didn't have the courage to ask them directly.

"All right," said Mr. Weston, "but just for a bit." He took his wife by the elbow and led her out of the living room. When Weston stood between Charlie and his wife, she completely disappeared.

Once the parents were out of sight, the girl sat down on the edge of the couch and began to weep, a wet snuffling noise. Charlie sat beside her, careful not to get too close. She cried for about a minute, and Charlie looked down at the rug, which was rust-colored with an Egyptianish design. Then Charlie checked his watch and when a minute was up, he said:

"You know who the dead girl was. She came to borrow your ID so she could get a job. You didn't know she had anything wrong with her so you gave her what she needed. You were being nice, just doing her a favor. You're not responsible. In a day or so we'll learn the girl's identity and it will be clear to everyone that you've been lying. If you tell me her name right now, then you'll never be bothered about this again."

The girl stopped crying and glanced at Charlie. Gray tearstains dotted her white blouse. "Is that really true?"

"Sure it's true. The girl's family doesn't even know she's dead. What will it look like when it becomes clear you've lied, that you've caused her parents unnecessary strain and worry and kept them from claiming their daughter's body?"

Annie Weston took a deep breath, then spoke all in a rush. "She's the cousin of a boy I know. She's from Fort Edward. Her name's Lynn Schorr. I don't know her father's name. She told me her parents wouldn't let her get a job and that she needed to save the money for college.

I didn't know she was sick." The girl put her face in her hands again. Standing up, Charlie patted her shoulder. It felt warm and bony.

"It wasn't your fault. Thanks for telling me." He walked across the living room and into the hall. Mr. Weston came out of the kitchen when he heard Charlie at the door. He looked at Charlie almost fearfully.

"I must have made a mistake," said Charlie. "In any case, your daughter won't be troubled again."

Fort Edward was a small town about ten miles southeast of Glens Falls. As he drove the red Renault down through Hudson Falls and over to Route 4, he thought about the girl he had known as Annie Weston. Had she known there was something wrong with her brain, thin blood vessels or whatever? Presumably, if she had to get the job without her parents' knowledge, she had known something was the matter. She had been so gentle, Charlie thought, the kind of girl who had easily broken his heart in high school—a shy smile and bottomless blue eyes. And he found himself feeling sorry for Joe Riklin, who must have liked her, maybe even loved her, and now was running away or hiding someplace thinking he had killed her.

If Victor had taken Riklin's picture and that happened to be the only decent picture of Riklin available, then possibly Riklin had run down Victor to make sure the picture didn't end up in the hands of the police. But even as he thought this, Charlie knew it was farfetched. If Riklin had a record, then presumably the police had lots of his pictures. Several years earlier, when Charlie had been chief of security of Lorelei Stables, he had made a point of hiring only ex-cons, and pictures, he knew, were the one thing ex-cons had in great supply.

On the other hand, possibly the picture was of Riklin and the dead girl together. That certainly would be damning evidence if Riklin thought he might be charged with her death. Even if Riklin hadn't been photographed, he still might have searched Victor's office at the hotel and also the detective agency. But that had been done almost too professionally, by someone who was used to doing illegal searches, and, presumably, whoever had done it had found the other roll of film. Someone had run down Victor and three different places had been searched. It was possible that four different people were involved. It was also possible that Riklin had nothing to do with any of it.

Only one Schorr was listed in the Fort Edward phone book, a Henry Schorr who lived on Maple Street. Charlie drove over to the address, which was a tall white Victorian house with long narrow windows. The front yard was bordered with red, yellow and purple flowers, and by the corner of the porch an older man in a green shirt and green work pants was on his hands and knees poking at the dirt with a trowel. As Charlie got out of his car, the man stood up and looked at him, wiping his hands on his pants. It was nearly six-thirty and the lowering sun shone full on the white front of the house, making it sparkle and reflecting off small prisms in several upstairs windows.

"Are you Mr. Schorr?" asked Charlie, fishing several business cards out of the side pocket of his seersucker jacket.

"That's me. What can I do for you?" The man was about sixty and had a small white mustache. He continued to wipe his hands on his pants, then reached out and took the two cards which Charlie handed to him. He looked from one to the other with almost an anxious expression, as if he were expecting bad news. He had a thin face with deep blue eyes. Just like his daughter, thought Charlie.

"Do you have a daughter by the name of Lynn? Blond, blue eyes, sixteen years old, about five foot six or seven, quite slender."

The man handed the cards back but didn't speak. His face, which had been questioning and anxious, seemed to age about ten years. The wrinkles appeared to deepen and turn downward. "She's dead, isn't she," said Mr. Schorr. It wasn't a question. "When did it happen?"

Charlie felt stricken for the man. Over the years, he had broken the news of death to several hundred people. It had never gotten easier. "In Saratoga. She was working as a maid in the Bentley. It was an aneurysm in her brain. I'm afraid you'll have to go down and make an identification. I knew her a little. She seemed like a wonderful person."

"She was wonderful," said Mr. Schorr almost angrily. "But she was also a fool. She knew she was sick. She'd had several small strokes. She knew she shouldn't exert herself. I told her and told her. She left here about three weeks ago while my wife and I were out shopping. She'd written a little note saying she'd be all right and not to worry. My wife wanted to look for her, but what was the point? She'd just go away again. She always said she didn't want to live like a cripple. We did all we could."

The man covered his face with his hands. He cried silently with his shoulders raising and falling—an almost violent movement which seemed to contradict the silence of his grief. Looking toward the house, Charlie saw a white-haired woman staring down from an upstairs window. At first her expression was wondering, then she too burst into tears before disappearing into the room. The white curtains swayed where she had been. A few seconds later the front door was thrown open and she ran across the wooden porch and down the steps, hurried across the yard. When the man heard her, he turned and they put their arms around each other, still crying.

Charlie stood with his hands hanging uncomfortably at his sides, trying not to watch the couple. The woman was probably in her mid-fifties. She wore a blue denim skirt and a light blue blouse. Her white hair was straight and just reached her collar. Her earrings were small chains of red beads, and as she cried they shook back and forth. Charlie turned away to look at the flowers which surrounded the house and yard in an orderly border. He liked flowers but knew the names of only the most obvious ones—roses, violets, dandelions. He had planted some violets out at his cottage on the lake but had no time to take care of them and now they were choked with weeds.

When Charlie looked back at the man and woman, they had stopped crying. The woman had a small green handkerchief and was wiping tears from the man's cheeks. Seeing that Charlie was observing them, they turned to face him, the man keeping his arm around the woman's waist. "I'm sorry for this," he said. "We knew it was coming, we've known it for five or six years. Even so, it doesn't make it easier to bear."

"She wanted to be like other girls," said the woman.

"Everyone liked her," said Charlie clumsily, then added, "Do you mind if I use your phone? I'll find out when you can claim her body." He wanted to say more, but couldn't think of the words. "I can't tell you how sorry I am," he said after another moment.

"The phone's in the living room," said Schorr. "I'll show you." He led the way toward the house while his wife remained behind. The inside of the house was very neat and old-fashioned with soft Victorian sofas and chairs upholstered with a flowered print material, the same flowers that bordered the yard.

"Did your daughter have many friends up here?" asked Charlie.

Schorr seemed surprised by the question. "We disapproved of her going out much because of her health. We tried to be her friends, as well as being her parents, of course."

"Did she ever mention the name Joe Riklin?"

Schorr appeared to think. His hair was thin and his scalp was pink from the sun. "I don't know the name. Should I?"

"Not necessarily. He was a friend of your daughter's and I wondered if he'd met her in Saratoga or had known her before."

"Was he her boyfriend?"

Charlie nodded. It sounded like such an innocent term.

Schorr passed his hand over his brow, then shook his head. "She'd never had a boyfriend before."

He showed Charlie the phone, then left the room. On the mantel was a picture of the girl Charlie had last seen naked and dead at the bottom of a laundry hamper. In the picture she was looking coquettish with her head tilted to one side. The sun shone on her blond hair and her mouth was open slightly as if she were about to speak, to utter some greeting or word of comfort.

Charlie got through to Peterson right away. "The dead girl's name is Lynn Schorr," he said. "She's from Fort Edward. I'm at her parents' house right now. I told them she was dead. You want to talk to her father or send someone up here or tell me where he can call about the body?"

Peterson didn't answer for a moment. Again Charlie

heard his thick breathing, as if he was trying to breathe through a sock. Then there was a long exhalation. "Charlie, just how did you find out about this?"

"I happened to be up in Glens Falls and just stumbled onto it."

There was another pause. " 'Happened'—Charlie, you never just happen to do anything."

"What can I say, chief?"

"Charlie, you're not going to start meddling in police business, are you?"

Charlie chose not to answer. "Have you found out who ran down Victor?"

"We're working on it. Novack's been checking out Victor's apartment. You were right. It seems to have been searched."

Charlie rolled his eyes toward the ceiling. He generally thought of himself as a patient man but he knew that wasn't true. Had he any patience he would have stayed with the police department, one more local boy to offset the FBI types whom Peterson favored.

"But those offices, Charlie, Novack thinks you're wrong about that. Maybe you've been upset. Come on, Charlie, you plan to meddle in this?"

"If you arrest the person who ran down Victor, you won't have to worry about my meddling. Have you found Joe Riklin?"

"No, he must be hiding somewhere, but, Charlie, you got to realize we're working on this as hard as we can. You can't turn it into a personal vendetta."

Charlie listened to Peterson's breathing a little longer. He wondered what Mrs. Peterson thought about it and if it kept her awake at night. "Give me one reason why not," he said at last.

5

There were twenty photographs of Mrs. Heinz—including both profiles and even one of the back of her head as she was walking away. She was a large woman in her late forties with a teasing smile and soft features as if her face had been cut from a huge marshmallow. Dark curls cascaded over her forehead, and her perfect false teeth appeared expensive. Despite the smile, Charlie felt Victor would not have been happy with her.

Charlie was in a back room of Henry Perkins's photography studio looking at the contact sheet from Victor's roll of film. It was shortly after eight in the evening. Henry was in the darkroom printing up the only two photos that seemed likely to be useful. As for the others, besides Mrs. Heinz there were three of the moose's head over the fireplace in the hotel lobby, six of the honeymoon couple who had spent the weekend at the hotel, two of Raoul looking grand, two of Charlie's mother looking charming and one of Charlie himself looking irritated, not to say aggravated.

Charlie had forgotten the picture. Victor had snapped it as Charlie was coming on duty the previous evening. Charlie had just walked through the revolving door and was making a kind of face, wrinkling his nose, squinting at the camera and forcing his mouth into a smile. This surprised Charlie, who liked to think he kept his face a perfect blank. It was a round face with a small bump of a nose, a nose that Charlie thought resembled a toe but here looked more like a grape. He was also slouching, which he found somewhat offensive since he had always believed he kept his back straight and stood as tall as his five feet eight inches would allow. His graying hair was mussed and his jacket untidy. Had Charlie not known the picture was of himself, if it had been a picture of a stranger, then he would have made this person a suspect, some violent character who could have easily run down Charlie's best friend.

The door to the darkroom opened and Henry Perkins emerged holding two eight-by-tens by their corners. "They're still wet," he said. "I'll put them on the table."

Charlie had been in first grade with Henry Perkins. In fact, they been together all through school, even graduating together. Then they had gone into the army—Charlie being stationed in Germany and Henry remaining in the States. Someplace down south, Charlie thought. They had never been pals, but they were close acquaintances, and Charlie liked being with someone he had known for forty years. Perkins had a triangular face and was nearly bald. His chin came to an abrupt point, and once during fourth grade Charlie got him to dip it in ink and try to write with it. Even though Perkins was middle-aged, when Charlie looked at him, he could see all his different faces, ranging back to 1939 when he wore knickers, had his light brown hair parted in the middle and answered to the name of Perky Perkins.

Charlie walked over to the table. The two pictures depicted almost the same scene but from slightly different angles. Both starred the same honeymoon couple featured in the other six pictures, but in one they were on the left and in the other they were on the right, while if the pictures were put together and the couple made to overlap, what emerged was a panorama of the entire bar at the Bentley, complete with ten other people.

"I can make that into one long picture if you want," said Henry. "The two shots must have been taken within seconds of each other. I used to take landscapes like that, all three hundred and sixty degrees, then make a big circular picture. It was almost like being there."

"Sure," said Charlie. "Can you do a couple? Peterson will want one."

As Henry Perkins went back into the darkroom, Charlie bent over the table. He felt particularly attentive because he knew that here was probably the person who had run down Victor as well as whoever had searched the two offices and apartment.

Could it have been the honeymoon couple? That seemed unlikely, since they had eagerly let themselves be photographed. They were young and wore party hats. The man, a thin-faced youth with slicked-back hair, was lifting a cigar with his left hand as he embraced his new wife with his right. She, a beautiful girl whom Charlie recognized as a recent Skidmore graduate, was embracing her husband with her left arm while lifting a glass of champagne with her right. She had the high cheekbones and perfect features of a model. The man too had those same perfect features, so their part of the picture resembled an advertisement, as if they were selling cigars or champagne or the prospect of good times. The young man wore a tuxedo and the woman a low-cut gown and a diamond necklace which glittered in the light from the flash. On the table before them were more glasses, a packet of cigarettes, the champagne bottle and a stuffed toy rabbit with a ribbon around its neck. As far as they were concerned, they were alone in the room, and the other ten people who had been trapped, as it were, in their wedding celebration looked on with amusement, indifference, irritation and, interestingly, fear.

In any case, the honeymoon couple could almost certainly be ruled out. Who else could be ruled out? Presumably, the bartender. Charlie had known him for years and had even employed him despite his long record for car theft and a fondness for driving high-performance automobiles at speeds well above one hundred miles per hour on the Northway between four and six in the morning. His name was Eddie Gillespie and he had a big smile for the camera as he stood polishing a glass behind the long Victorian bar. Most recently he had worked for Victor breaking down motel-room doors as Victor prepared to take hasty pictures of the occupants.

The waitress, also, could probably be ruled out—an attractive Skidmore junior who had been snapped pouring beer into a customer's glass. And that particular customer could be ruled out, since Charlie knew him as a local lawyer. The woman with him was another familiar face. As Charlie recognized her, he felt a little blip of pleasure, since she was rarely in Saratoga or even in the United States. She was an equestrienne by the name of Artemis, a small dark-haired woman in her late thirties who mostly lived in Vienna, although she had a house in Bennington and stabled several horses at a farm near Cambridge. Charlie thought her immensely distinguished. She was staring across the room with an expression of curiosity and concern.

And there was Joe Riklin. At first Charlie didn't recognize him, since he was pushing a cart of dirty dishes toward a door at the left side of the bar and was scowling back over his shoulder. How thin-faced he was, how pointy

and fast-looking, as if always in a hurry. Charlie wondered
what Lynn Schorr had seen in him. But it wasn't an unkind
face, just impatient. Perhaps the scowl indicated he was
unhappy to be in the picture, but maybe he was just critical
of the honeymoon couple, for whom there seemed no past
or future, as if this one moment of celebration could be
stretched out forever. If Riklin's face were blown up, it
would be quite clear, and possibly he hadn't wanted that.
Possibly all the other pictures of him, those in the hands
of the police for instance, were old and inaccurate. If
Riklin believed he had killed Lynn Schorr, even accidentally, and believed he would be accused of murder, then
he might have tried to get this picture. Still, it seemed
unlikely he would run down Victor to do it.

At the bar were three men seated on stools and turned
to face the camera. The two on either side were young
and reminded Charlie of the policemen Novack and Tidings. They had that same lean and professional look. Men
who never overate or indulged themselves, who constantly
exercised and tended to their bodies, who prided themselves on their hardness, their inability to be taken by
surprise. Men with thin lips and small flat ears, well-
defined jaws and narrow eyes. Both were well dressed in
dark suits and had expensive haircuts, although Charlie
guessed that "haircuts" was no longer the accurate word.
Actually, they also reminded Charlie of the photograph
of Jesse James on the wall of his office, an abrupt birdlike
face, perhaps a blue jay or crow, surveying the landscape
for some dead thing to peck at and pluck.

The man between them was elderly, also dressed in a
dark suit, and appeared apprehensive as he looked directly
at the camera. He was leaning back against the bar and
rested a bottle of Budweiser on his knee. He had long
gray hair combed straight back across his head, a neatly

trimmed gray mustache and a heavily lined thin face. Charlie
thought he must be in his mid-seventies, perhaps older.
He also thought he recognized him, but he couldn't find
a name or even an event which made the man click in his
head. The face appeared rough and windburned as if he
had spent a lot of time outside, and his cheeks were sunken
with two indentations the size of golf balls. Charlie kept
staring at the man, trying to will him into memory, but
all he came up with was a picture of the bank robber and
escape artist Willie Sutton. But Sutton was short and wiry,
not long-boned like the man in the picture. And Sutton
didn't have so much hair. And even Willie the Actor couldn't
have faked this one, since he'd been dead for half a dozen
years. But once Charlie thought of Sutton, then he was
stuck and the bank robber's name kept returning again
and again as he stared at the photograph.

That left just two more people, or rather one and a half,
but before Charlie could study them more closely, Henry
Perkins emerged from the darkroom with two pictures.
Each was about ten by fourteen, and they curled at their
edges as Henry put them on the table.

"Pretty neat. They overlapped perfectly. You can see
the whole back of the bar just like a wide-angle lens."

Charlie sometimes thought Henry didn't believe in the
world until he first saw it on celluloid, as if the picture
authenticated real experience, making it believable. This
new picture was lighter and clearer. Charlie was drawn
immediately to a man and woman seated at a table on the
far right. The woman was crying and was in the act of
lifting her hands to her face as she stared at the camera
with what was certainly fear. She wore a dark dress and
her dark hair was like a frame around her pale frightened
face—a thin face but pretty, with a straight nose and large
full lips. The man was to her left and only partly in the

picture, his head being missing except for the tip of his chin. But from his body, he looked like a large man with a slight belly. He wore a dark blazer and gray slacks. His hands were folded on the table near a glass of wine. They were long thin hands. The kind of hands that Charlie imagined pianists to have, and on the little finger of his left hand was a large ring with a stone of some light color, maybe pink or yellow.

"Can you get this guy's face?" Charlie asked.

"I tried," said Perkins. "The chin was the best I could do. The woman looks sad, doesn't she?"

"And scared," said Charlie.

A few minutes later, Charlie was on his way over to the hospital. It was nearly nine and he knew he'd be late for work, but he still wanted to ask Victor about the picture. Charlie was hoping for a quiet night and the possibility of a nap on the cot in Victor's office.

Victor was asleep. Charlie stood in the doorway, undecided whether to wake him or tiptoe back down the hall. The Hungarians had all gone home. Again Charlie was struck by the pallor of Victor's face. The cast on his broken arm and shoulder was raised as if he were warding off a blow. His left leg was lifted high off the bed. Charlie thought Victor had a kind face, although he knew many people disliked him. He wondered how long it would be before there were complaints from the nurses. Within the lipstick heart drawn on his cast, the initials A.G. had been crossed out and replaced with P.R.—V.P. + P.R.

Charlie had just backed out the door when Victor opened his eyes. The two men looked at each other for a few moments without expression, then Victor said, "I'm not happy here, Charlie. There's nothing good to eat and my body hurts."

"Is there anything I can get you, maybe a milkshake or a piece of apple pie?"

"Nah, my stomach's fucked up from the pills. I'd just puke it. At first I thought I was lucky the guy who hit me didn't run over me, now I'm not so sure. I got to be here for a long time. Can you imagine having sex in a rig like this? It'd fuck up your back for sure. You find the guy that did it?"

"Not yet," said Charlie, unrolling the picture. "Tell me about this—do you recognize these people?"

"Hey," said Victor, taking hold of one side of the picture as Charlie held the other, "that's pretty snazzy. Did I take that?"

"Henry Perkins stuck two of the pictures together."

"The happy couple is Peter or Paul Irving and his newly wedded wife Patricia. I must of taken a dozen of them. They're from Utica, like I said, and were up for the weekend. You think they ran me down? I don't trust people who smile so much."

"What time did you take this?"

"About eight o'clock. They were waiting for a table in the restaurant. Eddie Gillespie, the waitress, that guy Riklin, the fellow sitting at the table is a lawyer, the rest I don't know. You think Riklin ran me down?"

"It seems unlikely. What about those three men at the bar? Does that old man look familiar, by any chance?"

Victor squinted at the picture. "Never seen them before."

"Were they around long? I mean, were they staying at the hotel?"

"That I can't tell you, but I have the feeling they only came for dinner. He's a tough-looking old bird, isn't he?"

"What do you mean?" Charlie was still standing next

to Victor, holding the left side of the picture. He bent over slightly to get a better look.

"He looks like he's knocked around a lot."

"You hear anything they said?"

"Not a peep, but I think the old guy was showing them the layout. Those other two look pretty tough themselves, karate salesmen or those guys who expand their chests and break chains."

"What about the woman who's crying and the man she's with?"

"Don't know 'em. I noticed her right away, of course, a real looker. Mature in a way I like them. But she seemed, you know, nervous, what they used to call neurasthenic."

"What about the man?"

"That I can't say. What the hell, all you got's his chin."

"But what did he look like, how old was he?"

"Maybe he was your age or a little younger. I can't put a face to him."

"Was the woman trying to cover her face so she wouldn't be photographed?"

"Hey, Charlie, I was concentrating on the wedding couple. These other people, I didn't see them till later."

"Did they all stay in the bar?"

"Beats me. This Irving guy and his fresh mate wanted some pictures of them standing in the lobby by the stairway, and I was happy to oblige. Boy, if he was the one who ran me down, I'll really be pissed. Who's the dolly with the lawyer?"

"Her name's Artemis. She's a friend of mine."

"She's the one who stands on horses' backs?"

"The very same."

"She seems to be staring pretty hard at that crying woman. Maybe they're wearing the same dress. Females can be pretty touchy about that sort of thing."

When Charlie rolled up the picture and said he had to get back to the hotel, Victor protested that he was bored and needed someone to talk to.

"I was supposed to be at work ten minutes ago."

"Not even a quick game of gin rummy?"

"I'll play you a game tomorrow."

"That's called a brush-off, Charlie. I don't like lying here thinking about my life. It can't stand that kind of scrutiny."

As Charlie drove back to the hotel he kept thinking of the old man in the photograph who reminded him of Willie Sutton. Both had a jauntiness which for Sutton could take the form of reckless daring. One time he single-handedly robbed a bank on 110th Street between Broadway and Amsterdam by knocking on the door before the bank opened and telling the guard he had to use the bathroom. The only catch was that he was wearing a policeman's uniform. On another occasion, dressed up as a Western Union delivery boy, he showed up at a bank before opening with a fake telegram. Was the man in the picture like this, a criminal, or was it just the jaunty quality that seemed familiar?

Charlie parked the Renault and hurried up the front steps of the Bentley. He was almost a half hour late and still had to change. Suzanne stood at the desk. She glanced at him, then looked away. Four elderly couples in golfing togs were lined up to sign the register.

Charlie paused by the desk. "Did Peter or Paul Irving and his wife check out by any chance?"

Suzanne didn't look at him. She was wearing a dark blue velvet suit that made her look like Little Lord Fauntleroy. "Peter Irving. They left this morning. Raoul is waiting to see you. He's in his office."

Groaning, Charlie passed around the registration desk,

then through the anteroom to a door with the word "Manager" written across the frosted glass. Charlie knocked.

"Just a minute," called Raoul.

Ignoring the request, Charlie opened the door. Raoul was changing out of his pinstriped suit. He stood by his desk, balancing on one leg and pulling on his pants. He turned to see Charlie, then had to hop to keep from falling. "I said wait," he said.

"Guess I didn't hear you. Suzanne said you wanted to see me." Charlie wondered what it was about Raoul that filled him with a desire to be bad. He wondered if he had been born Raoul, baptized Raoul. He wondered why he had the constant expression of someone sucking on a lemon. He had a very thin mustache and his dark hair was slicked back with a prominent widow's peak which came to an aggressive point. He reminded Charlie of the actor Don Ameche—not in his role as Alexander Graham Bell but in his more usual one of disappointed lady's man.

"I heard from Suzanne that you've been bothering the maids and I wondered if you had an explanation." Raoul had a high-pitched voice as if he were slightly choking.

"Bothering?"

"Interfering with their work."

"I wanted to see what they knew about the dead girl."

"Wouldn't that be better left to the police?"

"It would take longer that way. Now we know her death was an accident, know her real name and that there's nothing to hurt the hotel." All his life, Charlie thought, he had been slightly on the other side of authority—in school, the army, the police force. Even talking to Raoul he was aware of his complete willingness to deceive and prevaricate just so he'd be left alone.

"I still don't see why you couldn't have let the police handle it," said Raoul, threading a brown belt through the loops of his tan slacks. "After all, you're only night hotel manager."

"I thought it would be faster. I'd heard you were frightened about the hotel's reputation and I thought I could help."

Raoul went to a mirror and began tying his tie—it was blue with a design of small white poodles. After a moment, he said, "So, are you going to stop this pseudo-police work and get back to the business of the hotel?"

"I intend to find the person who ran down Victor."

"Can't Chief Peterson do that?"

When Raoul saw that Charlie wasn't going to answer, he took a pair of silver-backed brushes and began brushing his hair, further dramatizing his widow's peak. "I'm not sure that's legal, Charlie. Certainly I can't permit you to do anything that might hurt the hotel."

"I'm a licensed private detective and I have a client."

"And who is your client?"

"Victor." It seemed to Charlie that although he had known all along that he wanted to find whoever had run down Victor, it wasn't until this conversation that his resolve was entirely established in his mind.

"Charlie, you can't be both a private detective and the night manager of the Bentley." Raoul was looking at Charlie in the mirror as he continued to brush his hair.

"There's nothing you can do about it. I'm here as a favor to my mother, and as soon as the season is over, I'm quitting. You can criticize and complain, but you can't fire me."

Raoul put the brushes back in a wooden box and closed the lid with a snap. "One favor, Charlie—that blue suit you wear each night. Get it pressed, will you?"

As Charlie walked to the door, Raoul called after him,

"By the way, your mother wants to see you. She's in her suite."

Before seeing his mother, Charlie went into his little office, which was down the hall from the kitchen, and changed into his blue suit. Then he inspected himself in the mirror. Maybe it was a little wrinkled, but not badly, not so he thought anybody would notice. Then he noticed a gravy stain on the lapel. Maybe he really was a slob after all. He spat on his fingers, then rubbed at the stain. After a little work, he was able to reduce it to a smudge. Tomorrow I'll get it cleaned, he thought, adding that he should probably even get another suit. But what could he do with two suits?

Suzanne was still at the desk. The lobby was full of ballerinas, part of the New York City Ballet, which was to begin performances the next week—long, leggy girls who took Charlie's breath away.

"I have to talk to my mother," Charlie told her. "Do you mind hanging on for another minute?"

She nodded but made a face to indicate she didn't like it. Charlie crossed the lobby, threading his way between the dancers, then climbed the great staircase with its red carpet and brass railings. At the top was Mabel Bradshaw's suite, which she had designed and decorated herself, guided by notions of beauty that derived, Charlie thought, primarily from Mae West.

Although his mother had always been flamboyant, for much of her life her flamboyance had been curtailed by her poverty. She had married Charlie's father, a gambler, right out of high school, became a mother a year later, then a widow at twenty-two after her husband decided to cope with $25,000 in IOUs by putting a bullet in his head. From then on she had had a series of bad jobs—for years working as a maid in the Grand Union Hotel. After that closed in 1952, she worked as a waitress, saving her pennies for what was originally intended to be a modest Victorian guest house called Happy Haven or the Wayfarers Arms. But instead of putting her pennies in a bank, she had invested in fractions of racehorses—trotters and pacers that raced the small tracks through New York and New England.

She must have been good at picking them, because as time went on she had owned more and more of the horse until she wound up with half a horse named Ever Ready for whom she quit her waitressing job and began touring the country. Then, after two years, she sold Ever Ready for a large chunk of cash, which she took to Atlantic City and substantially increased. Charlie had always believed that in his mother's relationship with his father she had played the victim, but presumably she had also learned quite a bit about blackjack, roulette, poker, craps and those other pastimes to which her husband had dedicated his life. When she returned to Saratoga the previous year she was no longer interested in buying a tourist home and naming it Shady Nook or Bideawee. This, after all, was the 1980s. She had to have a big Victorian hotel and name it the Bentley. She meant to be a great lady.

Charlie rapped lightly on her door, in the middle of which was a brass nameplate with the words "Mabel Bradshaw Prop." A muffled voice told him to enter, and he pushed the door open. The room was done mostly in red: red rugs, red silk hangings, red settees and overstuffed chairs and sofas, red wallpaper with black vertical lines. But set against the red were the thirty or so green plants that hung, perched, balanced and flowered from one side of the room to the other.

Mabel Bradshaw was seated at a dressing table painting

her nails. She was a large woman—busty, blowsy and blond—and wore a red silk dressing gown with an ermine collar. For most of Charlie's life she had been as thin as a rake with mousy brown hair shaped in severe waves, but after she made her money she decided to become another person. Although in her mid-sixties, she looked fifteen years younger, and people intent on pleasing her often said she must be Charlie's sister, even his younger sister. But even though she could seem foolish, Mabel Bradshaw was no fool, and behind the mascara and false eyelashes was a sharp and critical eye.

As Charlie entered, his mother reached out a hand to him. "Dear Charlie, how tired you look."

Although Charlie knew his mother bore him in maternal regard, he was often suspicious, since her ideas for his future seemed to differ radically from his own.

Charlie kissed her cheek, then tried not to sneeze as some powder got in his nose. "Raoul said you wanted to see me."

"Isn't it a tragedy about that girl? Raoul said you were involved."

"Only in the solution end. I thought it might have something to do with Victor getting run down."

"Poor Victor. I've sent him flowers." Not only had Mabel Bradshaw's appearance changed, but her accent had become inexplicably southern—broadened vowels and missing terminal r's. "And did it concern him?"

"Apparently not."

"And I suppose you still must find out who did it?"

"That's right." A heart-shaped box of chocolates lay open on the dressing table. Charlie took one and bit into it, hoping it would be a caramel. Instead, it was some jelly mixture and Charlie wished he could put it back. He held the remaining portion loosely in his hand, and when his mother's attention returned to her fingernails, he tossed the candy toward the wastebasket. It hit the rim and bounced onto the rug. Charlie retrieved it, then dropped it in the basket.

"If you're not going to eat all of it, then I wish you hadn't taken it in the first place," said his mother.

Charlie nodded and tried to keep his face a blank. It amazed him how they always seemed to fall into a child-parent relationship despite his forty-nine years. He imagined being eighty and his hundred-year-old mother telling him what to eat and asking if he had brushed his teeth.

"Raoul's afraid that you might create bad publicity for the hotel. Is that a danger?"

"Not that I can see. I'm just asking a few questions."

"Personally," said his mother, blowing on her nails, "I think any publicity is good publicity unless we have an actual murderer in our midst. Is there any chance of that?"

"Not unless it's Raoul himself," said Charlie.

"Then do what you want," said his mother, looking up at him. "Just don't upset your cousins, and try to be nicer to Raoul. He told me that you didn't like him."

"How peculiar," said Charlie, then he nodded and smiled and tried to look as if everything was all right, as he remained irritated with himself for being unable to throw off the heavy yoke of being a child. As for his cousins, they were three respectable Saratoga businessmen who believed that Charlie's one purpose in life was to tarnish the family name. Charlie had been raised with them and even loved them, but if he never saw them again he'd be perfectly happy.

It was a quiet evening. Charlie checked in half a dozen new guests, answered questions about local restaurants and nightclubs, handed out schedules to the harness track and upcoming events at the Performing Arts Center. He sent up fresh towels to a guest who seemed to spend all his time in the tub. He answered complaints about the champagne. He arbitrated a dispute between an assistant cook and a waitress who had let some food get cold because it was eleven p.m. and at eleven p.m. she always meditated for twenty minutes. The cook knew it, everybody knew it, meditation was her way of life, she said.

Around midnight, he wandered into the bar to talk to the waitress and the bartender, Eddie Gillespie. He had Victor's photograph and hoped they could help him with the identification. Although the general motif of the hotel was Victorian, the bar was solid Art Deco with lots of black and white and angular bits of decoration. In fact, thought Charlie, angles seemed to be what Art Deco was all about.

The bar was empty except for a table of ballerinas drinking strawberry drinks and lounging over their chairs like solidified rivers of plastic. Charlie called over the waitress, whose name was Bridget, and asked Gillespie to bring him a Rolling Rock, wondering if he'd ordered the beer because Raoul had said that hotel employees couldn't drink on the job. Also, Raoul thought beer was low-class. Charlie unrolled the photograph on the bar and Bridget leaned over his shoulder. A dark wave of hair fell forward, half-obscuring her face.

"I look bored," she said. "If Raoul saw that, he'd give me a lecture about being cheerful."

"Not me," said Eddie Gillespie. "Look at that smile. I should get a raise." He did a little drumroll on the bar with the tips of his fingers, then spun on his toes so his artfully tousled black hair flickered and shone. He was an athletic young man who maintained an almost romantic relationship with a series of Nautilus machines at a local health club.

"What about the others?" asked Charlie. "Do you know those men seated at the bar?"

"They were just here for a couple of drinks," said Eddie. "I thought they were doing a lot of arguing."

"They'd asked for a table in the restaurant," said Bridget, "then changed their minds."

"What were they arguing about?" asked Charlie.

Eddie poured a little Vichy in a glass, then added a wedge of lemon. "I wasn't paying attention," he said, sipping the Vichy. "But the younger guys seemed to be complaining. I had the idea they were making fun of the older one, although he didn't seem to mind."

"What kind of tip did they leave you?"

"Nothing at all."

"That old guy strikes me as familiar," said Charlie. "You seen him around before?"

"Not me," said Eddie. "They were complete strangers. On the other hand, I know what you're saying. He looks familiar. Maybe he's been on TV or something."

"What about you, Bridget?"

"I'd never seen them before either. But the old guy was nice. I'd gone to some trouble to get them a table for dinner and when they canceled the old guy slipped me five dollars."

"What was your impression of them?"

"At first I thought the old guy was an uncle or something," said Bridget. "Then I decided they hardly knew each other."

"Those other guys were pretty tough," said Eddie. "Ex-Vietnam gone mean."

"You mean they were crooks?"

"Not necessarily, just tough, that's all."

"What about the woman who's crying? Was she staying at the hotel?"

"I think they just came in for drinks. They too left right away," said Bridget.

"What about the man? What did he look like?"

Gillespie tugged at his chin. "I don't know, sort of regular-looking. In his mid-forties, pretty well dressed."

"Did he have a beard, mustache? Did he wear glasses, was he bald, did he have a hook nose, straight nose, thin-lipped, full-lipped?"

"No," said Bridget, "Eddie's right. He was pretty regular-looking—except he was getting bald. Maybe a little heavyset, a regular face, not bad-looking, but not handsome either. And glasses, maybe he wore glasses. I'm not sure."

"How tall was he?"

"About six feet," said Eddie. "He was getting a little flabby, like he used to play ball, then let it go and was starting to get fat."

"What about that ring he's wearing—do you remember the color of the stone?"

"Yellow," said Bridget. "Bright yellow."

Charlie finished his beer, thought about having another, then decided against it. What he wanted most was to go to sleep. No dreams, no tossing and turning, just sleep. "And what about Riklin?" he asked. "You have any idea where he might be hiding out?"

Bridget had gone over to the table of dancers to give them their check.

"What kind of trouble is he in?" asked Gillespie.

"Basically, no trouble at all. The girl's death was accidental. I figure he panicked, thought he'd be blamed for it, put the body in a laundry hamper, then disappeared.

The police still think he ran down Victor, but that's unlikely. The only problem is if the police catch him, then it might get rough. So I thought it'd be better if I could find him first, just to keep his head from getting bashed in."

"He's a pretty good kid," said Eddie. "Got a temper, but he's okay. I guess I've known him since he was about seven. My best friend here in Saratoga, Bobby Lang, he's got a younger brother named Raymond and Raymond is Joe Riklin's best friend. So when I'm over at Bobby's house, I sometimes run into Joe. He was pretty hot on that maid. Can you imagine being with a girl and having her die on you? Even if you didn't like her much, it'd be depressing."

"Where can I find this Lang?" asked Charlie.

"Raymond and Bobby share a sleazebox over on the west side on Franklin Street right across from a Gulf station. That's where they work. Bobby's a pretty good mechanic, and Raymond pumps gas. I bet Raymond knows what Joe's up to. They're pretty tight. Just don't get me in trouble, okay?"

"One other thing," asked Charlie. "This old guy, could he be an ex-con?"

Eddie again looked at the picture, bending over the bar to stare at the old man's face. "Maybe you got something there. Sure, he's been in the joint. He's got that gray quiet look."

6

At noon the next day, Charlie was sitting at the end of his rickety dock dangling his feet above the water. It was warm and sunny and Charlie could feel the warmth on his bald spot. Out on the lake were a half-dozen boats with solitary fishermen—older men, presumably retired, who wouldn't catch anything and to whom it didn't matter. Charlie sipped a cup of coffee and criticized himself for not getting up an hour earlier so he could get into the Saratoga YMCA and swim his beneficial mile. As it was, he felt the fat globules fastening and increasing on his body, puffing him up to twice his present size. No wonder Doris had dumped him for the science teacher. Who wanted to be courted by the Pillsbury Doughboy?

Charlie had gone home from the hotel that morning at six. It had been a quiet night except for a dog that had sneaked through the lobby and started barking up on the third floor. In any case, Charlie had slept about four hours on the cot in Victor's office, which made his sleeping late this morning even less forgivable. One of Charlie's respectable cousins always maintained that a mentally healthy person needed only four hours sleep a night, and while Charlie didn't really believe this, part of him felt that his own requirement of eight or more hours was a sign of neurosis and spiritual turpitude.

Charlie had brought the photograph with him onto the dock. Unrolling it, he looked at it again. Was the old man an ex-con? If so, then possibly Peterson would recognize him. The jaunty quality was a kind of attentiveness, as if he were ready with a wisecrack or argument. His head was tilted to one side and there was a twist to his mouth. Again Charlie thought of Willie Sutton, whom the New York City police had once called the Babe Ruth of bank robbers, although considering that Willie had spent thirty-five years in prison the nickname seemed misplaced.

Then Charlie looked at the crying woman and again wondered why she was crying, looked at the man who was with her and wondered about the significance of the ring with the yellow stone. And there was Joe Riklin looking over his shoulder as he pushed a cart of dishes toward the kitchen. Best settle with him before dealing with the others. The pair with the old man looked tough enough not to care two cents about running down someone. But why try to kill Victor just to get this photograph? Why did it matter?

Half an hour later Charlie was driving into Saratoga to see Chief Peterson. The car windows were rolled down and the smell of fresh-cut grass was everywhere. As he drove up Union Avenue, he looked over at the track being made ready for the races in August—the stands being painted, red geraniums being planted in their black kettles. This year, Charlie decided, he would approach his betting systematically—get a book, learn about the horses. Even so, he knew it would do no good, that he'd continue to bet according to a whim or foolish idea like putting five dollars on the horse that nodded or blinked in his direction. It was for suckers like me, he thought, that betting was invented.

When Charlie entered Peterson's office, he found the police chief hanging a frame with four blue ribbons on the wall behind his desk. Peterson raised, trained, bred and exhibited Irish setters and his office was full of trophies, ribbons and plaques celebrating his success. He took this so seriously that Charlie often felt the real reason Peterson was such an eager defender of law and order was just to make sure that nothing disturbed his dogs—high-strung creatures that seemed constantly ill at ease.

"I have those pictures," said Charlie, "the ones that someone half-killed Victor to get." He handed Peterson one of the long photographs. The police chief looked at it as if he couldn't imagine what Charlie was talking about.

"Just one picture?" asked Peterson. "Weren't there others?" Peterson walked to the window to look at the photograph in a better light.

"That's the only important one, but I brought the contact sheet so you could see for yourself." Charlie handed Peterson the sheet of pictures. "That woman is a Mrs. Heinz. Victor is interested in her. Have you found any trace of Riklin?"

"We're still looking," said Peterson. "That's a pretty good likeness of him here."

"Do you know any of those guys sitting at the bar?" asked Charlie. "I thought the old guy looked familiar."

Peterson studied the photograph. He had thick bushy eyebrows, which Charlie thought he made as bushy as possible for their ominous effect. "Never seen them before. You really have Eddie Gillespie working for you? I wouldn't let him within a mile of a cash register of mine."

"What about the woman who's crying?" asked Charlie. "Is she familiar?"

"No, the only people I know are Riklin, Gillespie and that lawyer, Frankie Schwartz. Who's that woman he's with?"

"Her name's Artemis. She's an equestrienne."

"How'd you get these pictures?" asked Peterson.

Charlie explained how Victor had left the film at the Backstretch and how Henry Perkins had developed it.

"These are evidence, Charlie," said Peterson. "You should of brought me the film right away. How come you had it developed?"

"Because I wanted to see the pictures."

"Charlie, this film is police business and you've no right to be fooling with it. You have everything here, all the pictures and negatives?"

"Sure," Charlie lied.

"Look, Charlie, I know you're worked up about Victor, but we'll get this guy Riklin. It's only a matter of time."

Peterson walked back to his desk and began fiddling again with the frame containing the four blue ribbons. He couldn't get it exactly straight.

"Did you talk to the dead girl's parents?"

"Yeah, they made the ID on the body last night. A funeral home in Hudson Falls is picking her up this afternoon."

"When's the funeral?"

"I don't know, later this week. What do you care?"

"I liked her," said Charlie. "I'd like to go. You know the name of the funeral home?"

"I'll get it for you."

"One other thing," said Charlie, moving toward the door. "If I were you I'd run a check on that old fellow. I think he's an ex-con."

Peterson looked skeptical, then resigned. Too many times he had dismissed Charlie's hunches and then regretted it. "Maybe I will, but look, what's he doing? Having a beer, talking with his friends. Where's the trouble?"

"Some people went to a lot of trouble to get this film," said Charlie, "and I don't think it was Mrs. Heinz. If the guy's a crook, it would seem worth your while to find out."

Five minutes later Charlie was driving across town to visit Raymond Lang, who Gillespie had said was Joe Riklin's best friend. He found him at the Gulf station on Franklin in the process of changing a tire. He was a dark-eyed young man in a green uniform and a yellow cap with a patch showing a bulldog and the words "Mack Trucks." Charlie gave him his two cards, then stood back while Lang looked from one to the other. A marmalade cat emerged from the office, walked over to Charlie and began rubbing against his legs. It made Charlie realize that he had forgotten to feed Moshe.

"So what d'you want with me?" asked Lang. His hands were greasy and the grease got on Charlie's business cards.

"Well," said Charlie, "I've got a small problem. Joe Riklin works at the hotel . . ."

"Who'd you say?" asked Lang, giving the greasy cards back to Charlie. They were standing in one of the three bays of the garage.

"Joe Riklin."

"Gee, I'm afraid I don't know him."

Charlie reached down and scratched the marmalade cat behind the ears. Already, his eyes had begun to water. "That's funny. I heard you'd been best friends since you were both three years old. Why don't you listen to me before you start getting protective? Riklin thinks the police want him for killing his girlfriend. As it happens, her death was accidental. She had weak blood vessels in her brain and had a kind of stroke. Actually, the police are looking for him for running a guy down on the street yesterday morning, but I don't think he did that. What I want is to clear this up so I can get on with some other stuff—that means taking Riklin downtown, settling this, then getting him back to his job at the hotel so we don't have to hire someone else."

"Joe doesn't even have a car," said Lang. "He's got an old Vespa that he buzzes around on. What do you mean, the girl's death was accidental?" Lang poked the cat with his work boot and it took a swipe at his toe.

"Just what I said. The walls of the blood vessels were too thin. She had what's called a berry aneurysm. She was born with this condition and it was only a matter of time before something happened. I figure Riklin's blaming himself. He probably thinks he killed her."

"That's true enough," said Lang. "They were together in bed and she just died. Joe really liked her, I mean like he loved her."

"So where is he?"

Raymond Lang didn't answer. A bell rang twice and Charlie looked to see an old Ford drawing to a stop in front of the gas pump. Lang leisurely walked out to the car, spoke to the driver, then walked back to the pump. Charlie glanced around the garage. He found waiting in garages one of the most boring things in the world. The marmalade cat continued to rub against his legs. Charlie decided he'd have to go over to Victor's apartment after leaving here and feed Moshe, maybe change his cat box as well.

When Lang returned, Charlie said, "If the police find Riklin, they'll probably hurt him. They'll even put him in jail. If I'm the one to find him, he'll be back at his job this afternoon." Charlie hoped that was true.

Raymond Lang nudged the cat again with his boot and

it ran under a workbench. "You know Eddie Gillespie, don't you? He used to work for you."

"He still does. He's a bartender at the hotel."

"But in that detective business, he did some work there. Eddie says you're a good guy, even though you used to be a cop."

"Anybody can make a mistake," said Charlie.

"You see," said Lang, "I'm worried about Joe. He's pretty moody. He's all by himself in this cabin and if he keeps thinking he killed this girl, well, I'm afraid what he might do."

"Where's the cabin?" asked Charlie.

"Just one thing. If you're lying, if Joe ends up in jail, then you better watch your back. I don't care who your friends are."

"Where's the cabin?" Charlie repeated.

"Up past Lake George near Crane Mountain. I'll show you on the map."

Crane Mountain was fifty miles northwest of Saratoga and twenty miles west of Lake George. Charlie had once climbed it as a kid with some hardy Boy Scouts. The blackflies had begun on him at the bottom of the trail and the mosquitoes started about ten feet later. Near the top was a clear lake where he'd been able to wash the crushed bugs from his body, and at the very top was a watchtower with a wonderful view which Charlie would have appreciated more had his eyes not been almost swollen shut.

The cabin where Joe Riklin was hiding appeared to be on the west side of the mountain and not very far up. Charlie was wearing his blue seersucker jacket and broken-down loafers. He figured he was good for a quarter-mile walk, no more.

As he drove he kept glancing at the photograph on the

seat beside him. Again and again he was drawn to the old man. He was certain he had seen the face before but in his memory it was a younger face. If the man was an ex-con, then perhaps he had been involved with the gambling and rackets in Saratoga during the twenties and thirties. Even Willie Sutton had been pressured by Dutch Schultz to join his gang. Schultz was the biggest fence in New York City, which was how Sutton got to know him, since at that time he was robbing jewelry stores. Schultz was also on the board of directors of the syndicate that ran Saratoga's casinos and nightclubs. He had controlled a huge number of crooks, bank robbers, prostitutes and other lawbreakers until he tried to put a contract on Thomas Dewey and the rest of the mob decided he was too dangerous to have around. Even Charlie's father had been forced to pay him money for about a year, and Charlie wouldn't have been surprised if this old fellow in the picture had been in league with him too.

Charlie drove along a blacktop county road looking for a dirt turnoff to his left which Raymond Lang had said would take him to the trail leading to Riklin's cabin. Technically, the cabin belonged to his uncle, but Riklin had free use of it. Before leaving Saratoga, Charlie had stopped to feed Moshe, and his nose was still running. He had no tissue or handkerchief and was forced to blot his nose on the road map. The day had remained sunny and all the windows of the Renault were rolled down.

The turnoff was in the middle of the woods. Charlie proceeded along the dirt road, really no more than a track, until he could go no farther, then he parked and got out. There was no sound except for the nagging of a squirrel and a few distant crows. Charlie searched around in the dirt until he found the tire tracks of what he guessed was Riklin's Vespa. He followed the tracks along the trail until they disappeared. Already the blackflies had formed a cloud in front of his face. He slapped at them with two hands, and whenever he crushed one he felt a vindictive pleasure.

The cabin was about a mile uphill from where Charlie had parked, and by the time he reached it he was tired and sweating and had at least a dozen bug bites which he knew would plague him for several days. It was a small log cabin, one room and a loft, with a screened-in porch and a fieldstone chimney on the left side. Charlie climbed the steps to the porch and knocked on the door. No answer. Trying the knob, he found the door was unlocked. He gave it a push and it swung open.

"Hello?"

As yet, he hadn't decided on a plan of attack. Since Riklin had done little that was wrong, it seemed inappropriate to sneak up on him, even if Charlie could have gotten through the woods unheard. On the other hand, if Riklin believed he was wanted for murder, then he might be scared and dangerous. It seemed to Charlie that a sort of bumptious obviousness was his best ploy—all innocence and surprise.

Charlie stepped into the middle of the cabin, which was furnished with a cot and a couple of chairs. Someone was clearly staying here. Clothes were scattered around, as were food wrappers and an empty container of orange juice. On a table was a box of corn flakes, evaporated milk, bread, cheese, several cans of Pabst and a bag of sugar.

Charlie went back onto the screened porch to wait. "Hello," he shouted again. "Joe Riklin, I want to talk to you!"

Next to the cabin was something covered with a gray tarpaulin. Charlie went down the steps to look. Pulling the tarpaulin aside, he found an old and rust-colored Vespa. At least Riklin was still nearby.

Charlie turned away and as he did so there was a flash of movement as somebody dropped through the air. He crouched and spun around, just as Riklin landed in front of him. He had been on the porch roof, and if Charlie had been any slower, Riklin would have landed on his back.

"Jesus," said Charlie. "You nearly scared me to death."

Then he saw that Riklin had a hunting knife, and just as he noticed it, Riklin slashed at him. Charlie jumped backward. To his right along the side of the cabin was stacked wood for the fireplace. Grabbing a branch about two feet long, Charlie swung it toward Riklin, forcing him to retreat.

Riklin looked furious. He wore jeans and a jean jacket, and although Charlie knew he was eighteen, he looked younger. He was clean-shaven and Charlie guessed he never needed to use a razor. His red hair hung down to his eyes and he stood in a crouch, moving the knife back and forth across Charlie's stomach.

"I'm not going to jail," said Riklin in a flat voice. "I'll kill you first."

"Why should you go to jail?" asked Charlie. He held the branch in both hands and kept parrying Riklin's moves with the knife. All the birds had stopped chirping, and the woods seemed completely still.

"Don't play dumb with me. You're Bradshaw, the big detective. You want to arrest me for murder."

"No, the girl had a birth defect, something wrong with the blood vessels in her brain. Her death was accidental."

"You're lying."

"Talk to her parents. Her name was Lynn Schorr. Did you know her name was Lynn?"

"She'd told me. What d'you mean, her brain was bad?" There was an urgency in Riklin's question. Charlie guessed he'd been living with the thought that he had killed Lynn Schorr for about thirty-six hours.

"Not her brain, it was the blood vessels. That's why her parents wouldn't let her get a job, why she had to get a fake ID and run away. Call her parents, call the police, you can even call the coroner, but stop being stupid out here in the woods." The blackflies were swarming around Charlie's face, but he didn't want to let go of the branch. Even though Riklin seemed to have a trace of doubt, he was still angry.

"The real charge against you," continued Charlie, "is for running down Victor Plotz yesterday morning on Broadway—hit-and-run, attempted murder. The police are pretty eager to tie you to that one."

Riklin stopped swinging the knife. "Who the hell's Victor Plotz?"

"The hotel detective. He was snapping pictures in the cocktail lounge Saturday night and got a good likeness of you."

"But why should I run him down?"

"In order to get the picture. Someone ran him down, stole his camera and searched his apartment. The police think that after the girl died you panicked and decided to remove all evidence of yourself. You remembered those pictures Victor was taking and went after them."

"That's stupid. What am I going to do, hit him with my Vespa?"

"So where were you yesterday morning?" Charlie knew he could knock the knife from Riklin's hand but he decided to wait.

"I came out here. I figured I could hide here for a month or so, then get up to Canada."

"What happened with the girl?"

"I don't know. We were in her room. Both of us, we were asleep. She'd set the alarm for six so I could get out without anyone knowing. The alarm went off. I woke up and looked at her. She was dead. Her eyes were open and she was looking at the ceiling. So calm, you know, like nothing was bothering her." As he talked about it, the anger left his face and he seemed about ten years old. He also looked tremendously sad.

"Why'd you put her body in the laundry hamper?"

"Because she was supposed to start work at seven. If she wasn't there, they'd come looking for her. I figured if I put her in the hamper that'd give me more time to get away. I didn't know what had happened but I was sure I'd get blamed. The other girls, they knew we were sleeping together. I mean, I loved her, I wanted to marry her. She didn't want to. She liked me fine but she just didn't want to get married."

"She was only sixteen," said Charlie. Cautiously, he swatted a mosquito that was biting his cheek. Riklin didn't seem to notice.

"So what? Lots of people get married that young. But she wanted to go back to school in the fall. I figured I'd go up to Glens Falls and get some kind of job so I could keep seeing her. I know what you're thinking, that she wasn't serious. But she was, we were both serious. We were going to wait and after she graduated, we'd get married. I was even going to go to the community college. Did she know she had something wrong?"

"That's what her parents said."

"She kept saying we didn't have any time. I didn't know what she meant. She was nice, you know. I told her I'd been in jail, that I used to steal cars. But she told me I'd grown up, that I wasn't that kind of person anymore. I don't know, I never thought about it. But I wasn't going back to jail again, that I can tell you for sure."

"What did you do after you left the hotel?"

"I snuck out the back, then I rode over to Schuylerville to see this guy who used to be a teacher of mine, Mr. Lasorella. He's okay—I mean, I can trust him. I told him what'd happened and asked what I should do. He gave me breakfast. It was his idea I should see the police. He didn't pressure me, he just said that's what I should do. I said I'd think it over, but there was no way I was going to let the cops get me. So when I left I bought some stuff and came up here."

"What time did you leave his house?"

"Around nine."

"So you don't even have to worry about running down Victor. You were with this teacher when it happened."

"Yeah, that's what I've been telling you." Riklin had stepped back a few feet and held the knife at his side.

"Look, why don't you come with me to Saratoga. We'll talk to Chief Peterson and get this straightened out. Then you can go back to the hotel. You want that job or you want to lose it? Suzanne's pretty unhappy with you."

"I'm not going anywhere."

"Don't be foolish. Her death was an accident and you've got an alibi for Victor. You've nothing to worry about."

"I told you," said Riklin, "I don't like jail. I'm not going anywhere, and now I got to figure what to do with you." The soft quality left his face and he raised the knife a few inches.

Now it was Charlie's turn to get angry. Swinging the branch, he flung it at Riklin's feet so the boy had to jump not to be hit. "So stab me, then you'll really be in trouble. I already said you won't go to jail. I spent twenty years as a cop; I know. We'll see Peterson and it'll be all right.

Either kill me or let's get out of here. The bugs are driving me crazy."

Even as Charlie was shouting he was thinking of the old man in the photograph. Maybe Riklin knew a little about him. Or maybe there was someone else in Saratoga who could help. He didn't think Riklin would stab him. The boy had calmed down and it would take a lot to cold-bloodedly stick a person with a knife.

"What are you waiting for?" shouted Charlie. "Either stab me or let's go!"

"Stop yelling," said Riklin, putting the knife in a sheath at his waist. "You sound just like my fuckin' aunt."

7

Maximum Tubbs was the very definition of dapper as he walked across the small dance floor to where Charlie was sitting. He was a small man, about the size of a steeplechase jockey, and wore a three-piece dove-gray suit which exactly matched his thick silver hair. Charlie thought he carried his seventy years as if they were a trifle.

Charlie had asked Tubbs to meet him at the bar of the Bentley around ten Tuesday evening. He had come on duty an hour before, then had worked frantically arranging the room assignments for thirty members of the Westchester Ballet Club who were arriving by train the following Monday for the opening of the New York City Ballet.

Earlier that evening Charlie had had to deal with problems surrounding Joe Riklin. Peterson at first wanted to book him, charging him with hiding the body and not reporting the death. This had been in Peterson's office, where Charlie had shown up with Riklin around six o'clock. On hearing that Peterson wanted him in jail, Riklin would have fled had not Charlie kept a grip on his arm. Charlie knew that Peterson was irritated that he'd circumvented the authorities by finding Riklin himself and showing he was, on occasion, better at police work than Peterson's professionals.

It wasn't that Charlie approved of Riklin's decision to hide the body and run away, but he understood the young man's fear and consequently protested his arrest so strongly that Peterson had agreed to turn Riklin over to Charlie's custody while he discussed matters with the district attorney. At the moment Riklin was back busing tables, and every time he passed through the bar he would give Charlie a big grin.

Charlie was happy to see Tubbs. There was an eagerness about the man that cheered him. Although Charlie was not related to Tubbs, he saw him as part of his immediate family in a way that he never did his respectable cousins. Tubbs had begun gambling in Saratoga in 1931, and at this late date probably even he was unsure if his name had originally been Maxwell or Maximilian. Whenever he gambled, he bet to the limit, which was why he was called Maximum to his face and less flattering names behind his back. He had won and lost several fortunes and didn't care as long as he had money enough to continue. He had gambled in Saratoga when it was legal and gambled now that it was illegal, which had led to his friendship with Charlie, who had arrested him about twenty times during his years as a policeman.

Maximum Tubbs had known Charlie's father, had even been friends with him, at least to the extent that two gamblers can ever be friends. He would describe his father's quick laugh and willingness to bet on anything— how long it would take a fly to land on a sugar cube or whether he could pitch a penny down a woman's cleavage. Maximum had also known Dutch Schultz, Lucky Luciano, Owney Madden and even Arnold Rothstein, losing to and winning from them all. For this reason, Charlie had thought he might recognize the old man in the photograph.

"Say, Charlie," said Tubbs, "what're you doing in a phony-baloney dump like this?"

"I don't know," said Charlie defensively. "My mother owns it. What's wrong with it anyway?"

"The 1930s, you know, they came and went a long time ago. I mean, you hear this shit about the new Saratoga, all it is is a bunch of stores and restaurants and nightclubs pretending to be something else. It's what they call packaging. That's what Saratoga is about these days: packaging, turning the whole place into a fucking commodity. Like this bar and all this Art Deco shit, it's packaging, make people think they're not just having a drink in a bar, they're having a meaningful experience, so instead of charging them a buck for a Budweiser, you charge 'em three bucks for the experience with a beer thrown in." Tubbs took a handkerchief out of his back pocket, wiped off the stool next to Charlie and sat down.

"You been down in your luck?" asked Charlie. "Losing a few card games?"

"Nah, I just feel I'm being priced out of this burg. Even the guys I shoot craps with have college degrees. It's like everyone's pretending to be at a costume ball. Least the harness track's about the same, just people betting on horses and no frills—your good old blue-collar horse race." Maximum Tubbs flicked a speck of dust from his sleeve. "So I gather you got a problem. What can I do for you?"

"You want something to drink?"

"Sure, give me a three-dollar Bud."

Charlie called over Eddie Gillespie and relayed the order, then he unrolled the photograph on the bar. "Who's the old guy?" he asked.

Tubbs took a pair of gold-rimmed glasses from the inside pocket of his suit coat, perched them on the tip of his nose and leaned over the picture.

"Well, well, well," he said after a minute. "I figured he was dead."

"Who was dead?"

"Hey, you took his picture right here, right on this very stool."

"Victor took it," said Charlie somewhat impatiently. "Who is he? Do you know him? I mean, I almost recognize him but I can't think of the name."

"I never knew him personally, although I saw him probably a half-dozen times. His name's Tommy Polanski. He's a crook but not a bad guy. He used to be a bank robber, also he knocked over a couple of armored trucks. And he escaped from the joint a couple of times, too, although only once did he stay out awhile."

"Just like Willie Sutton," said Charlie half to himself.

"A little bit," said Tubbs, "except Sutton had brains and a sense of humor. Polanski just wanted to be a big shot. Like he wanted people to think he was hot stuff. Can't figure it myself. I mean, he must have spent thirty years in jail."

"I remember some of it," said Charlie. "In fact, I bet I've got a picture of him." As a hobby, Charlie read and collected information about great outlaws of the past, and included in his collection was a shoebox full of photos of desperadoes living and dead: Bonnie Parker smoking a cigar, the corpse of Baby Face Nelson held up by a half-dozen cops and someplace, maybe, Tommy Polanski.

"Wasn't there something about ballistics and a cop getting killed?" asked Charlie.

"That's right, that was his big piece of bad luck. He

and about four other guys knocked over a bank in Albany in the late twenties and a cop was killed. They swore they didn't do it, but you know how it goes. I guess they nearly got the chair but instead they ended up with life terms. Polanski was sent to Dannemora. Around 1935 he manages to break out and just at that time ballistics tests are coming in and an appeal from one of the other robbers shows the cop was killed by another cop's gun. So they all get their sentences reduced and are eligible for parole, except not Tommy Polanski. He's already on the outside, has knocked over another half-dozen banks and done a Brink's truck. He's able to stay out about six years, then he's picked up around 1940, '41, just walking down the street. Some cop makes the ID and that's that. They got him in Utica of all places. So now he goes to Attica and he's there twelve or fifteen years before he gets a parole. He comes out and starts doing banks and armored trucks again. He does these snazzy, well-planned jobs but, you know, after a couple of years someone squeals and by the late fifties he's back in Attica again. And that's the last I know. To tell you the truth, I thought he'd died there.

"I ran into him here in the thirties. Some of the big racketeers were giving him protection, so he was around off and on. Then I guess he became too hot so they told him to get lost. He was a quiet kind of guy, although he could tell a good story. It's funny, what he really wanted was attention. He wanted other crooks to think he was the real article. He had two older brothers in the rackets. One got shot up driving a beer truck in Albany in the twenties. The other landed in prison for knocking over a grocery store. Tommy was just following in the family tradition. When he got out of jail in the fifties I guess he never thought about going straight. Some guys I knew said they'd seen him in Saratoga, but I never ran into him. All the cops were on the lookout for him. No one wanted him around."

"You know who those other men are?" asked Charlie, pointing to the picture.

"Nope, they're too young for me. Maybe they're cops—they got that tough look about them."

"What do you think Polanski was doing in Saratoga?"

"Beats me, but he used to spend a lot of time here. Maybe he was just checking out the old place."

"Was he dangerous?"

"Not that I know of. The only shooting was that cop in Albany, then I guess he winged a guard in a Brink's truck. He liked to do these jobs that were like big jigsaw puzzles, jobs that everyone else thought couldn't be pulled off."

Charlie told Maximum Tubbs how Victor had been run down on Broadway and how someone had searched for the roll of film.

"Seems out of character for Polanski. Smacking a guy with a car, you gotta be pretty desperate. Maybe it was one of the guys with him. The question, of course," said Tubbs, finishing his Budweiser, "is why they wouldn't want their pictures taken, which suggests a range of possibilities and one pretty big one."

"Like what?" asked Charlie, already knowing the answer.

"Like maybe they got a job in mind."

"Isn't Polanski too old for that?"

"He's not so ancient. Maybe he's got five years on me, and I can still shuffle a deck and know where I've put the aces. Anyway, it depends what you're looking for. If what you're after is respect, then perhaps you never give up."

* * *

Wednesday morning when he got home from the hotel around six, Charlie fetched the box of photographs from the back of his bedroom closet and began looking through them. Here was Jesse James lying in his coffin, the Wild Bunch posing for a formal photograph in Fort Worth, John Dillinger in sailor's uniform while serving aboard the battleship *Utah*, Al Capone playing gin rummy with a guard on the train to Leavenworth.

The sun was bright over the lake and Charlie took the pictures out to the dock along with a glass of orange juice and an English muffin. Charlie guessed he had five hundred pictures, and after looking through them for half an hour, he found the one he wanted: Tommy Polanski, age thirty or so, sought for numerous robberies and for escaping from Dannemora, pausing in his flight from justice to have a formal photograph taken in Poughkeepsie. He stood, it seemed, on a sort of stage. Behind him was a painted backdrop of foliage—rosebushes presumably, but badly done. He wore a dark suit and had one hand in his pocket and the other on the globe of the world. Glittering on his tie was a diamond stickpin. Mustache, thin face, thick black hair, chin tilted up and his lips set in a wide grin, his eyes far apart and crinkled at the edges with good cheer as if he had just thought of a joke. To Charlie there was nothing mean about the face like Capone's hired killers John Scalise and Albert Anselmi or crazy like Clyde Barrow or vicious like Piker Ryan of the New York Whyos Gang. Still, the face had an obsessive quality, as if this was a person who would define a course of action, then stick to it no matter what.

Walking back to his cottage, Charlie got the picture Victor had taken on Sunday to compare the two faces. Forty-five years had done Polanski a lot of damage but hadn't beaten him. His face still had that obsessive quality, yet now it seemed more stubborn—the set of his jaw, the way his teeth were clamped shut, but even with that anxious expression there was still humor and a readiness to laugh. Charlie also saw pride in the face, and dignity as well. His dark suit with its narrow lapels was out of fashion but still impeccable, and it fit him perfectly. Again Charlie wondered what Polanski was doing in Saratoga and who his companions were. As always Charlie then looked at the other faces: the honeymoon couple, Artemis and the lawyer, Eddie Gillespie and Riklin, the crying woman and the man with the yellow ring. Then he realized it was nearly seven and he was exhausted. He had stripped his bed the previous day in order to wash the sheets and had forgotten to make it again. No matter, he'd sleep on the pad. He got undressed and pulled the blankets over his head. The room was bright with morning sun. Sometime, he thought, he'd like a job where he kept regular hours.

Six hours later Charlie was laboriously pulling his body back and forth across the swimming pool of the Saratoga YMCA. Too many days without regular exercise was making him feel as if he had surrendered entirely to the forces of entropy. He imagined becoming one of those fat people who are confined to oversized wheelchairs and wheeze dreadfully. Charlie was not a particularly fast swimmer but he was stubborn, and after finishing the seventy-two lengths that made up a mile, he hauled himself out of the pool and returned to the locker room to shower.

About a dozen men were either preparing to swim or had just finished. Charlie knew most of them, had known them for years and in several cases had known them all his life. He liked that, liked sharing a sense of history with someone. As Charlie dressed, he exchanged greetings and small talk. Several of the men knew Victor and asked Charlie to take him their best. This fabric of behavior often struck Charlie as frighteningly thin, since there were times in the past when he had done something or had been accused of doing something which had made these men think they'd be endangering their good names to be seen talking to him. So although Charlie enjoyed this loose camaraderie, he didn't put much faith in it, nor did he really believe it.

Leaving the Y around one-thirty, Charlie drove down Broadway to the hospital to see Victor. That morning while Charlie slept, rain clouds had moved in over the Hudson River Valley area, and occasionally from the west came the rumble of thunder.

Victor was watching a quiz show on the TV and leafing through an old *Playboy*. He seemed poised on the very brink of fury and boredom. Strung up to hooks and pulleys by one leg and one arm, he appeared to be dangling over the bed rather than lying within it. He hadn't shaved and his face looked grizzled. Within the lipstick heart drawn on his left shoulder, the second set of initials, P.R., had been crossed out and replaced with E.B.V.—V.P. + E.B.V.

"Hey," said Victor, "so you finally found time to visit your old buddy. No flowers, no chocolates? Shit, Charlie, at least you could of brought a vibrator so I could buzz myself into oblivion—a vibrator and a bottle of hootch, that's my idea of a hot hospital date. Fucking nurses won't come within three feet of me anymore. They say I got itchy fingers. Hell, these fingers aren't itchy, they just hungry."

"I'll bring some chocolates later if you want." Charlie sat down on the chair by the bed. On the table was a great bouquet of yellow and red flowers. "Who sent these?"

"Your mother. She wants me to get well soon. Probably she's got more chores for me to do."

Charlie didn't say anything. He wanted to ask Victor about the night he'd taken the photographs and to tell him about Tommy Polanski but decided to let him gripe first.

"You know who else came up to see me?" asked Victor with a sly look. "Your ex-girlfriend Doris."

Charlie found himself becoming alert, as if he'd been given a little poke with a pin. "What'd she say?"

"Not much, just that everything was the same at the bar and shit like that. I asked her why she didn't dump her science teacher and go back to old strong and steady Charlie Bradshaw, but she told me to mind my own business. She's a cute girl, Charlie. Too bad you blew it."

"Lay off, Victor."

"Vic."

"Okay, okay, you think I like it that she's seeing some other guy?"

"Too bad I'm laid up," said Victor, "or I'd go bust his nose for you. It's your own fault for falling in love. There's nothing that fucks up a good sexual relationship any faster."

Charlie unrolled the photograph of the bar scene and held it in front of Victor. "Tell me more about those guys sitting at the bar."

"Jesus, Charlie, you just don't quit, do you."

"What was the old guy like? Talkative, quiet, joking?"

"They were all talking but there wasn't any real excitement. The younger guys seemed pretty bored and were humoring the oldster."

"Did you hear them laugh?"

"No laughter, no jokes. The old guy seemed to be showing the place off and the other two weren't very interested. You find out who he is?"

Charlie tossed the other photograph of the young Polanski onto the bed. "Tommy Polanski," he said.

"And who's that supposed to be?"

"A bank robber. I don't mean like the Barkers or the Dillinger or Pretty Boy Floyd—guys who'd rush into a place and scare everyone half to death. Polanski, I think, saw himself as a problem-solver. He would find some impossible bank and then, against all odds, he would rob it. Willie Sutton was like that, also maybe half a dozen others. You see, there are two kinds of bank robbers. The Jesse James kind that blast their way in and out. And the Gentleman George Leslie kind who use their wits, who sneak in and crack the safe, guys with foolproof plans. You could call them the overt and covert styles of bank robbery—"

"Jesus, Charlie, what kind of crap is this? 'Overt and covert'—either you're a bank robber or not. Seems fairly simple."

Charlie gave Victor a patient look. "I remember one time Polanski took a big bank in Albany that had three armed guards. He did it with one other guy and a female accomplice. You know those little pellets of fake blood that actors use? Right before closing the woman starts screaming, bites into the pellets so blood's pouring from her mouth; then she flings herself on the floor like she's having a fit. The guards run over, and while they're distracted, Polanski and the other guy get the drop on them."

"Sounds like a real joker," said Victor.

"Another time he wants to crack the safe of a big jewelry store but the safe was kept in a well-lit front window while right across the street was a police station. Polanski got some art student to do a painting of the safe, then propped up the painting in front of the real safe with about three feet between so he could just squeeze in and break it open. Nobody noticed it was a painting until the store opened in the morning and the manager found everything gone."

"Doesn't sound so covert to me," said Victor. "So what's he doing in your mother's hotel?"

Charlie looked down at the two photographs. "That's what I was hoping you'd tell me."

"Well, as far as I noticed him, he was just a backdrop to the billing and cooing of the honeymoon couple. But if I were you, I'd pay attention to the other two guys. Polanski might be quick-witted but he's still pushing eighty and if he's hoping to knock over the Adirondack Trust and if I was bank manager, then I wouldn't be too worried. I remember he was pretty shaky on his pins and those other guys had to support him when he walked. In traction he's not, but he won't win a footrace. None of them liked my business with the camera, but the young guys gave me what the passion writers call venomous looks."

"Did they say anything?"

"No, they were just pissed."

"Have you had any more thoughts about the woman who's crying and the man with the ring?"

"Not really. The woman was upset from the moment I first saw her—not because of me but in general. She was nervous and didn't want to be there. The guy kept talking to her quietly, and I hardly noticed him. She would of been pretty if she hadn't had all those tears in her eyes."

"What color hair did the man have?"

"Don't trick me, Charlie. You know as well as I do he was almost bald."

"And the person who ran you down?"

"He was wearing a hat. Shit, it might of been a broad."

Charlie took the pictures from the bed. "Well, I'm going

to see Peterson. Maybe he can trace Polanski. Maximum Tubbs thought he was either dead or in jail."

"Seems like the same thing to me," said Victor. "Get me some more skin mags, and don't forget to feed Moshe."

Charlie stopped by Victor's apartment to feed the cat on his way to police headquarters. Consequently, when he entered Peterson's office, there were tears in his eyes and he was snuffling slightly. Peterson was with Tidings and Novack. They looked up with irritation when he walked in; then, when they saw Charlie appeared to be crying, their expressions changed to surprise.

"What's eating you?" asked Peterson. The three men were grouped around a map laid out on Peterson's desk.

"Cats," said Charlie, blowing his nose. "I'm allergic to them."

"What cats?" said Peterson, glancing around his office.

"I've been feeding Victor's cat," said Charlie. "Have you identified that old guy in the picture?"

Both Novack and Tidings looked at Charlie with disapproval. In their minds, the world was divided into clear categories of people and behavior, and one of their roles as policemen was to see that the lines were not crossed with impunity. It seemed to them that Charlie had no respect for such separations—wandering into Chief Peterson's office without knocking was an example of this. To Novack and Tidings this was unforgivable, and deep in their hearts they meant one day to punish him. Charlie of course knew this and it depressed him.

"Jesus, Charlie, don't you know I got more important stuff to deal with than some old fart in a photograph. That liquor store by the Grand Union got knocked over last night, and so was a liquor store in Ballston Spa. Same people did it."

"Kids?" asked Charlie. Watching out for kids had been his job in the youth bureau, and he still worried about them.

"No, an older guy, white, maybe in his thirties."

Charlie's interest faded. "The old man in the photograph is Tommy Polanski. That name mean anything to you?"

Peterson assumed a thoughtful expression as if he had misplaced his keys or couldn't find his pen. Novack looked down at his hands and made fists.

"You mean the bank robber?" asked Tidings.

"That's right. I've got his picture." Charlie put both pictures on the desk on top of maps of Saratoga and Ballston Spa with the liquor stores circled in red. "See, it's the same guy."

The three policemen looked at the photographs, trying not to appear interested but interested all the same.

"The last I knew," said Charlie, "Polanski was in Attica, so I wondered if you had any more recent information."

"How does it concern you, anyway?" asked Tidings.

"I'm night manager of a big hotel and we often have a lot of money in the safe. If a famous bank robber is in Saratoga, and especially at my hotel, then I want to know it."

"Nah," said Peterson, putting his arm around Tidings's shoulder, "Charlie's still trying to find out who ran down his buddy and he's got a new lead. You're really a bulldog, Charlie."

Charlie looked down at his broken-down loafers. "When I used to work here, we'd get a list each summer of pickpockets, crooks, gamblers, con men, safecrackers, jewelry thieves—all the guys who were making their way toward Saratoga for the summer events. Here I've identified a famous bank robber for you. You should be grateful."

"Charlie, he must be eighty years old."

"Maybe so, but the men with him look healthy. If I were you, I'd show the picture to the clerks at those liquor stores."

"The robber had a stocking over his face," said Peterson, still looking down at the photograph. "Okay, Charlie, I'll find out about this Polanski and try to get an ID on the other two. But I tell you, I bet Victor wasn't knocked down by anyone in this picture. What kind of guy is he, anyway? He mocks people, bad-mouths them, flirts with their wives, makes fun of them. Hey, I'm not saying I approve of hitting old Victor with an automobile, but I can see how someone might be driven to do it."

8

"Why did I rob banks?" wrote Willie Sutton. "Because I enjoyed it. I loved it. I was more alive when I was inside a bank, robbing it, than at any other time in my life. I enjoyed everything about it so much that one or two weeks later I'd be out looking for the next job. But to me the money was the chips, that's all. The winnings. I kept robbing banks when, by all logic, it was foolish. When it could cost me far more than I could possibly gain. . . . And yet, banks continued to have such a strong appeal for me that I never was able to pass one without automatically, almost unconsciously, looking it over. Much in the way that a man with an entirely different kind of compulsion might take that hard, appraising look whenever he passed a pretty woman."

It was still Wednesday afternoon and Charlie was sitting in the office of the detective agency glancing through Willie Sutton's autobiography, *Where the Money Was*. Rolled out on the desk was the photograph of the bar. Charlie had weighted it down at the corners with an ashtray and a .38: a snub-nosed Smith & Wesson Chief's Special. As Charlie read, he occasionally glanced at Tommy Polanski's face, wondering how he would respond to Sutton's remarks.

"The line between a bank robber and a lawyer is a very thin one," Sutton wrote. "In robbing a bank I always planned the job carefully, leaving nothing to chance. It's the same thing in trying a case. 'Preparation is everything,' lawyers say. Once you're inside the bank, you have to see everything, guard yourself against everybody. . . . In both professions, it helps to be a little paranoid."

Looking at the picture, it almost seemed that Charlie could see Tommy Polanski nod in agreement. These were the truths of serious skulduggery. Sutton, Polanski and a dozen others like them didn't rob for economic reasons but for emotional ones. It was like a drug, even despite the punishment of years in prison. And so it seemed reasonable to Charlie that Polanski might be planning another crime, and if that was true, then either he or one of the men with him could have been disturbed enough by Victor's picture-taking to try to steal the film, no matter if it meant running Victor down on the street in broad daylight. Yet even as he looked at Polanski, Charlie's gaze slid across to take in the crying woman. What had happened to make her cry so?

Around four-thirty Charlie returned to police headquarters to see if Peterson had learned anything about Polanski. He found the police chief alone in his office with Tidings. They were standing by Peterson's desk and looked startled when Charlie walked through the door.

"Charlie, the city of Saratoga pays my secretary a good salary," said Peterson, "and one of her jobs is to let me know when somebody wants to see me. And yet you keep sneaking past her."

"I wasn't sneaking," said Charlie, "I just didn't want to bother her." Actually, the secretary had been listening to a Walkman and her eyes had been closed.

"It's her business to be bothered." Peterson raised himself up on tiptoe and linked his hands behind his back. Tidings wandered over to the window. He was so thin and doglike and quick-looking that Charlie wished he could see him run.

"What'd you find out about Polanski?" asked Charlie, still standing by the door.

"He got out of Attica in 1978. He's been living with his sister down in Schenectady since then."

"You have her name?"

"Blanche Siegel."

"What about an address?"

"What are you planning on doing, Charlie?"

"I thought I'd pay him a visit."

Tidings turned from the window. "Hey, Bradshaw, this is police business. What right d'you have to see him about anything?"

"Are you planning to see him?" asked Charlie.

It was clear from Tidings's expression that he had no such intention. "We can't go bothering the guy just because he's an ex-con, you know better than that."

"Then it won't hurt if I talk to him."

"What do you plan to talk to him about?" asked Tidings.

"Someone tried to kill Victor with an automobile just because he took some pictures. If Polanski is planning a job, then maybe he didn't want anyone to know he was around here."

"For shit's sake, Charlie," said Peterson, "the man's seventy-eight years old."

"He's still a professional thief."

"And he's never been known to hurt anybody," said Tidings. "You just going down to Schenectady and bother this old guy who probably wants no more than to die in peace?"

"I want to talk to him only because he's in the photograph. Now are you going to give me the address or do I get it someplace else?"

"Okay, okay," said Peterson. He turned back to his desk, wrote something on a sheet of paper and handed it to Charlie.

"You run a check on those other two guys?" asked Charlie, folding the paper and putting it in his breast pocket.

"Not yet."

"What about Polanski's sister? What's her background?"

"I have no idea," said Peterson.

"You find the men who robbed the liquor stores?"

"We're still working on it."

It occurred to Charlie that Peterson was about to lose his temper. "How much did they get?" he asked.

"All told about fifteen hundred," said Tidings. "You going to try and solve that one too, Bradshaw?"

"You're a little touchy, aren't you?" said Charlie. "I was just curious."

"You're never just curious," said Peterson, pushing both hands back through hair. "You've always got some goddam little plan. Go find your antique bank robber and get the hell out of here."

As Charlie went down the stairs, he wondered if he should be angry with Peterson. But he had known Peterson too long and such anger was nonfunctional. Still, it didn't cheer him. If anything, it made him more determined. He decided to grab a sandwich, then drive down to Schenectady. Again he began to think of Willie Sutton.

"A professional thief," wrote Sutton, "is a man who wakes up every morning thinking of committing a crime the same way any other man gets up and goes to his job."

Instead of going to the hotel, where he could have eaten

for free, Charlie decided to drive to the Backstretch, telling himself he didn't wish to see Raoul. Even as he thought this, he knew he was lying, since there were at least fifty other places he could have gone. Doris started work at five and there would be no way to avoid her. But then, perhaps he didn't want to avoid her, perhaps he would ask her to go out with him. It had started to sprinkle, and Charlie hurried down Broadway to get his car. What would happen if he asked Doris to dinner? Unfortunately, he already knew the answer.

The Backstretch was crowded with men and women who had just gotten off work, and half a dozen spoke to Charlie, asking what he'd been up to and where'd he'd been hiding himself. The owner, Berney McQuilkin, bought Charlie a beer. He knew about Charlie and Doris and said no more than that it was good to see him. Charlie found an empty stool at the corner of the bar and ordered a rare cheeseburger with fries. Doris had nodded to him when he came in but she was busy waiting on tables and had no chance to come over. She wore a white blouse, a khaki skirt and a pin that said "No Nukes" right above her heart. Charlie thought she was beautiful.

After Charlie had received his cheeseburger and was nearly finished eating, Doris asked McQuilkin to take care of the customers for a minute. Then she sat down beside Charlie.

"How's Victor?" she asked.

"Better. It was nice of you to go see him."

"Do they know when he can go home?"

"I guess it won't be for another several weeks and even then he may need someone to take care of him. I'm going to try to get him a room at the hotel. I don't think my mother would mind." Because of their changed relationship, Charlie found it difficult to look Doris full in the face.

"What about the person who ran him down? Have you learned anything about that?"

"No, but the film Victor left here was what they were after." He went on to talk about the picture of the bar, the honeymoon couple and all the possible suspects. Then he told her about Joe Riklin and the dead girl, Lynn Schorr. He even told her about Polanski and compared him to Willie Sutton and told her how Willie Sutton had once said, "Hell, I was a professional thief. I wasn't trying to make the world better for anybody but myself."

As he talked he became less shy, even animated. Once he noticed himself in the mirror and saw he was smiling. It was easy to talk to Doris; he wanted to talk to her more often. Consequently, when he'd finished telling her about Polanski, he said, "By the way, I'm not working Thursday or Friday night. Is there any chance we could have dinner?"

Doris looked down at her lap and seemed embarrassed. "No, Charlie, I told you I don't want to go out anymore."

All the doors of possibility clicked shut. "You mean because of your science teacher?" Charlie tried to keep the irritation out of his voice.

"Partly, but there are also ways that we're just different and they're the sort of differences that bother me."

"What differences?" asked Charlie, who was afraid she might be talking about personal hygiene or that he was overweight.

Doris turned her stool so she was facing forward, not looking at Charlie. She had a box of matches and kept moving it around on the bar. "Well, for one thing, there's a way that you're outside of life. I'm not sure how to say this but it's like you're on the periphery, on the outside looking in. You sort of skirt the perimeter, asking questions and wondering what it's like instead of diving in and becoming a part of it. Maybe even living out at the lake is an example of that. You live out there and watch Saratoga from a safe distance."

"Is that why you won't go out with me?" asked Charlie, uncertain what Doris was saying.

"That may be one of the reasons. I mean, what makes you good as a policeman or a detective is that you're curious and ask questions, but then you do the same thing with life itself, as if you're in a store deciding whether to buy or not to buy. You can't do that with life. You have to jump into the middle and take what comes."

"I don't think I'm like that," said Charlie, wondering if he really stayed at the perimeter of life and what that meant.

"I'm not trying to insult you," said Doris, still not looking at him. "I'm not even making a criticism. I'm just describing. It's always seemed there was a way you don't live in the real world and then I decided you didn't want to live in the real world, you didn't trust it, so you hang back at the edge like a sort of wallflower. Well, I love the world and want to be a part of it and I want the man I love to be a part of it too. Do you understand what I'm saying?"

Charlie wanted to ask if there was some kind of course he could take or book he could read, but the question seemed foolish. Instead he just nodded, even though he didn't understand, and shortly Doris had to go back to work and a few minutes after that Charlie left the Backstretch feeling more depressed than ever.

It was just five-thirty and there was still time to drive

down to Schenectady before he had to be back at the hotel. First, however, he swung by the Bentley to pick up Joe Riklin. He wanted the company and he didn't want to think about what Doris had said. He didn't know what he could do about it or how to change himself. As for Riklin, Charlie had noticed that whenever Riklin thought no one was looking, he seemed sad, and Charlie guessed he was grieving for Lynn Schorr. Because of his feelings for Doris, this made Charlie particularly sympathetic.

Riklin was pleased to be asked and happy to stop busing tables for a few hours. Getting him out of the hotel, however, wasn't as easy as Charlie had hoped. Raoul didn't approve. When Charlie and Riklin were leaving the dining room, Raoul stopped them.

"Where are you going with Riklin?"

"I need him for some other work."

"He's a busboy. His work is here." Raoul's dark hair was perfectly slicked back and Charlie realized he probably kept it in place with Vaseline. The high half circles of forehead outlined by his widow's peak seemed glossy and bright.

"I've just promoted him," said Charlie as the idea sprang into his mind. "He's my assistant."

"What do you need an assistant for? You don't do enough work to need one."

Charlie decided he had to be pleasant and tried thinking forward to that happy time in September when he could be free of the Bentley. "You've got Suzanne as an assistant. So I'm taking Riklin."

"I won't permit it. Who's going to bus the tables?"

All three were standing at the door of the dining room and people had to squeeze around them to get in. The tables were round with white tablecloths. In the center of each was a little vase of fresh flowers. Charlie didn't know their names—there were yellow flowers and some red and purple ones as well.

"I don't care if you won't permit it. You can hire another busboy or have one of the others work overtime. Saratoga's full of kids who'd leap at the job."

"There's no time to train anyone new," said Raoul. His eyes were so dark as to be almost black. Looking into them, Charlie was surprised to see how much Raoul disliked him.

"I'm sorry if you don't like this, Raoul, but you know our relationship. I mean, there's nothing you can do about it. I need an assistant and so I've hired Riklin. Is my mother around?"

"She's taking a nap."

"Tell her I might be back a little late but no later than ten. Maybe you can keep Suzanne around until then."

Whenever Raoul grew extremely angry, his face became paper-white. It was like that now. "Do you realize how irresponsible this is?"

Charlie held up a hand to calm him. "There's a good chance that someone's going to try and rob our safe. These are men with guns, Raoul, and they will put little windows in you. You might consider I'm trying to do something about it."

"Are you serious?"

"Of course I'm serious." He turned and walked across the lobby with Riklin a few steps behind him. It irritated Charlie to lie and be deceitful. He disliked the kind of person he became around Raoul and Suzanne and Peterson. Maybe he really did live on the periphery, maybe he had no idea what life was about.

As they were descending the front steps of the hotel

toward Charlie's Renault, Riklin said, "I don't want to get you in trouble, Mr. Bradshaw."

All of Charlie's immediate responses seemed cynical, and he thought that's what he disliked most about Raoul and his troop: they made him cynical. To be cynical, thought Charlie, meant you always had a barrier between yourself and everything else; you could never respond naturally. Maybe that's why he stayed on the outside, as Doris had said, just so he wouldn't become too cynical.

"How can you call me Mr. Bradshaw," said Charlie after a moment, "when you tried to stick me with a knife? My name's Charlie."

Riklin brushed his red hair away from his eyes. "Am I really going to be your assistant?"

"Sure, there's lots of stuff you can do. What do you get now, two hundred a week? I bet the hotel can manage two-fifty—is that okay?"

Riklin nodded, then remained silent. In fact, he had been mostly silent with Charlie, as if he hadn't defined him clearly to himself and wouldn't be able to talk to him until that definition had been made. They got into the Renault, and Charlie drove south on Broadway. It wasn't until they reached the Northway that Riklin spoke again.

"So why are we going to Schenectady?"

"I'm trying to find a bank robber," said Charlie. The sun was in his eyes and he fished his dark glasses out of the glove box.

Riklin leaned back and appeared to think about what Charlie had said. "How come?" he asked after about a minute.

"Well, it's complicated. You know that night my friend Victor was taking pictures? There were three men seated at the bar, and the one in the middle, the old one, used to be a bank robber—banks and armored trucks were his specialty. He got out of Attica in '78 after twenty years inside. Not much of a specialty, if you ask me. Anyway, Victor got run down by someone who wanted his camera, or rather the film. And I'm guessing the person was after those pictures that Victor had taken in the bar, and maybe this old bank robber had something to do with it, either him or the guys with him."

Riklin continued to stare ahead. He had sharp features, and his profile, to Charlie's glance, looked like a series of points. "One of those guys was carrying a gun," said Riklin.

"You saw it?"

"He had it in a shoulder holster. I was sweeping up some stuff in front of him and when he leaned over to say something to the old guy, I caught a glimpse of it. Couldn't tell what it was, though."

Charlie was impressed. "You make a good assistant night manager. Anything else about those guys?"

"Just that they treated the old man pretty bad. I mean, they kept making fun of him. He thought the hotel was, you know, impressive, and the other two thought there was nothing special about it. But they were the kind of guys who don't think there's nothing special about nothing."

Charlie pulled into the center lane to pass a semi. The rain had stopped but the pavement was still wet and he had to turn on his wipers. "I know policemen like that," he said, thinking of Novack and Tidings. "I call them the great unflappables, people who pride themselves on never being taken by surprise, never being excited or sad, never deviating from a kind of cool in-between place. There're lots of people like that. They're called professionals. What about the woman who was crying—do you remember anything about her?"

"No, just that she was sad."

"Was the man being mean to her?"

"Not at all, he was trying to comfort her. I thought they were really in love, you know, the way they kept touching each other and looking at each other. Then she started crying and he tried to help her."

"You know about love?" asked Charlie, teasing a little.

"I think so," said Riklin seriously. "I mean, I loved Lynn, although it took me a while to figure out what was wrong, to understand what I was feeling."

"How would you describe it?" asked Charlie.

"It's when you like and think more about the other person than you like and think about yourself. I don't just mean you want to fuck her, although there's that too of course. But it's like you don't want there to be a division or barrier of skin between you."

Charlie thought that seemed about right. "And the crying woman and the man with the ring, they were like that?"

"That's how it seemed to me," said Riklin, looking at Charlie for the first time. "But scared too, excited and scared at the same time."

9

Blanche Siegel had moved from Schenectady two years before. Charlie knocked on the doors of several of her neighbors. Someone had died, he told them, and left Blanche some money. Eventually a young woman who was holding a baby under her arm as one might hold a basketball gave him an address in Troy. As Charlie walked back to his car he wondered if his ability to lie so easily was another example of how he was an outsider, someone who lived on the perimeter.

Riklin was leaning against the Renault eating a Good Humor bar from an ice-cream truck that was ringing its bell half a block away. A few drops of ice cream had fallen onto his jeans jacket, and he dabbed at them with his thumb. "I got you a toasted almond," he said, tossing the ice-cream bar to Charlie. "They're my favorite." He flicked his head trying to shift the weight of red hair from his brow. It was a habitual gesture that had little effect on the hair, which remained stuck to his forehead as if with glue.

They climbed back into the Renault. Charlie steered with his knees as he took the paper off the ice cream. "What does it mean to be an outsider?" he asked.

"It means not having enough money," said Riklin.

Blanche Siegel had an apartment on the north side of Troy just off River Street. Charlie knew Troy mostly as the childhood home and final resting place of Old Smoke Morrissey, the Congressman and prizefighter who brought big-time gambling and horse racing to Saratoga in the 1860s. Other than that it was the home of the Freihofer Bakery, maker of his favorite cookies.

"You want me to wait in the car?" asked Riklin.

"No, you come too." They climbed the steps to a four-story red brick apartment building and Charlie pushed the buzzer next to Blanche Siegel's name. He waited, then pushed the buzzer again. Just as he was about to give up the door was opened by a round-faced old woman whose chin was only slightly higher than Charlie's belt.

"Are you Blanche Siegel?" asked Charlie as politely as possible.

"Depends what you want," said the woman. She seemed to be in her mid-seventies. Dressed in a bright yellow pantsuit and yellow running shoes, she appeared ready for anything.

"Well, actually, I'm looking for Thomas Polanski. Is he here?"

"You can't know him if you call him Thomas, not even his mother called him Thomas. No, he's not here. He hasn't been here for a month. Is Tommy in trouble?" She asked the question not with anxiety but mild interest, even pride.

"I'm not sure."

"Are you a policeman?"

"A private detective." Charlie gave her one of his cards, and she held it up first to her left eye, then to her right.

"I don't know if he's alive or dead," said Blanche Siegel. "Given his health he should be dead. I've told him, of course, but he won't listen. 'Why do I want a long life?' That's what he says, and I tell him it's his duty. Reverend

Patterson says it's our duty as Christians to live as long as possible, but Tommy isn't a Christian and never was."

"What's wrong with him?" asked Charlie. He stood by the door and Joe Riklin stood a few steps below him jiggling some keys in his pocket and looking at the red brick buildings. Out in the street half a dozen kids were playing stickball.

"Sick, that's what's wrong with him—sick in the body, sick in the head, sick in the soul. Everything about him is eaten with sickness. I've tried to help him. I've let him live with me. I've fed him and washed his clothes, but what does he care about any of that?"

"How is he physically sick?" asked Charlie.

"Don't you know? He's got cancer. They took out his lung in January, but d'you think it made any difference? The day after the operation I went to see him and there he was smoking like a chimney. Then the doctor came in, saw the cigarettes, took them into the little bathroom and poured water over them. Tommy didn't even blink. The moment the doctor was out the door he gave me two dollars and told me to get him a pack of Luckies. I didn't but he got them anyway. He doesn't care if he gets better. Even when he got home he'd sit around smoking or be down at some bar that he likes. To tell the truth, I think he misses being in jail. That's his home, not here. All those years I drove way across state to see him in prison and now he'd just as soon be back there again."

The old woman was still holding the door open and talking into Charlie's stomach. Although it had stopped raining, drops of water kept falling from the roof and onto Charlie's head. He unrolled the long photograph and held it up. "Your brother was in Saratoga last weekend. You have any idea what he might have been doing?"

Blanche Siegel peered at the photograph. "How do you expect me to see that without my glasses? You'll have to come inside. Don't mind the mess and don't knock anything over."

Her apartment was immaculate and filled with china figurines which Charlie vaguely thought came from Germany. At least the little red-cheeked boys wore lederhosen and cocked hats with feathers. He and Joe Riklin stood in the doorway. The room had been designed, Charlie thought, for someone under five feet tall, and he felt certain that if he entered, he would break something. After a moment he edged his way across the room past several round tables filled with figurines—fawns and badgers and chipmunks on one, windmills on another—and sat down on a soft love seat covered with a violet satin material.

In the meantime, Blanche Siegel had put on a pair of black horn-rimmed glasses with gold flecks and was studying the photograph. "That's Tommy all right. What's he doing in a fancy place like that?"

"I was wondering the same thing," said Charlie. "You know the men he's with?"

"Never seen them before. Are they cops or crooks? I can never tell. Tommy's not supposed to drink either. No drinking, no smoking, no fooling around, and in bed no later than ten. Looks like he's breaking all the rules. What about that couple with the champagne—what're they doing?"

"They just got married."

"Silly faces," said Blanche Siegel. "It won't last. What's that woman crying about?"

"I don't know," said Charlie.

"Poor thing."

"What's your brother been doing since he got out of prison?"

"Absolutely nothing. I don't mean to be hard on him, but he hasn't known what to do. He's been bored silly. He gets up, watches television, eats lunch, watches television, takes a nap, watches television, eats dinner, watches television, goes to bed. Sometimes he goes out to a bar where he's got some friends. Ex-convicts mostly. It seems he can't talk to a person unless the person's been in jail. Sometimes he goes fishing, he likes to go fishing. He's got a friend with a boat. I've tried to get him to go to church with me but he won't go."

"You think Tommy might try and rob another bank?" asked Charlie, deciding he'd just try out the question.

"That's plain silliness. He can hardly walk. That's why he doesn't go out more than he does. It hurts him to move his legs and he can't get his breath. He's too old. He might like to rob a bank but he's too old and worn-out. Our grandfather lived till he was ninety-three and he could have robbed a bank just fine, but Tommy's a wreck. To tell you the truth, I thought he'd gone someplace to die. He's a proud man, don't you know? Sometimes the police will come and ask something and he's as rude as can be. He doesn't let them forget that he hates them. And in prison too, he could have been out a lot earlier if he wasn't so proud. They don't like proud men in prison. Even reporters, a reporter will come to talk to Tommy and he sends him packing. He hates being old and weak but he doesn't complain. He just grits his teeth."

"What did he take with him when he went?"

"Clothes mostly, about a suitcase full. He snuck out when I was at church."

"Did he leave a note?"

"Yes, I'll show it to you." Blanche Siegel lifted the lid

of a small china box with pictures of blue flowers, took out a piece of paper and handed it to Charlie.

Smoothing the paper out on his knee, Charlie read, " 'I'm tired of living like this. Thanks for everything. Love, Tommy.' "

"Your brother like anything about being in the joint—you know, prison?" asked Riklin, still standing by the door.

"He liked some of the people. For years he fought it. They put him in solitary and wouldn't let him work. They had someone follow him around all the time. Then bit by bit he settled down. Maybe he got to like the routine."

A few minutes later Charlie got the name of the bar where Polanski often went and the name of the friend he saw there: Frank Hensley. Then Charlie wrote down the number of the hotel and asked Blanche Siegel to call if she heard from her brother.

"I won't hear from him," she said. "I won't hear till it's time to bury him. I'm the last one left. You know, as a little girl I used to wonder what my job was in the family, what chores were mine, like washing the dishes or taking out the trash. Well, my job was to bury them. I buried them all."

As they drove over to the bar, Charlie said, "Why did you ask about prison?"

"Because I hated it. I mean, I was only in a kids' prison but I still hated it. It was too noisy and you could never be by yourself and the sex was all weird. But some people liked it and that always surprised me."

The bar was named Jack's and it was located near the bridge to Green Island. Outside was a red-and-blue neon sign like a theater marquee and inside a dozen men were watching the Red Sox play Milwaukee on a flyspecked color television stuck over one end of the bar. Charlie asked the bartender where he could find Frank Hensley, and the bartender pointed to an elderly man seated by himself with his back to the television. Charlie and Riklin walked to his table.

"Do you mind if we join you?" asked Charlie.

Hensley slowly looked up him. He was what Victor would call half in the bag. Bald with a heavily lined face and a fat red nose, he wore a green-checked sport shirt with the buttons unevenly buttoned so his whole body seemed lopsided.

"Buy me a beer and a shot and I don't give a fuck what you do," said Hensley.

Charlie nodded to Riklin, who went back to the bar to get the drinks. "You want anything, Charlie?"

"Just a beer, I guess." Charlie gave Hensley his card.

"Don't ask me to read anything," he said. "You a cop?"

"A private detective."

"Well, I don't have the jewels and I ain't seen any kidnapped little boys. Does that take care of it?"

"Not really," said Charlie, sitting down. "I was wondering what you could tell me about Tommy Polanski."

It seemed to Charlie that Hensley grew somewhat more attentive. "Does Tommy have the jewels?" he asked after a moment.

"What jewels?"

"Just a joke." He remained silent and hunched over the table until the drinks arrived, then he tilted back his head, drank the shot, took a mouthful of beer and swilled it around between his cheeks before he swallowed. "So what d'you want Tommy for?" he asked.

Charlie unrolled the photograph on the table. "Tommy was in Saratoga with some other men over the weekend. I wonder if you know what he was doing there."

Hensley bent over the picture, then took a Zippo lighter

from his pocket, lit it, and moved it back and forth about six inches over the table. In the glare of the flame Hensley's nose looked as bright as a maraschino cherry. "Tommy looks all right, looks like he's having a fine time. What do you want him for?"

"The man who took this picture was run down by a car the next day and someone tried to steal the film. I thought Tommy might know something about it."

"Tommy never hurt anyone in his whole life," said Hensley.

"What about the men with him?"

"The last time I saw Tommy was in this bar exactly one month ago. Then he left and I haven't seen him since."

"You know where he went?"

"Don't have the foggiest."

"Do you know why he went?"

"Get me another shot," said Hensley. As Riklin went back to the bar, Hensley continued to study the photograph. Charlie remained silent, looking at the old man. He wondered how long he'd been in prison and what he'd been in for. When Riklin brought back the whiskey, Hensley drank it down as quickly as he had the first.

"You want to know why he went?" asked Hensley. "Because he was bored. It's as simple as that. He was bored and he knew he was going to die. Not like I'm going to die or you're going to die. He's got cancer, even after his operation he had cancer, and he didn't want to sit around and let it eat him. He wanted to do something."

"Do what?" asked Charlie.

"Beats me. Maybe he just wanted to have a good time in Saratoga, take in some races."

"Where'd he get the money?"

"People like Tommy always have a little money tucked away."

Charlie sipped his beer. "You recognize those other men, don't you? Who are they?"

"I never talked to them."

"Who are they?"

Hensley lowered his forehead to the table so that it rested on the photograph, right on top of the honeymoon couple laughing into the camera. "I don't know them, I don't know anything about them," he said in a muffled voice, "but one of them was in here once talking to Tommy. I tried to sit down but Tommy wouldn't let me." Hensley raised his head and looked at Charlie. He looked sad, as if suddenly struck by the fact of his age and all the wasted time. "Afterward I asked Tommy what the guy wanted and he wouldn't tell me. We were friends, you know, we talked about everything. So when he wouldn't tell me I laughed and said he was probably after him for not paying his taxes or something like that and Tommy said no way, the guy wanted something from him, and I said, 'What could he want from an old fart like you?' And you know what he told me? He told me one single word."

"What?" asked Charlie.

"Expertise, that's what he said. They wanted his expertise."

"Did he say what he meant by that?"

"No, that was the only word he said. Then a few days later he took off. Didn't even drop in to say goodbye. I know, he was a crook and robbed banks and did all sorts of shit, but to tell you the truth he's one of the best guys you'd ever hope to meet. He'd lend you money, he'd worry whether you're happy or unhappy, he'd stand you a drink and he'd laugh at your lousy jokes. A good friend, you know what I mean?"

"Sure," said Charlie. "You served time too, didn't you? What were you in for?"

"I was what they call a paper hanger. Bad checks. Pure piss-ass stuff. But Tommy, he's the real article. He's not afraid of anything."

It was eight-thirty by the time Charlie and Joe Riklin left Troy and drove across Route 7 to the Northway. Charlie was silent at first, thinking about what Frank Hensley had said and then worrying that he'd be late for work.

"So what did you think?" he asked after a while.

Riklin was scrunched down in his seat with his knees up on the dashboard. "I'd say he's planning to do a job and those two guys in the picture are going to help him do it."

"Where's the proof?"

"I don't need any. I just know it."

"I guess I feel the same way," said Charlie.

"Hell, he doesn't even care if he goes to jail. He'd just as soon do some dopey holdup so they'd put him back inside."

"I don't think that's true," said Charlie. "I mean, I agree he doesn't care if he goes back, but if he goes back, he wants to do it after something big. He wants people to know he still has what it takes to knock over a bank."

"Fuckin' Adirondack Trust," said Joe Riklin, grinning, "or that big bank in Glens Falls. Shit, don't I wish I could see it happen. I'd love to sit on the curb and watch."

"They won't do a daylight robbery," said Charlie. "I mean, if that's what they're planning, why need Polanski's 'expertise'? No, it's going to be more complicated than that."

Charlie's first stop back in Saratoga was police headquarters. It had begun to rain again very slightly, more like mist than rain, and the streetlights were each surrounded with a yellow nimbus. Peterson had gone home and Emmett Van Brunt was on duty.

"You can't just bother him, Charlie," said Emmett when Charlie told him he wanted to call Peterson. "The chief's been real busy. You ought to let him rest." Emmett sat behind his desk with his large red hand covering the black telephone.

"I want to tell him something."

They were in Emmett's small office, which was made smaller by ten slot machines recently confiscated from somebody's basement. Riklin was fooling with one, tugging at the arm and obviously wanting to put in a coin.

Emmett glanced uncomfortably at Riklin. "It can wait, Charlie. Call him tomorrow. I don't want you upsetting him now. I won't give you his number."

"That's okay," said Charlie, "I remember it well enough." He reached for the phone and dialed as Emmett knitted his brows. When Peterson answered, Charlie asked, "You busy, chief? This is Charlie. I got something to tell you."

There was a silence, then a slow exhalation of breath. "What is it, Charlie?" Peterson's voice was less raspy on the phone, more melodious somehow. It reminded Charlie of Johnny Cash, or maybe some other country-western singer.

"Polanski's disappeared. He went off a month ago with those young guys in the picture. One of them carries a gun. I talked to Polanski's sister and a friend of his. Everything points to the fact that he's going to pull a job. Those young guys hunted him out to get his help. Is there any chance you can get an ID on them? You still have the picture, don't you?"

"It's on my desk. Can't this wait, Charlie?"

"Sure, there's probably no hurry," said Charlie. He was surprised to find himself angry. "But if these guys rob the Adirondack Trust and it turns out someone's been warning you about it, it won't look good if you've been dragging your feet."

There was a pause. "Those are pretty hard words, Charlie. Why are you bothering about this?"

"I want to find out who ran down Victor."

"And you're going to turn everything upside down to do it, right?"

"If I have to."

"Okay, I'll give Emmett a call," said Peterson. He breathed deeply again, half exasperation, half sigh.

"He's right here," said Charlie, handing Emmett the phone.

Joe Riklin was still inspecting the slot machines. "How d'you make these work?" he asked.

Emmett Van Brunt stood with his back to them, saying, "Sure, chief, I'll get on it right away."

Charlie looked at the nearest machine—an old one with lots of chrome and curlicue designs. "You need a silver dollar or a special slug."

"I got one of those," said Riklin, digging into his pocket. "Someone tipped me a silver dollar just the other night." He put the coin in the slot and pulled the handle. The wheels with their pictures of fruit began to spin. Emmett turned and stared at them as he continued nodding at whatever Peterson was saying.

The spinning wheels stopped on one cherry, then a second, then a third. There was a rush and a jingle and a flood of coins poured onto the floor.

"Hey!" shouted Van Brunt.

Joe Riklin scooped up several handfuls and put them in the pockets of his jeans jacket.

"Let's get out of here," said Charlie, scooping up a handful for himself. "This is against the law," he added.

They hurried out of Emmett's office and down the stairs.

It was nine-thirty by the time Charlie and Joe Riklin entered the lobby of the Bentley. Suzanne was at the desk. Without looking at Charlie, she said, "Your mother wants to see you." She wore an emerald-green gown with shoulders so padded that they were like green epaulets.

"Fine," said Charlie, not thinking it was fine at all. "Show Joe what you do at the desk, will you? I've hired him as my assistant."

Joe had taken off his jeans jacket. On his left shoulder was a ballpoint-pen tattoo of a heart surrounding the words "No regrets." Suzanne stared at it, then looked up at Charlie as if he'd done something unbelievably stupid. "This kid?"

"That's right. Don't be too hard on him, okay?" He turned and trotted up the stairs to his mother's suite.

As he knocked on the door, Charlie prepared himself for criticism. He had been told that a successful hotel manager was someone who did not call attention to himself, whose good deeds shone forth like the sun through the clouds. As for Charlie, his hair was always messy, which he attributed not to slovenliness but to the ill effects of chlorine in the YMCA pool. But then there were buttons missing from coats and shirts, cuffs that were frayed, shoes that needed polishing, occasional dirt under the fingernails, until the accumulated weight of small sins bowed his shoulders and made him once more grateful that he lived out at the lake and not in town where the forces of virtue and righteousness could plague him with greater attention.

When Charlie entered the suite, he found his mother, Raoul and two of his successful cousins, Jack and James, seated at a table covered with a green felt cloth and sipping drinks from little glasses. Hanging above them was a renovated gas lamp with a green glass shade.

"There you are," said his mother cheerfully. "How nice you're not too late. Come join us. Would you like something to drink?"

"Beer, I guess," said Charlie, feeling he'd said the wrong thing.

Charlie's cousin Jack owned a successful hardware store in downtown Saratoga and was a man on whom fortune consistently seemed to smile, blessing him with good looks, a beautiful wife, intelligent and sensible children. He was a year older than Charlie, and when they were growing up he was always mentioned as the person whom Charlie should be more like. It would have been simple if Jack was unpleasant, but mostly he was friendly and helpful, giving Charlie old clothes, old baseball mitts, old girlfriends. Charlie liked him, and the fact that he sometimes wished Jack would get a cavity in one of those perfect teeth or have something turn out, oh, not badly but just not so well filled Charlie with guilt.

His cousin James was originally a carpenter, then he owned a construction company and at the moment he was known as a developer. As he moved up, his name had changed from Jimmy to James to J.W. He was five years older than Charlie, had been president of a number of fraternal organizations and was now something important in the Rotary Club. For more than forty-five years he had taken a keen interest in Charlie's moral well-being. All three of the cousins were over six feet and looked very athletic, although Charlie had never known them to exercise. All three were not the sort of men to eat between meals, fall victim to unfortunate crushes or put off till tomorrow what should be done today. As these details swept through Charlie's mind, he found himself again picking up his discussion with Doris—wasn't the existence of these men reason enough to live out at the lake and wasn't it brave of him not to have moved away altogether?

Charlie sat down at the table. "What's up?" he asked.

"Charlie," said James, "we feel you may be jeopardizing by your behavior a position of financial security that it has long been our hope you would someday acquire." James had thick silver hair and Charlie sometimes wondered what he did to it to make it so shiny.

"Your mother's a great woman, Charlie," said Jack. "If I was a betting man, I'd have never thought she could have raised the money for this hotel, renovated it and made such a success of it. Yet here it is, a grand venture, another bright spot for Saratoga to be proud of."

"What they're saying, Charlie," said his mother, nibbling a square of Dutch chocolate, "is they think you're messing up and that you'll get the hotel in trouble. Every day Raoul has another complaint, and mostly I've been ignoring them but this business about taking a busboy with a long record of theft and assault and making him your assistant seems rather hostile."

"He dumped a girl's naked corpse in a laundry hamper," said Raoul, who looked serious and even melancholy. But Charlie wasn't fooled. He knew Raoul was having the time of his life. Victor had once described Raoul as the kind of person who let his Grape-Nuts soak overnight, and as time passed Charlie increasingly understood what that meant.

"A dead girl, Charlie," said James, "and you've made this man your assistant?"

Charlie glanced around the table. No one had brought him his beer. "He loved the girl and he panicked. Besides, since he hasn't been charged by the police, you have no right to charge him either. Besides that, there seems to be some confusion about my place in the hotel. I'm here to do my mother a favor. I don't particularly like the job and I don't plan to keep it, but I'll do it until Labor Day and that's it. Why would I want it? Why would I be happy smiling and nodding at people and getting them fresh towels and adjusting the temperature in their rooms and helping them into their beds when they get drunk?"

"It's a good job, Charlie," said James. "It commands respect."

"And what's this business about the hotel going to be robbed?" asked Jack. "Surely you were joking, Charlie."

Jack was pointing his chin toward Charlie. It was square and red and always reminded Charlie of half a brick. "My friend Victor took some pictures in the bar. In one of the pictures were several men with criminal records, and one was carrying a gun. Victor was then run down and someone tried to steal the film. I'm just trying to find out who did it." Charlie paused and folded his hands before him on the green felt. He wondered why he always felt the need to exaggerate, make the case stronger than it actually was.

"But Charlie," said Jack, "you're the night manager of a hotel, and Raoul has said that this private detective work is interfering with your job. Can't you let Peterson handle it? After all, he's our chief of police."

"Peterson and I disagree as to why Victor was run down," said Charlie, "so I thought I'd poke around a little."

"Chief Peterson is a personal friend of mine," said James, "and I'm sure he has this under control. To be rushing around with your own investigation, well, Charlie, it seems somewhat Boy Scoutish, don't you think?"

"Let me tell you how things stand," said Charlie. "Victor is my best friend and I want to see that the person who tried to kill him gets caught. That's my priority. I don't think this has interfered with my job, but if you feel it has, then I'd be happy to quit. Let Raoul take over the whole thing and give my job to Suzanne."

Looking at the four faces, it seemed to Charlie that Raoul was trying not to smile, while his cousins were trying not to look shocked. As for his mother, he couldn't tell what she was thinking. She wore her red dressing gown with the ermine collar and was idly poking at her nails with an emery board. Then she raised her head, glanced at Raoul and her nephews, then looked at Charlie and smiled.

"I don't want you to quit," she said. "You stay here until Labor Day. Raoul just gets too upset too easily. But try not to tease him in the future, all right?"

"What about Joe Riklin?" asked Raoul.

"He stays too," said Mabel. "He's colorful; I like him."

10

"To tell you the truth, Charlie," said Victor, "I feel like an old fart. When my wife was dying I had to spend a lotta time in the hospital and it sort of turned me against them. And now here I am fuckin' wired to the ceiling, for crying out loud."

"Aren't the nurses nice to you?" asked Charlie. It was one-thirty Thursday afternoon and Charlie had just come from swimming only to find Victor somewhat depressed, not to say gloomy.

"Sure, the nurses are swell, that's part of the trouble. I mean, I'm just a lump they fell sorry for. To tell you the truth I didn't start feeling sorry for myself until they did it first. So it's sort of their fault, if you see what I mean." The third set of letters, E.B.V., drawn within the lipstick heart on his cast had been crossed out and replaced with a fourth set: V.P. + L.W.

"Would you prefer them to be rude and angry?"

"Not too rude, but I've always thought girls look prettier when their eyes flash. Which reminds me, how you doin' with Doris? Got her back in the sack yet?" Victor managed a weak leer. The bandage around his head had been trimmed, and gray tufts of hair stuck out from the sides like rudimentary earmuffs.

"That's over, I guess. She thinks I live on the perimeter of life."

"What's that supposed to mean?"

"It means that I'm afraid to get involved in the world, that I'm an outsider."

"Hey, you taken a good look at the world lately? Who can blame you?"

Charlie sat up a little straighter in his chair. The creases in his khaki pants looked like lazy lightning bolts. On the other side of the white curtain, the Hungarian was declaiming something that Charlie thought might be poetry. "So you think I'm an outsider too?" he asked.

"Well, they'll never elect you mayor, that's for sure. I don't know if I'd call you an outsider. Let's say you'd been born a lemming. When the time came for those other lemmings to leap into the sea and drown, you'd stay up on the cliff watching it all happen. Then, after a while, you'd wander home, have something to eat and think how strange it all was. Hey, Charlie, you're my friend. I wouldn't let you be my friend if you were a creep. No way."

"Would you jump into the sea?" asked Charlie. He tried to remember what a lemming looked like. Something like a pudgy mouse, he thought.

"You kidding? I can't even fuckin' swim. Forget it, I'd be right up there with you. Never mind Doris—once I'm outta here I'll introduce you to some ladies who won't care if you're in an iron lung as long as you can show 'em a good time." Victor paused and tried to insert his hand under the cast on his shoulder so he could scratch. "So tell me what you been doing. You catch the guy that tried to squash me?"

"Not yet, but I thought maybe you could give me some advice."

"Like what?"

"I think the person who ran you down was involved with this old bank robber I was telling you about. And I think they're all up here somewhere preparing some kind of crime."

"What kind of crime?"

"That's what I don't know. The old guy, Tommy Polanski, used to rob jewelry stores and banks. He's even robbed Brink's trucks. One time he put on the uniform of a Brink's guard and just got in the cab of the truck as it was leaving the bank. Then he forced the driver to go to a warehouse, where he and some buddies cleaned out the back. With banks, he's dug tunnels, he's gone through the roof. He even went into one in broad daylight dressed as an Arab prince with robes and everything. What I don't see is what he's going to do in Saratoga."

"Are you sure he's after something here?"

"Either here or Glens Falls. But most likely here. I think he has a thing about Saratoga. He used to spend time here in the twenties and thirties. He gambled a lot. He went to the races. The place means something. I mean, I think that's why he showed up at the Bentley, just because it looks like one of those old places. He wants to do something big that'll make the front page so his friends in prison can read about it and be impressed."

"What about the guys with him?" asked Victor.

"I think they just want the money. They know Polanski has a talent for organization and precision and they're simply buying it. But Polanski doesn't care if there's money involved or not." He went on to tell Victor about Polanski's lung operation and trouble with cancer. "He probably figures he won't live that long anyway," Charlie concluded.

"What about the Adirondack Trust? Could he take that?"

"I don't know. It's right across from the police station.

I mean, you couldn't pull a Dillinger on it. You'd have to sneak in. Peterson is alerting all the local banks, sending them copies of the picture. He doesn't think anything will happen, but neither does he want a nasty surprise."

"Okay," said Victor, "so this Polanski disappeared about a month ago. What's he been doing ever since? Planning the job. Well, why haven't they done it? Either they haven't finished planning or they're waiting for something. You figure they been strolling around Saratoga for a couple weeks, at least until I took their pictures and got run down. Now they're probably laying low. So where are they hiding? In a motel? Check them. In an apartment? Check them too. Did Polanski have any friends up here? Find out. Shit, Charlie, you know the score. You don't need to ask my advice. You're just trying to cheer me up, that's all. Make me think I got some purpose while I'm tied down to this hospital bed."

"That's not true," said Charlie, who had already told Joe Riklin to start calling places between Albany and Lake George—motels, hotels, cabins, rooming houses—anyplace that had short-term rentals. "I need your help. But I agree they must be hiding someplace. There've been two robberies of liquor stores recently and I wouldn't be surprised if these fellows were involved."

When Charlie left the hospital a little later the first thing he did on reaching his office was to telephone Doris to see if they could have coffee together before she went to work.

"I don't think we have anything to talk about," she said.

"I wanted to ask you more about my being an outsider," said Charlie. He felt he should let her know what Victor had told him about lemmings.

"I've already said what I thought."

Charlie was seated at his desk at the detective agency staring at the picture of Jesse James. Jesse had had what Charlie considered a simple life—no doubts, no complications. "You sure you can't think of anything else?" asked Charlie.

"No," said Doris. She was silent a moment, then added, "I'm sorry, Charlie, but we just don't have anything to say to one another."

Hanging up, Charlie thought of the basic imbalance between the person who wanted to end the relationship and the person who didn't. Nothing he could say or do would make any difference. He had no power. Romantically speaking, he had already been discredited.

For a minute or two, Charlie stared out across the street to the window of a dentist's office. In the past, the dentist's assistant would occasionally notice him and wave. She was an attractive blonde in her mid-thirties. Today the office appeared closed. After another moment, Charlie turned back to the telephone and called Blanche Siegel in Troy. No, she hadn't heard from her brother. No, she didn't remember the names of any more of his friends.

"Did he know anyone up in Saratoga?" asked Charlie.

"Tommy knew people everywhere," said Mrs. Siegel. "Saratoga, Utica, Rochester, you name it. I've never known a man with so many friends."

"You can't remember any names in Saratoga?"

"He used to talk about Lucky Luciano, but that was some time ago."

Afterward, Charlie called up Jack's Bar in order to talk to Frank Hensley. But Frank hadn't come in. This was odd, the bartender said, because Frank was usually in by noon. Maybe he had a cold.

"Maybe," Charlie said.

Replacing the receiver, Charlie went through the yellow

pages and made a list of all the banks in the Saratoga area;
then he spent ten minutes staring at the wall as if hoping
the name of the right bank would suddenly appear there.
After that, he took a book from the belly drawer of his
desk. It was called *Box Man* and was the memoir of Harry
King, a safecracker on the West Coast who'd been a few
years older than Polanski.

"When I'm stealing," wrote King, "I'm always eating
at the best places. I enjoyed the food—but mainly it's
because policemen never go to the best places. They can't.
So that's the best place to go and eat. If you want to drink,
go to the best cocktail lounge in town. There won't be no
bulls there. So you avoid any heat."

After reading a little, Charlie went back to staring at
the wall. He was still staring at the wall when the phone
rang. It was Joe Riklin.

"Charlie, I think I found them," said Joe, speaking
quickly. "Except they already moved out and there
weren't three of them but six."

"Six?"

"That's right. It's one of those places on Route 9 on
the way to Glens Falls. You know, a bunch of run-down
cabins. It was the sixty-eighth place I called. You want to
go up there?"

"My car's in front of the hotel. I'll meet you in about
two minutes."

Charlie hurried to the door, then paused and went back
to get his .38, almost embarrassed for thinking he might
need it. But the fact of six men impressed him, not because
of the danger but because of what it said about the scope
of what they might be planning.

The cabins were seven miles north of Saratoga. They
were dirty gray, with cracked windows, rusted screens,
missing shingles, and probably hadn't seen a drop of fresh

paint in forty years. There were thirty of them in a wide semicircle set back from the road. The owner said he had a similar place in Florida near Apollo Beach. Both places were called the Forget-Me-Not, and pictures of the flower had been painted on the cabin doors.

"Five months in one, five in the other and two months in Europe for the wife," said the owner, a chubby man in his sixties named Bellamy. "Name a place and I bet we been there."

"Dachau," said Joe Riklin.

"Just to see the exhibits and buy some p.c.'s."

"So these guys who stayed here," said Charlie, "you get any sense of what they were like?" They were in the office, which was decorated with postcards from former guests who had written back to thank Bellamy for having such a swell place. From another room came the sound of a television—the intense yet hushed conversation of a soap opera.

"They were just young guys, 'cept for the old fellow. They'd hang around during the day playing cards. Then they'd go to the trots at night."

Charlie unrolled the photograph on the desk. "You recognize anyone in this picture?"

Bellamy bent over it. He was balding and had some kind of scalp disease; the top of his head was marked with red spots. "Those fellows at the bar, they're the same ones."

"You sure?"

"Hell, I saw them every day for two weeks. What's wrong with the lady who's crying?"

"I don't know," said Charlie. "You ever talk to these people?"

"Nope. Once I started talking to the older man. Seems he used to visit Saratoga a long time ago. But then one of the others came and got him. They kept to themselves, I'll say that for them. No noise, no bothering their neighbors. They had three cabins down on the far end. Even did their cooking there. You're not supposed to of course, but I never said anything. Sometimes a couple of them would be outside working out, you know, push-ups and sit-ups. Like they were soldiers."

"What kind of car were they driving?"

"Had a Ford van and a VW, both pretty old."

"You have the plate numbers?"

"Sure, they wrote them down when they registered." Bellamy looked through a card file. "Here it is," he said.

Both vehicles were registered in Massachusetts. Charlie wrote down the numbers. At the top of one card was the name Peter Hobson, at the top of the other was Mitchell Cary. "And who are these names?" asked Charlie.

"One's the old fellow," said Bellamy, "and the other was this guy here." He pointed to the man seated to the left of Polanski in the picture. "I can't remember which was which, so don't ask me."

"That's okay," said Charlie. "And when did they leave?"

"Just this Monday. They'd figured on staying longer but had to go unexpectedly. A death somewhere, the young guy said."

"You clean their rooms already?"

"Sure, they been gone three days. What kind of place do you think this is?"

"You find anything? I mean, did they leave anything behind, a piece of paper or some clothing?"

"Well, they cleaned it up pretty much themselves, swept and tidied, but you know I did find one thing."

"What's that?" asked Charlie.

Bellamy opened the drawer of his desk, removed something and stretched out his hand to Charlie. Then he opened his fingers to reveal a bullet. It was large and Charlie guessed it was for a .45. Instead of the slug being rounded and torpedo-shaped, it had a flat point.

"What kind of bullet is that?" asked Riklin. "It looks weird."

"It's like the kind made by Webley for their service revolvers," said Charlie. "It's called a Manstopper."

"Found it under the bed," said Bellamy. "Gave me a start, I can tell you."

Charlie took the bullet and rolled it around in his hand. "Could it have been there before they came?"

"Sure, it's possible," said Bellamy. "We always clean but I guess we could of missed it. I just don't think we did, that's all."

Back in Saratoga, Charlie dropped Joe Riklin off at police headquarters to give Peterson the bullet, the license plate numbers and the descriptions of the six men. He didn't think it would amount to anything—the plates were probably stolen—but at least it should convince Peterson that something serious was afoot. Afterward, Riklin was to start calling motels again, then drive down to Troy to find Frank Hensley and see if he could remember anyone Polanski had known around Saratoga.

For his own part Charlie decided to seek out Maximum Tubbs and ask his advice. Maybe he would have a sense of what Polanski was after. Tubbs, however, was often difficult to locate and it wasn't until Charlie had visited a dozen bars and a few floating card games that he found him in the early evening shooting craps with five other men in the back of a Gulf station on the west side of Saratoga.

"Sit down, Charlie, and make an investment," said Tubbs.

He and the other men were seated in a circle on overturned boxes. Their playing floor was a large sheet of
cardboard.

"It'd be more like a withdrawal," said Charlie, nodding
to the other men, several of whom he had arrested once
or twice as a policeman.

"That's not what your father would say," said Tubbs.
"He'd sit right down and laugh and tell stories till all his
money was gone or he'd wiped us out." Tubbs was dressed
in a three-piece light brown suit and had covered his particular cardboard box with a white handkerchief. He held
the dice in his delicate pink hands as if they were as fragile
as soap bubbles.

"And what did it get him?" asked Charlie.

"Now, Charlie, you sound like your cousins. He took
his chance and it didn't pay off. At least he didn't have
to get old."

It occurred to Charlie that he was now ten years older
than his father had been when he shot himself. The thought
amazed him. His father had been almost a kid.

"So what do you want if you're not going to gamble?"
asked Tubbs. He had turned back to the table and was
slowly shaking the dice. The other men stared at his hand
as if Charlie didn't exist.

"I need to talk to you."

"How long?"

"Maybe an hour."

"It must be serious." Maximum Tubbs stopped shaking
the dice and gave them to the man on his left. "Okay, I
can quit for that long." He counted out the bills on the
floor in front of him, then wrapped them in the white
handkerchief. "There's two hundred and thirty-seven dollars there, boys. I expect to find it here when I get back."

Five minutes later Charlie and Maximum Tubbs were

seated in a booth at the Backstretch, where Charlie had gone, he was certain, just to torment himself. It was eight o'clock and relatively quiet. Doris was seated at the bar talking to the owner, Berney McQuilkin. She had nodded to Charlie when he came in but hadn't spoken or smiled. The walls of the Backstretch were covered with the pictures of prizefighters with inscriptions saying "My pal, Berney, a helluva swell guy" and "To Berney, my best buddy, thanks for the laughs." The handwriting on all the pictures was the same and Doris had once told Charlie that Berney McQuilkin had written the inscriptions himself. Above Charlie's booth was a picture of Spanky Skoyles crouched down with his gloves guarding his narrow jaw. His one chance at the middleweight title in the late thirties had evaporated when he had gotten mixed up with a young North Carolina girl and had been shot in the arm by her father. Maximum Tubbs sat acrosss from Charlie on a white handkerchief. He always sat on a white handkerchief.

"Okay, Charlie," said Tubbs, "what's the story?"

So Charlie told him. He told him how the old man in the picture was indeed Tommy Polanski. He told him about talking to Polanski's sister and Frank Hensley. He told him how Polanski and five other men had spent the past two weeks at the Forget-Me-Not. He told Maximum his own suspicions and ideas, what he thought about Polanski's desire for respect and not wanting to be forgotten, how Polanski had cancer and probably didn't have long to live, how the young man had come looking for Polanski wanting his expertise. He told about the discovery of the bullet, the Manstopper. Charlie talked for twenty minutes. Then he paused and looked around. Doris was joking with someone whom Charlie didn't recognize. Berney McQuilkin was scratching his belly.

"What seems obvious," said Charlie, "is that Polanski and these other men are planning a job. Maybe it's the Adirondack Trust, but I doubt it. They're not the kind of guys to take that risk. Whatever it is will require genius, absolutely cool nerves and the timing of a trapeze artist. Given all that, I can't think what it could be."

Maximum Tubbs had been sipping Saratoga Vichy through a straw. Now he fished out the straw and bent it in half. "I'll think about it," he said. "Actually, I have a faint idea what they're up to. I expect it's a 1930s sort of crime—nothing to do with drugs or computers or real estate scams. You know, I been remembering Polanski. He was on the lam but he was still hanging out around Saratoga. In another life he might have been an inventor—someone who liked facing insurmountable problems. Maybe a mountain climber, maybe an athlete. No, it would have to be something that took brains. Tommy was proud of his brains. Maybe he could have been a Houdini. That's who he probably admires, Houdini."

"What's your idea?"

"I want to give it more thought. But I'll tell you what, you pick me up at that crap game at exactly eleven-thirty and maybe I'll be able to show you."

"Show me?"

"Sure, don't you want to see for yourself? Now drive me back to that Gulf station. Those dice were hot."

After dropping Maximum Tubbs off at his crap game, Charlie drove to his office. Joe Riklin showed up ten minutes later. He had called the rest of the motels and had found no trace of Polanski. He had also driven down to Troy, looking for Frank Hensley, but Hensley had apparently disappeared.

"They're probably just waiting," said Charlie, seated in the swivel chair behind his desk. "Waiting for the right day. Most likely one of them is staying here in town. I wouldn't be surprised if they were keeping an eye on us as well."

"How would they know about us?" asked Riklin. He was drinking coffee from a Styrofoam cup. A long strand of red hair kept falling across one eye and he brushed it aside with the back of his hand.

"Polanski may be in contact with Hensley and Hensley might have told him. Also, they've probably been nervous ever since Victor was run down."

"You think they'll decide against doing a robbery?"

"I don't know. What often catches a guy like Polanski is being too clever, thinking he can get away with something no matter what, thinking the cops are too dumb or too slow."

Riklin nodded toward the picture of Jesse James on Charlie's wall. "Who's that guy? He looks familiar."

"Jesse James."

"He looks like a bird," said Riklin. "Isn't it odd for a private detective to have a picture of Jesse James on his wall?"

"I don't think so," said Charlie, surprised. "His family was from around here, even though he was born in Missouri."

"Was he the first bank robber?"

"No, although he and his men were the first organized gang to rob a bank: Clay County Savings in Liberty, Missouri, February 13, 1866. They got sixty thousand dollars and some nonnegotiable bonds."

"How big was the gang?"

"Ten men. One of the bank tellers was named Greenup Bird. I've always thought that was a strange name. No, the first bank robbery took place on December 15, 1863, in Malden, Massachusetts. A drunk by the name of Eddie

Green went into the bank and saw that the only person around was the owner's seventeen-year-old son. So Green shot the kid twice in the head and took five thousand dollars. Of course, when he started spending the money, he was arrested right away. They hung him two months later. There are two kinds of bank robbers—those who bust in and those who sneak in. Jesse James, Eddie Green, the Dalton brothers and John Dillinger—they were all busters. Polanski, Willie Sutton and George Leslie, who was called the king of the bank robbers, were sneakers. Leslie had a degree in architecture from the University of Cincinnati, but then he moved to New York and started robbing banks. That was over a hundred years ago. He'd get the bank's architectural plans and figure the best way to sneak in, then he'd crack the safe. They figure he made twelve million from robbing banks. He even robbed the Saratoga County Bank in Waterford. Then he retired and worked as a consultant, devising plans for robbing banks. In six years, he supervised the robbing of about fifty banks and made twenty thousand dollars a job."

"What happened to him?" asked Riklin.

"Oh, he got involved with someone else's girlfriend and got shot in the head."

"Love always fucks you up," said Riklin.

"Isn't that the truth."

"How come you know this stuff?"

"It's comforting. It's a world where everything's clear—no gray areas, no confusion. I like that. I mean, Jesse James might have been a sadist, but he knew what he wanted and he didn't fool around."

When Charlie picked up Maximum Tubbs at the Gulf station at eleven-thirty, the old man was gleeful, or at least as gleeful as someone who has been gambling steadily for sixty years would allow himself to be. Even on the black vinyl seat of the Renault, he sat on his handkerchief.

"Five hundred smackers, Charlie. Not like the old days, but it pays the rent and buys the bacon."

"So where are we going?" asked Charlie.

"Drive over to Nelson Avenue. You know that motel on the corner of Nelson and Gridley right by the harness track? Drive over there."

"A motel?"

"We can park there."

"What kind of robbery is this?" asked Charlie. He crossed Broadway, then turned onto Spring Street, bordering Congress Park. It was a warm night and the windows were down. The moon, which had been full several days before, was looking lopsided as it rose to Charlie's left above the Caffe-Lena.

"You'll see. I'm not promising anything, Charlie, but if I was Polanski and had a gang of five men, this is the job I'd try and pull off."

Charlie drove up Union Avenue, then turned right on Nelson. After several blocks, the houses became more scattered. On his left were the grounds of Saratoga Race Track, which would open in August. They reached the motel and Tubbs told Charlie to park facing Nelson Avenue. Charlie did as he was told. The motel was full of people from the harness track—owners, trainers and drivers, which in harness racing often meant the same thing. The races had ended about half an hour before, but Charlie could still see the lights over the roof of the motel. Then, just as he was looking at them, they went dark.

"You ever go to the harness track?" asked Charlie.

"Not me, too many germs. I like to keep my gambling limited to a few people. You want to play a little cards while we wait? It might be ten or fifteen minutes."

"Can't afford it. Tell me something about my father."

"I already told you all I remember."

"Tell me something anyway."

Maximum Tubbs thought a moment. From the motel came the sound of disco music and laughter. "Did I ever tell you about the time your father won a Chinese girl in a poker game?"

"Tell me again."

"Well, for a while your father was playing cards with a bunch of Chinamen who owned some stores in town. One night he's playing and there's one poor stiff who's finally down to his store or his daughter. I guess he owned a laundry. So he bet the daughter in a game called Black Maria and lost. When the game was over, the daughter followed your father home. 'Go away,' he kept saying. 'Go home, the deal's off.' But she followed him anyway. She was about fifteen. Poor girl didn't even have any shoes. Your mother was real pissed. I guess you were just a baby. For a week this girl slept on the couch in your apartment. She didn't clean, she didn't sweep the floors, she only cried. So your father hunts out the Chinaman and gets him to play again. 'I don't have any money,' said the Chinaman. 'I'll lend you some,' your father said. So your father lent him a stake and they started to play. Your father was always straight, never cheated or fooled with the cards. The Chinaman won his daughter back, plus a little money to get her some shoes. It was the only time I saw your father rig a game. After that, he didn't play with Chinamen anymore. 'Too risky,' he said."

They sat in silence for about five minutes. Charlie stared across the road into the woods near the backstretch of the flat track. He thought of the young Chinese girl sleeping on his parents' couch and how his father must have worried.

"Okay," said Tubbs, "here it comes."

Charlie saw flashing lights to his right and heard the roar of a motor. A Burns armored truck shot by, heading toward town. Ten feet behind it was a Saratoga patrol car, a blue-and-white Plymouth. Both vehicles must have been doing over sixty. Charlie caught a glimpse of the guards in the truck and two policemen. Then they were gone.

"That's got the money from the harness track," said Tubbs. "Maybe four hundred thousand, maybe more. It goes by here every night."

11

Saratoga Harness opened in the summer of 1941, shortly after pari-mutuel betting became legal in New York State. Although the meet that first year was only twenty-six days, the track had grown steadily and during the last year there was racing on 203 days. The crowd averaged about three thousand but had gone as high as fourteen thousand. It was especially big on those nights when there were free giveaways—Jacket Night, Pitcher and Tumbler Night, Sport Bag Night, Digital Watch Night—evenings when the first seven thousand paid admissions received a little bonus. Charlie was interested to see that a Jacket Night was scheduled for the following week.

The record handle or total money wagered for a single night was half a million back in 1975. The average handle for the previous year was $220,695 with the highest being $425,464 for a night in the middle of August. The total handle for the year had been $45 million, of which $1.2 million went to the state, $100,000 to Saratoga Springs and another $100,000 to the county. Certainly, the total handle was not in the Burns International Security truck which Charlie had seen speeding into the Adirondack Trust, since some money had to be paid back to those lucky people with winning tickets. On the other hand, neither had the track started with no money at all, so presumably the Burns truck was carrying at least $300,000 and possibly as much as $500,000, which would also include the money from paid admissions and the concessions, restaurants and souvenir stands.

Friday morning Charlie went out to the Raceway just to look around. It was deserted except for the maintenance people cleaning up after the previous night. Out on the track, a large yellow grader was smoothing the surface. The Raceway had an energetic, no-nonsense look about it with its white buildings and red-and-gray-striped roofs. Even though some pennants were flying from the roofs, it had none of the pizzazz of the flat track. Where the flat track was colorful and romantic with its gingerbread decoration and thousands of flowers, the Raceway was plain and pragmatic, dominated by the great wall of glass enclosing its indoor grandstand so the fans could be warm and comfortable even in midwinter.

Charlie sat on the top row of the bleachers and looked out at the green tote board, before which a pattern of shrubbery spelled out the word "Saratoga." Flanking it were a pair of horseshoes made from the same shrubbery, while in front stood a Civil War cannon. Around the far side of the track grew a border of trees. Far to the left was the stabling area with room for nearly a thousand trotters and pacers. It was a sunny day, and as Charlie leaned back, putting his elbows on the railing behind him, he wondered why he hardly ever came here. There were all sorts of stories—that the front-runners blocked the trailing horses, that it was harder to glean necessary information from the past-performance sheets. But Charlie's main reason was the lack of magic. Going to the flat track, wandering through the paddock before a race, catching the eye of a horse and following it to the walking ring and out to the track—it was like falling in love, whereas betting on a trotter was more like a real estate deal. Harness racing was not the sport of kings but of small businessmen. It could be exciting and Charlie had lost money here, but he'd never lost his heart.

Still, a lot of money changed hands, and as he walked back across the huge parking lot to his Renault he wondered about Tommy Polanski. After the last race, the money was counted, bagged and put in the Burns truck. Then it was rushed into the bank about two miles away with a police escort. During August, there were usually two police cars, one in front, one in back. But now in June, when the town wasn't swollen with tourists and racing fans, one police car was thought sufficient. The route led mostly through the city, the only open area being that stretch of Nelson Avenue between Wright Street and Crescent along the grounds of the flat track. There was even a gate right by the clubhouse turn with two white pillars and a twelve-foot chain-link fence. That was one place a truck might be robbed. Another was farther up by Lincoln Avenue, or perhaps it could be stopped as it turned onto Union Avenue or even Circular Street. Even so, it seemed crazy to try to stop a truck containing three armed men followed by a patrol car with two policemen.

But that very impossibility, thought Charlie, could get under Polanski's skin and itch and nag at him, teasing him to figure out how it could be done. It was, as Maximum Tubbs had said, a 1930s kind of crime. It was something that would appeal to Polanski, and if he had really come to Saratoga with five men hoping to win back his reputation as professional thief extraordinaire, then it seemed to snatch an evening's receipts from the Saratoga Raceway would be a good way to go about it.

Charlie started the Renault. It was time to pay another visit to Chief Peterson. But Charlie was not pleased with Peterson. It seemed the police department was dragging its feet. Peterson would have been happiest if absolutely nothing happened in Saratoga—no racing, no ballet or rock-and-roll concerts, no Philadelphia Orchestra, no Skidmore, no historical pageants, no polo or Little League baseball, nothing but dog shows. As it was, Peterson liked to pretend he had everything under control. And one way of doing this was to discount the possibility that anything might go wrong. He was like the owner of a china shop, sitting with eyes shut, thinking that the fact he could see nothing made it all safe, yet waiting for the sound of breaking glass.

Charlie found Peterson alone in his office, seated at his desk with his chin in his hands and looking balefully at some papers spread out in front of him. Seeing Charlie, he squinched his eyes shut in an expression that Charlie could only describe as a wince.

"There's been another liquor store robbery," said Peterson, "out at the shopping center on Route 50. Got about eight hundred dollars."

"Same guy?" asked Charlie.

"Sure it's the same guy, you think it's a fuckin' fad? A young white guy with a stocking over his head and another waiting in a car. It's had Tidings and Novack running around all day."

Charlie sat down in the armchair in front of Peterson's desk. "You find out anything about Polanski?"

"Charlie, can't you hear? We been busy."

Charlie leaned forward and put his hands on his knees. Since it was his day off, he was wearing jeans. He liked wearing jeans. It felt like a political act. "Polanski and his five associates are planning a robbery, a big robbery, and if they get away with it, you're going to look pretty stupid."

Peterson stood up. He was wearing a white shirt and was in his shirt sleeves with his blue vest unbuttoned. Charlie guessed he owned a dozen three-piece blue suits, maybe more. "I don't want any offensive talk, Charlie. We've had plenty to do around here."

"You make an ID on those other guys in the picture?"

Peterson looked unhappy. "Yeah, one of them. His name's Ralph Bloom. He got out of Attica a year ago after a five-year stretch for dealing cocaine. He's a tough guy and they say he's killed some people. Now he's dropped out of sight."

"So he knew Polanski in Attica."

"Could be."

"You have the picture there? Which one is he?"

Peterson rummaged around his desk, found the picture and handed it to Charlie. "It's the guy on Polanski's left."

Bloom had a square face with carefully cut black hair like a movie actor or male model—wide brow, long straight nose, square chin, a wide mouth with narrow lips. His eyes, Charlie thought, were like the eyes of a lizard: hooded slightly and almond-shaped. They looked straight at the camera and seemed absolutely devoid of emotion. In his hand was a glass of something that might have been scotch and soda. Bloom wore a dark suit and in his lapel was a white carnation. Could this have been the person who ran down Victor?

"What about those Massachusetts license numbers that Riklin brought in?" asked Charlie, handing the picture back to Peterson. "You get anything on those?"

"Stolen plates. We're looking for them but nothing's turned up."

As Charlie talked, he took a felt-tip pen out of his pocket and began fiddling with it, making little black marks on his thumbnail. Then he wrote "yes" on one and "no" on the other. It seemed to say it all. "You want to know what kind of job they're planning?" he asked.

"Liquor stores."

"No, seriously. They're planning to rob the armored truck that brings in the money from the Raceway each night."

Peterson stared at Charlie as if he had spoken in Greek. Then he began to laugh, a guffawing laugh so that tears squeezed out of the corners of his eyes and he couldn't catch his breath. "That's good, Charlie," he said, "that's really good." Then he broke down again, bending over with his hands just above his knees.

Charlie waited and again thought how he disliked policemen. When Peterson seemed sufficiently calmed, Charlie said, "Polanski wants to do a big job. He's robbed armored trucks before. The men with him are counting on a big haul. Really, this is just the sort of crime they would do. For Pete's sake, chief, I'm telling you for your own good."

Peterson stood by the window breathing deeply. Across his blue vest was a small silver chain from which hung a miniature revolver. As he breathed, the revolver rose and fell. "Charlie, I believe you're sincere, I'll say that for you. But you know how impossible it would be to rob that truck? It's as tight as a drum. There are three men with guns inside and a car full of cops right behind. When they get to the bank, there are more cops to meet them. Let's say, for the sake of argument, someone tried to stop the truck. The men in the following car would immediately put out a signal and a dozen patrol cars would arrive in a maximum of two to three minutes. Well, let's say they still get the money and drive away. Where they going to go? Every main road will be blocked, every secondary road will be watched. They couldn't even get out of town. You think they might have a plane? There'd be police at the airport. Look, Charlie, we've thought of these things. It would be almost impossible to rob that truck, and if someone still managed to rob it, then it would be impossible to get away. We could have over two hundred cops in the area in ten minutes, over a hundred cars. We could have helicopters, bloodhounds, snipers, you name it."

"I still think it's going to happen," said Charlie, feeling less certain.

"You read too many of those history books. You're like this guy Polanski, you're living in the past. Jesse James doesn't hang out around here, Charlie. This is civilization. But maybe you have a point about this Polanski. Maybe he wants to do some jobs. Look, I'd be far more willing to pin the liquor stores on him. But maybe he'll try the truck. Who's to say, an old guy like that, crazy, sick with cancer, maybe he'll do something stupid. I'll tell you what, I'll have Emmett ride in the patrol car until we can get a line on the guy."

"Emmett?"

"Sure, he's a sergeant, he's got experience and he's a good shot. Other than that, I'll put two more men at the bank in town. And I'll notify the state police, sheriff's department and surrounding towns that there might be an attempt. Believe me, if anyone robs that truck, every road will be closed. But this is stretching things, Charlie. I don't have the manpower to do more. We're trying to cover these liquor stores. No telling when they'll rob another. They must be junkies. Why else would you take such a chance for so little money?"

Charlie wondered if he was right about Polanski. There

was nothing he could argue, no proof to put forward. After all, hadn't he done enough just to warn Peterson?

"It's a joke, Charlie," said Peterson. "This Polanski's a dreamer. They been probably up here going to the trots like the guy at the motel said. I mean, even if Polanski is crazy enough to want to rob the truck, is it believable he could find five guys who are just as crazy to help him? Jesus, Charlie, this is the real world, it's not a cowboy story."

"What about the bullet?" asked Charlie.

"Could of been there for five years, who's to say?"

"What about the stolen license plates and fake names?"

"Okay, okay, we're looking for them, but if they're ex-cons they're probably just paranoid. An armored truck, though, that's something else again. Come on, Charlie, stop this dreaming and let me get back to work."

As Charlie was driving over to his office, he happened to meet Artemis, the equestrienne, who had also been in Victor's photograph. She was driving north on Putnam and Charlie was driving south. When she saw Charlie's red Renault, she honked. Then they pulled up next to each other and talked through their open windows. Artemis drove a black Saab turbo, which Charlie thought of as classy.

"I've just gotten back to the States," said Artemis. "You must come for a visit." She wore a metallic-green leotard with long sleeves and stretched her hand across to Charlie, who tentatively shook her fingers. On her little finger was a silver ring with a horse's head with glittering red eyes. She had very precise features with a long narrow nose and flat cheekbones. A wave of dark hair fell across her high forehead.

"Have you been in Vienna?" asked Charlie.

"Yes, so boring. The lights, the applause, the galloping horses—the Viennese are like children. Delightful but with sugar around their mouths and sticky fingers."

A black Trans Am honked behind Charlie. "I saw your picture recently. You were in the bar of the Bentley. That's my mother's hotel. I wanted to talk to you about it." The car honked again.

"That funny man was taking them. Pictures are so difficult. One never knows what to wear." As she spoke, Artemis kept widening and narrowing her dark brown eyes so that her face was constantly busy.

"That was my friend Victor," said Charlie hurriedly. In his rearview mirror, he saw the man in the Trans Am hammering on his steering wheel in exasperation. "Do you remember anyone else in the bar? It has to do with a case I'm working on." The Trans Am started honking over and over again.

"Come and see me," said Artemis. "I've rented part of a stable in Cambridge." She gave him directions. "I'm there nearly every day with dear Phillip." Phillip was her horse.

"I'll try to make it this weekend," said Charlie. "I need your advice." Artemis waved and accelerated down the street with a roar.

When he got to his office, Charlie again unrolled the photograph from the bar: the honeymoon couple, Polanski and his two companions, the bartender, waitress, Joe Riklin, the lawyer, then Artemis looking at the crying woman, then the man with the yellow ring. Riklin had said the man and woman had been in love. What did that mean? He could hardly think, since just the very word led him to brood about Doris, making him wish he could lie down with his face to the wall. He tried to put Doris out of his mind and again concentrated on the man with the yellow ring or at least what he could see of him: hands, torso, chin—a balding and slightly overweight man in his early forties. Charlie wished he could see his eyes. Although he was 90 percent sure that Polanski was planning a robbery, he was less sure that he or his friends had run down Victor. It seemed unprofessional. It was a panicky gesture.

Charlie felt certain that Polanski himself wouldn't have run down Victor, since in his long career as a thief he had never been known for violence. As for Ralph Bloom and the others, he knew nothing about them. He suspected they had been the ones to search the two offices, but again, the search of Victor's apartment had been done by someone frightened and desperate. Well, the only way to discover if Polanski was responsible was to find him. The man with the yellow ring could come later.

Charlie again began looking through Harry King's memoirs, still hoping to find some clue to Polanski's behavior.

"When I used to steal why we'd go and visit other thieves, my old lady and I . . . and we'd sit up there and cut up what we call 'old-touches'—that's a phrase for discussing old capers, 'cuttin' up touches'—and we would get a great kick out of it. We'd go all through the old scores and discuss the ins and outs of it, the trouble we had with the safe or somebody asleep or in the joint or a means of entry or outrageous things that we found and things like that. And I can't honestly say that I have found anything to laugh about since I became a square-john. Everything's been so serious where I used to laugh a lot. I laughed when I fooled the bulls; I laughed when I pulled a good caper; I'd laugh when I'd sit with friends of mine and talk and I was happy go lucky. But since I turned a square-john why it's been all serious. It's been fightin' to understand and do like they do and I don't know."

* * *

Friday afternoon Charlie and Joe Riklin drove up to Hudson Falls for the funeral of Lynn Schorr. With them they took the three maids, Eunice, Millie and Trudy, who were silent on the way up and wept on the way back. The service was at the Lutheran church, and later they went to the cemetery. Nobody spoke to them or asked why they were there. Mr. Schorr saw Charlie but looked through him as if he were invisible. There were over a hundred people at the funeral, mostly teenagers, and this seemed to astonish Lynn Schorr's parents. Afterward, Joe Riklin spent about half an hour standing by her grave while Charlie and the maids waited in the car. Back in Saratoga, Charlie took Riklin over to Hattie's Chicken Shack for dinner. There were fancier places in Saratoga, but no place with more class. They had to bring their own wine in a paper bag, and Riklin got a little tipsy as he told Charlie about Lynn Schorr.

"She always listened to my stories," he said. "She never got bored or told me to shut up. And did you ever see her hands? The way they moved, they made me think of birds."

That Friday night between eleven-thirty and twelve, Charlie and Joe Riklin were sitting in the Renault, which was parked on Wright Street facing Nelson Ave. From where they were sitting, they could see up Nelson for several blocks. It was a warm night, although a slight breeze was blowing through the windows. From somewhere came the buzzing of cicadas.

"The trouble is," said Charlie, "that Peterson doesn't want to believe me. He doesn't like me and he wants me to be wrong, therefore he doesn't want to believe what I say. I'm not being paranoid, that's just a fact. I mean, if

I told him it was raining, his first response would be doubt. He wouldn't believe me until he was sopping wet and even then he'd find some reason to be angry."

"You know him better than I do," said Riklin. "To me he's just a hard-ass." Riklin had slid down in his seat and had his feet on the dashboard. Balanced on his stomach was a bottle of Stroh's beer and every now and then he took a sip or blew into the bottle to make a kind of foghorn noise. He had stopped talking about Lynn Schorr but still seemed to be thinking about her.

"It gets tiring to tell him stuff and not be believed. Like I go into his office with the best intentions in the world and he just scoffs at me. Well, I'm sick of it. Look out, here it comes."

They got out of the car and looked south down Nelson Avenue. There was no moon or streetlight. The nearest house, fifty yards away, was dark. The truck rushed toward them flashing its lights, while right behind it, roaring along with lights and siren, was the patrol car. Charlie guessed that both vehicles were going at least seventy. In the backseat of the patrol car sat Emmett Van Brunt, staring out the window and looking nervous. When he saw Charlie, he opened his mouth, but then he was gone and both vehicles became only noises retreating in the dark.

"If someone's going to try and rob that truck," said Riklin seriously, "then he's got all my respect and admiration."

Just then a blue Volkswagen shot by about a block behind the Burns truck. Charlie caught a glimpse of two young men inside and Connecticut plates.

"Come on!" he said.

Charlie jumped in the Renault and started it. Riklin scrambled in the other side. "You think it's them?"

Charlie didn't answer. He shoved the Renault into first

gear and roared around the corner onto Nelson. The Renault had never been fast, and Charlie heard the engine making strange popping noises. The VW was about three blocks ahead. Charlie accelerated as far as Union Avenue, where the VW had turned right. He thought of the Trans Am he had blocked that afternoon while talking to Artemis. That was the kind of car private detectives were supposed to have. When Charlie turned onto Union Avenue, there was no sign of the VW. For about five minutes he drove around the various side streets, but the other car had disappeared.

"Maybe it was just an innocent VW," said Riklin.

"Maybe."

Charlie drove downtown, where the Burns truck was pulled up to the white marble facade of the Adirondack Trust. Two patrol cars with flashing lights were parked nearby and several policemen were out directing traffic. Charlie noticed Emmett Van Brunt leaning against a lamppost on the corner. Wanting to see if he had noticed the VW, Charlie pulled up beside him.

Emmett didn't give him a chance to speak. "I hear I owe this night work to you, Charlie. Don't you know I got a wife and kids? Thanks a whole lot."

Emmett's black horn-rimmed glasses were sliding down his nose, and he jabbed them back in place with his thumb. Looking up at him, Charlie could feel the dislike streaming from Emmett like heat. He wanted to say something about the blue VW, then thought, What's the point?

12

Mabel Bradshaw was not a woman who had ever smoked, but now that she was the owner of a grand hotel, she not only smoked but affected a black cigarette holder about six inches long. Charlie thought she had started smoking only so she could use the cigarette holder, which also had rhinestones that sparkled in the light from the window. It was late Saturday morning and they were in his mother's suite having coffee and croissants. His mother was drinking espresso from a little white cup which had come with a bit of lemon peel. Charlie kept telling himself that here was a woman who had worked forty years as a waitress and a maid in hotels much like this one. Possibly she had even worked for this hotel, possibly she had cleaned this very room.

"The real reason Doris broke off your romance," said his mother, lighting another cigarette, "is that you lack dash."

"What's that supposed to mean?" It seemed to Charlie that people were always telling him that he lacked something.

"You're a kind of plodder. Sweet, generous, kind, but still a plodder. You lack fire and imagination." Mabel sipped her espresso, delicately holding the cup with her little finger extended. She was half reclining on a chaise longue covered with some salmon-colored material. Her bare legs protruded from her red silk dressing gown and she wiggled her feet, which were protected by a pair of fluffy white slippers. She had recently come from her bath and her hair was wrapped in a white towel.

"Charlie, what would you do if you had a million dollars?"

"Go away."

"But where would you go?"

"I think I'd buy a boat and live on the boat and fish. I'd have it down in Florida someplace, maybe the Keys. I've never been there. I'd fish and in the evening I'd read. Maybe I wouldn't even have it tied up at a dock but anchored offshore a little ways."

"But then how could people visit you?"

"They couldn't," said Charlie. "They'd have to stand on the shore and wave. Maybe I'd row over to get them in my dinghy or maybe I wouldn't. It would depend how I felt."

Mabel looked disapproving. "Does that sound like the kind of dream that could attract a woman?"

"Depends whether she liked fishing and reading. I don't know if I was trying to attract Doris. I just fell in love with her, that's all. It was like stumbling off a curb. It just happened. She said she was breaking it off because I'm too much of an outsider. I don't know, I'm tired of thinking about it."

Charlie was waiting for Joe Riklin, who had called that morning to say he had learned something that might be important. Riklin had been going through the microfilm of old newspapers up at the Crandall Library in Glens Falls, reading all he could find about Tommy Polanski, trying to discover the name of anyone who had known him.

Mabel Bradshaw's room was full of sunlight. Plants hung in the window and classical music tweetled on the radio. Charlie had come to ask his mother about Victor—if it would be okay if he stayed at the hotel after he left the hospital. She had been very generous about it, even suggesting that Victor had been injured in the line of duty as a hotel employee. In return, Charlie had to promise to be kind to Raoul and to dress neatly whenever he came to work.

"Your father had dash," said Mabel. "Rather too much, I'm afraid. And I had dash too, at that time. We lived high, never paid our bills. After he died, of course, there was no room for dash in my life. Your uncle was supporting us. I had to find work as a maid. Your uncle hated dash, and your cousins too for that matter. You're very unlike your parents, Charlie."

"Maybe my dash is the quiet kind," suggested Charlie.

Mabel put out her cigarette, then carefully wiped the cigarette holder with a tissue as she gazed at Charlie with motherly concern. "Have you ever had to kill anyone?" she asked.

"Fortunately not. I've shot at people and wounded them and hurt them in a variety of ways but so far I've been lucky not to kill anyone."

"You seem very quiet," said his mother, "one of those people who live always in reaction to other people, as if you never did anything on your own but always because someone else did something first. But I don't think that's true. Of course you're secretive, and as a boy you were a sneak, never saying where you were going or what you were doing. I bet you've had an exciting life. It's just hidden, that's all. Doris must have found that frustrating."

* * *

When Joe Riklin arrived five minutes later, he could hardly keep still, but he wouldn't say what he had learned until he and Charlie were outside. Joe was wearing jeans, engineering boots and a jeans jacket with the words "Big Trouble" spelled out on the back with silver studs. Raoul noticed him crossing the lobby with Charlie and slowly shut his eyes.

Getting into Charlie's Renault, Riklin said, "Polanski was friends with Irving Kramer. He'd been seeing Kramer a lot in the fifties before he was arrested. There was even talk that some of Kramer's money had come from Polanski, that Polanski had given it to him to invest. The district attorney looked into it but couldn't prove anything."

Irving Kramer was a wealthy old man who owned a lot of real estate around Saratoga. Charlie had heard that Kramer had had a wild youth, but in all the years Charlie had known of him, he was almost a recluse, living in one of the huge mansions on upper Broadway and cared for by half a dozen servants. In the thirties, he'd married a singer from one of the gambling clubs. She died in childbirth, and Kramer had given the child, a daughter, to his sister to raise. She had been brought up in California and Kramer apparently never saw her. He hadn't remarried and rarely went out, and his only entertainment appeared to be a monthly poker game which had been going on for over fifty years. Maximum Tubbs played in it, as did some other men of Charlie's acquaintance. Tubbs had described Kramer as a fearless cardsman who took constant risks, yet rarely lost.

"Let's drive over there," said Charlie. "All he can do is kick us out."

Kramer lived in a three-story Victorian monstrosity with four white pillars and an immaculately tended two-acre yard. Charlie rang the bell. Riklin stood a few feet behind him. As the bell sounded, a dog started barking within the house, a great woofing bark.

The door was opened by a thin, middle-aged man in a black suit who didn't speak but looked at Charlie and raised his eyebrows.

Charlie handed the man his card identifying him as a private detective. "I'd like to see Mr. Kramer," he said. The great woofing bark was louder and, if possible, even angrier. The expression "torn limb from limb" passed like a heavy bird through Charlie's mind.

"Mr. Kramer is not at home to visitors." The man held the very tip of Charlie's card as if afraid he might catch something from it.

"You tell Mr. Kramer that I want two minutes of his time to ask about Tommy Polanski," said Charlie. "If he refuses to see me, then I'll have to talk to the police."

"I'll give him your message," said the man. The dog continued to bark.

"I don't like dogs," said Joe Riklin.

"You want to wait in the car?"

"What makes you think he'll let you in?"

"He hates publicity. If he knows where Polanski is, then he'll let me in. If he hasn't heard from him, he'll send me on my way."

"You got it all figured out?" asked Riklin, looking into Charlie's face as if not sure whether he was serious.

Charlie watched a man riding a red lawn tractor cutting the grass on the other side of the circular driveway. He wondered how he knew what he knew. "I guess I've been doing this a long time," he said.

The man in the black suit opened the door again a moment later. "Mr. Kramer will see you for two minutes," he said.

Charlie and Joe Riklin passed into a great hall with a tile floor and a huge white staircase. At the bottom of the stairs was a black dog, which Charlie guessed was a mixture of mastiff and Great Dane with a little bear thrown in. It was lunging and barking and showing its teeth, while holding on to its collar was a small white-haired woman of about ninety pounds. It occurred to Charlie that he could die right here in this hall, eaten to death by this monster dog.

"This way," said the man in the black suit, turning left down a corridor.

They were led into a large room almost entirely lined with books. There was a fire in the fireplace, although it was a warm day, and before the fire sat Irving Kramer in a red leather chair with a Scottish shawl across his lap.

"Two minutes, Mr. Bradshaw, that's all I have for triflers. What's on your mind?"

"Earlier this week Tommy Polanski contacted you needing a place to stay. I want to talk to him."

"What's he done?" Kramer's head was as bald and his face was as needle-nosed as a baby bird's.

"Nothing, but the men with him are going to get him into a lot of trouble, maybe even killed. I'd like to see that doesn't happen."

"Is he planning a job?"

"A pretty big one." Charlie could hear the dog still barking out in the hall.

"Tommy's a great guy," said Kramer. "But he's old and he's got cancer and I think he's a little crazy. You're not going to arrest him for anything?"

"No, I'll just take him back to his sister's, if that's possible."

"What makes you think I know where he is?"

"He knows I'm looking for him and he doesn't want to

stay in a public place like a motel. He trusts you. He trusted you with his money and he'd trust you about finding him a place to hide out."

Kramer wrote something down on a pad. "I own a little house in Ballston Spa. When Tommy called, I said he could use it. I don't know anything about any job. He said he had a couple of friends with him and was in town to go to the races." Kramer had bright little black eyes that gave nothing away. Charlie guessed he was lying. For that matter, they were both lying.

"That's probably true," said Charlie, "but he's got five friends with him and I think they're here to rob a bank."

After leaving Kramer's house, Charlie decided to drive straight down to Ballston Spa, but as they wound their way back through Saratoga, he couldn't help noticing that Riklin seemed quiet, even nervous. "What's bothering you?" he asked.

Riklin had on a black leather motorcycle cap with a short visor. As he slouched in the seat, he pulled down the visor so it just touched his nose. "I been thinking, Charlie. These guys have guns. There're six of them. They're probably pretty desperate and wouldn't think twice about putting a bullet in us. Are we just going to walk up and knock on the door?"

"Don't worry, they won't be there."

"What do you mean?"

"Kramer had to tell us where Polanski was. If he hadn't, we could have looked up his property at the registry and found them ourselves. Then if there'd been a robbery, he'd have been in trouble. Maybe he'd even get an accessory charge stuck on him, plus having to put up with a lot of bad press. Better to play innocent and to tell us what we want to know. But I guarantee that the moment we were out the door he telephoned Polanski and right this second they're getting out of that house as fast as they can."

"Is that why you mentioned a bank robbery, just to put them off the track?"

"I guess so. It's best to let people think you know less than you do. Most likely Kramer knew nothing about any robbery. Polanski probably said he wanted to go to the races and Kramer was doing him a favor. But maybe Kramer was suspicious, who knows? However, the last thing he wants is something tying him to Polanski, something that would get his name in the papers."

"But you were bluffing him," said Riklin.

"That's right, but he couldn't afford to call me."

The house in Ballston Spa was a small cape at the end of a dead-end street. The doors were open and it was empty. Charlie and Riklin wandered through it. Empty beer cans were stacked in the kitchen and playing cards were scattered across the dining-room table. There were dirty dishes, dirty towels, mud on the floor, but no clothes or papers or personal effects. Nothing to show who or how many people had been there. This time there wasn't even a bullet. Charlie put his hand on the teakettle, then yanked it away. It was still hot.

He expected there were fingerprints, hair cuttings—all the telltale bits by which a man could be identified. But none of these men were being sought by the police, and Charlie could imagine Peterson's exasperation if he called to suggest that a state police lab crew be sent over to Ballston Spa. A few days ago he might have tried, but not now.

Joe Riklin appeared at the door. "Hey, Charlie, the guy across the street saw them leave."

Charlie went outside and saw a youngish man on Canadian crutches swinging his way toward him up the front walk. He had huge shoulders and thin hips and legs, giving him a wedgelike shape. Around his head was a red bandanna. His shirt was open and there were tattoos on his chest and arms. Charlie guessed he was an old biker and felt he knew too much about him already. Introducing himself and Riklin, Charlie gave the man his card.

"So you're a private dick. They must of known you were coming." He snapped the card with his thumb and handed it back to Charlie as he balanced on his crutches.

"Why do you say that?"

" 'Cause they left about ten minutes ago. Lit out like there was a fire under them."

The man had a round white face with a small black beard. Charlie could just see lots of little scars and pockmarks, like what you'd get from sliding across gravel. "You ever talk to them?" asked Charlie.

"Nah, they were too unfriendly. They moved in last Monday. An old guy and four or five others. From Connecticut, or at least their cars were, had an Econoline and a blue VW. A coupla times some of them'd be out here in the morning working out, you know, push-ups and shit like that. I'd come over but they'd tell me to get lost. You imagine that? Like I was a dog or something. Used to be a time when I wouldn't permit that kind of talk. I hope they're in trouble and I hope you get 'em."

Driving back to Saratoga, Charlie decided that Riklin should take his scooter down to Troy to see if he could find Frank Hensley while he went out to see Artemis in Cambridge, about twenty miles away. Charlie still had an unsettled feeling about the photograph, and he hoped Artemis could help him. Consequently, after getting a sandwich at the Spa City Diner, he dropped off Riklin at the hotel, where his Vespa was parked.

It had been sunny all morning but as Charlie drove out Route 29 toward Cambridge he could see some clouds to the north. Through the window he caught the smell of growing things from the fields and barns, and occasionally the smell of rain. He skirted by the orchards on the edge of Schuylerville and glanced at the obelisk commemorating the battle of Saratoga. As he had often done in the past, he resolved to climb it again before much more time went by. From the top one could see all the Hudson Valley between the Green Mountains and the Adirondacks. Crossing the Hudson, Charlie noticed several large boats tied up at the dock. During racing season as many as a dozen yachts were moored in Schuylerville. He continued over the hill past the Hand melon farms with their occasional crow-bangers—small explosive devices in the fields to drive away birds—through Middle Falls and Greenwich, then on through the open farmland to the ridge between Greenwich and Cambridge where the views were greatest and he could see all the way into Vermont.

Charlie kept thinking of what Peterson had said about how impossible it would be for Polanski to get away after robbing the Burns truck. He tried to find comfort in this but kept returning to what he imagined to be Polanski's hunger, his need to commit a big crime, to push away his uselessness. Then there was Ralph Bloom. Charlie imagined him doing his calisthenics each morning. How he must take pride in the hardness of his belly. He reminded Charlie of many Vietnam vets he had known: efficient and tough-minded young men, who cared little for past or future and were willing to risk everything on a single chance. No, maybe Bloom and the others wouldn't get away with the robbery, but Charlie still believed they would try.

* * *

What had always impressed Charlie most about Artemis was not her beauty or intelligence or ability to engage in witty conversation but that she could pace up and down on a horse's back as if she were pacing in front of her own fireplace. At the moment she was doing this while showing Charlie the grounds and garden of a small horse farm which she shared with a woman who owned a string of six trotters and trained as many more.

As Charlie walked across the lawn, Artemis walked beside him, although not really beside him. Really she was walking six feet above him on the back of Phillip and Phillip was walking beside him. Phillip was a thick rectangular horse, a cross between a locomotive and a loaf of bread and of a color that Charlie could only describe as pinkish. Charlie had once stood on Phillip's back and hadn't liked it. Artemis, on the other hand, spent most of her time on Phillip's back, often urging him into a slow gallop while she did handstands and backflips and somersaults. Now, however, she was simply pacing, walking back and forth while studying the photograph that Victor had taken of the bar, as Phillip ambled along the border of a bed of yellow flowers and Charlie stared up at Artemis, trying to determine what she was thinking.

"I don't really remember the men," said Artemis. "They were angry and said harsh things to each other. The older one seemed contented enough but the other two mocked him. I assumed they were his sons and were behaving in bad taste."

"Why his sons?" asked Charlie. Artemis was wearing a burgundy-colored running suit, and as she paced she occasionally kicked up one of her feet to a few inches above her forehead.

"I never heard the exact words, but the tone was too

rude to accept unless you were related by blood. You know that tone children can use? If you heard it from anyone else, you would simply walk away. And the older man seemed to tolerate it, not even to mind. Aha, I thought, here is some unfortunate fellow showing his offspring a bit of the glorious past and they're too cloddish to appreciate it. So they're not his sons?"

"No, they're thieves. I think they intend to rob the truck that carries the money from the harness track to the bank."

"Perhaps thieves are like a family," said Artemis. "They're mean to each other because they realize they have no hope but to stay together."

"What about the woman who's crying?" asked Charlie. "In the picture, you seem to be looking at her." The sun was behind Artemis and Charlie had to squint to see her.

"She and her friend were fascinating. They seemed very much in love, but she was terrified to be there. I had the feeling she kept urging him to leave, which they did very soon. I doubt they were in the bar more than fifteen minutes."

"Just long enough for Victor to take their picture."

"Yes. If she was terrified before, she was panic-stricken afterward. The man was very gentle and was clearly only trying to make her happy."

"Were they married?"

"I don't think so. That might have been part of the trouble. I didn't hear anything they said, of course. As she cried, he stroked her shoulder, touched her cheek."

"What did he look like?" asked Charlie. They were walking along the edge of the corral. Charlie was getting a crick in his neck from looking up.

"He was very normal-looking—glasses, a smooth face, going bald, a very kind expression. After your friend took those pictures, he looked furious. There was such a difference between his kindness and his anger. There always is, of course, but here the difference made him seem like another person."

"Could he have run down Victor?"

"I don't know, that's such a violent act, but I sometimes think anyone is capable of great violence if he feels pushed to it or feels the need is great enough. Not a real need but one of those awful imagined ones. Were they staying at the hotel?"

"No, they'd just come in off the street. I don't think they're from around Saratoga at all. I had Joe Riklin ask at some of the other hotels and motels but I couldn't get a clear answer. I mean, it's relatively easy to trace six men. A couple is much harder. And you think she loved him too?"

"Oh yes, she looked at him with great gentleness. They weren't young, you know. She must have been my age, and he was a little older. That's partly what fascinated me. There's nothing more exhausting than passion. I rather hope that part of my life is behind me."

"And that's what they had?" asked Charlie, wondering if he'd had passions or only infatuations.

"I believe so." They had come to the end of the yard. On the other side of the fence was an open pasture where about ten horses were grazing. Artemis turned Phillip around, then slowly bent over, putting her hands on Phillip's buttocks, and kicked up her feet so she was standing on her hands. It never seemed to Charlie that she had any bones.

"Tell me," said Artemis, "how is your friend Doris?"

Charlie experienced an ache which he interpreted as remorse and regret. "It's over. She's seeing a man who plays squash, teaches science at the high school and is an active member of the community."

"Did she break it off?"

"She told me I refused to commit myself to life, that I was too much of an outsider. I don't know what that means. I told myself I would change in any way I could, you know, just to keep her. But I didn't see what I could do and then, after a while, I didn't see any point. I guess she thinks I'm too much of a loner. Maybe I am. I'd hate to move back into Saratoga and join the Masons."

"You are rather peculiar," said Artemis, "but it's an attractive peculiarity. You should come to Vienna. I'll hire you to look after my horses."

"Horses terrify me," said Charlie. "It seems all they want to do is step on my feet."

"Yes, that can be a nuisance. Perhaps that's why I stay on their backs." Artemis stared down at Charlie for a moment, then changed the subject. "So tell me about this robbery. It must be exciting to rob an armored truck."

Standing in the shadow of the great pink horse, Charlie told Artemis what he knew about Tommy Polanski, Ralph Bloom and what he'd decided must be their plan to rob the Burns truck. He also tried to define what he thought of as Polanski's need to rob the truck, how he wanted to be taken seriously again. As for Bloom, he just seemed to be using Polanski, to be picking his brains.

"Do the police know about this?" asked Artemis.

"I keep telling Peterson whenever I learn something, but he's not exactly excited. He says Polanski's too old and the robbery too risky. There've been several liquor store holdups in the last week, and that's got all his attention. Actually, I wouldn't be surprised if Polanski wasn't responsible for those as well, you know, as a kind of red herring, keeping the police busy someplace else while he robs the truck. Peterson has put more men into protecting the truck and has alerted the state police, but the main reason he doesn't believe it is that he says the thieves couldn't escape."

"And why couldn't they?"

"Because the police could have all the roads blocked within five minutes."

"That would be no problem for me," said Artemis. Balancing on one leg with her arms outstretched, she looked like a hood ornament for an expensive car.

"What do you mean?"

"I wouldn't use the roads. Phillip and I would just gallop across the fields, although I'd probably use a horse a trifle faster than poor Phillip. We'd just travel in ways that cars couldn't go."

Charlie stopped and stared at Phillip. "Then the police would be in all the wrong places."

"That's right. Sad for them, but good luck for us."

"But Polanski and Bloom don't have horses," said Charlie. Even as he said it, he found himself thinking of their Econoline van. All along he had wondered why they should drive such a cumbersome and easily recognizable vehicle. "What they have," continued Charlie as the idea struck him, "is motorcycles."

"Faster than horses," said Artemis, "but just as practical and they don't need feeding."

"The trouble is," said Charlie, "that the roads would still be blocked. I mean, motorcycles would give them a head start but they wouldn't get far."

"Then they must be planning something else as well. If all the likely ways of escape are impossible, then you must look at the unlikely ways. That's what the circus is: making the unlikely seem likely. And that's what I do up here on the back of dear Phillip—I make the impossible seem easy."

"Polanski has a friend in Troy who has a boat," said Charlie. "They go fishing together."

"Then how simple: rob the truck, ride motorcycles across country to the river, then take a boat down the Hudson. If these bad boys don't do it, we really must do it ourselves."

An hour later Charlie pulled the Renault off Route 29 and into the small parking lot by the dock in Schuylerville. The water was gray and choppy from a northerly wind. Before leaving Artemis's stable, Charlie had telephoned Blanche Siegel in Troy. She hadn't been able to remember the name of her brother's friend who had a boat. She didn't know where he lived or how Charlie could find him.

"I know he's not from Troy," Mrs. Siegel had said. "Maybe Cohoes or Watervliet, maybe even Albany."

"Was it a small boat," Charlie had asked, "like a rowboat with a motor?"

"No, no, it was bigger than that. They could sleep on it with no trouble."

Charlie got out of his car and walked down the path to the water. The day had become cloudy and he regretted not bringing a raincoat. At the far end of the dock was a small red building, really a shack, where the dockmaster had his office. When the door opened and the dockmaster came out, Charlie realized that he knew him, had, in fact, arrested him about a dozen times for being drunk and disorderly until the man joined AA and changed his life. His name was Louie Sardo, and when he saw Charlie, he laughed.

"Can't touch me now, officer, I just celebrated my eighth birthday—eight years of no drinking, no hangovers and no miseries." Sardo was a big barrel-chested man with a curly black beard and black hair with streaks of gray. He wore jeans and a red T-shirt with the question "Having Fun?" printed across the front.

"I'm not a cop anymore," said Charlie, shaking Sardo's hand, then wincing as he felt his bones pinched. "I'm working for myself."

"Good way to go broke," said Sardo. "What can I do for you?"

Charlie described Polanski and the other men and said how he was looking for a large fishing boat that might have come up from Albany. They stood by a pair of gas tanks. From a Chris Craft tied up about ten feet away, a small blond boy kept sticking his tongue out at them.

"None of that rings a bell," said Sardo. "As for the boat, it could be anyplace. You don't have to tie up here. There're a hundred different spots if you wanted to do it without attracting attention." He had a rapid way of talking that was almost like laughter.

"What about renting a boat?" asked Charlie. "A fast one that I could get about one o'clock in the morning and someone to run it? It'd have to be a person who didn't scare too easily."

"Legal or illegal?"

"I think these men are going to try a robbery in Saratoga, then get across to the river on motorcycles. I want to follow them."

"When's this likely to be?"

"Well, it might not happen at all, but if it does then I think it will happen next week."

Sardo clapped a large hand on Charlie's shoulder. "I got a fast boat that's just dying for to be used. Besides that, I've some pretty big debts as far as you're concerned."

*   *   *

Just before midnight, Charlie drove over toward the Harness Track to see the Burns truck go by. This time he parked on Union Avenue, right by the corner of Nelson. He waited about ten minutes, thinking about Doris and Artemis. He wished he were the sort of person who could drop everything and go tend horses in Vienna. But he saw this as his town, the place he wanted to live. He knew if he moved away that his cousins, Chief Peterson, his ex-wife and perhaps several dozen other people would heave a collective sigh of relief. But that was no reason to go. Anyway, he needed a home, even though he considered such a need a sign of weakness. Wasn't it domesticity that had killed Jesse James? Every time Jesse had got the chance he'd tried to settle down, ending up at last in a small white house on a hilltop overlooking St. Joseph, Missouri. It was there the Ford brothers got him, Bob Ford sneaking up behind him as Jesse stood on a chair to straighten a picture. Jesse normally wore two gun belts, four guns in all, but he took them off when he got on the chair. Ford shot three times, then ran from the house shouting, "I have killed Jesse James! I have killed him! I have killed him! I have killed Jesse James!"

Charlie saw the Burns truck about two blocks up Nelson, flashing its headlights with the patrol car running at full code about ten feet behind it. Again, both vehicles were going well over sixty. Charlie thought how tiresome it must be for the people who lived along the road, although perhaps the siren wasn't used all the time. The truck made the turn onto Union Avenue almost on two wheels, and the tires screeched. Charlie could see the driver grinning. The policeman driving the patrol car was also grinning. Emmett Van Brunt sat in the backseat, nervous and very serious. This time he didn't see Charlie.

Starting the Renault, Charlie continued to wait. About a minute later, he saw a single bouncing headlight, then Riklin's old Vespa came into view. As he made the turn onto Union Avenue, Riklin saw Charlie and raised one clenched fist in salute.

13

"There's a saying in prison," Willie Sutton wrote:
" 'Don't serve time, make time serve you.' Everybody
says it, and hardly anybody does it. Most of the people
coming into jail are uneducated, unintelligent, and un-
interested in improving themselves. They live for whatever
diversion is fed up to them, a game of baseball, a game
of football, or a motion picture. By the time they leave,
they have become so dependent upon the institution to
feed them, clothe them, and tell them what to do that
they are unable to take care of themselves. I can almost
always recognize an ex-con at a glance by a certain lifeless
quality behind his eyes; something lost and vacant. Stir
crazy is what the prisoners themselves call it, and it can
give you the creeps. . . . For some reason, people are
under a misapprehension that everybody in prison is a
stand-up guy. Far from it. You have to know exactly who
you're dealing with; the rat quotient is very high."

It was Tuesday afternoon and Charlie was sitting in his
office reading Willie Sutton's autobiography. He had just
come from swimming and his hair was still wet. As he
read, he idly tugged at the damp strands so they squeaked.
From his place on the wall, Jesse James looked aloof and
disapproving.

For the past two days, Charlie had been a dutiful son, dutiful friend and concerned citizen as he waited for some sign of Polanski. Each night he drove out to Nelson Avenue and each night he saw Joe Riklin hurrying after the Burns truck on his Vespa. Turning back to the book, Charlie tried to imagine what damage thirty-five years in prison had done to Polanski and why, despite that punishment, he would decide to rob again.

"During the planning of a robbery, you are in a constant state of excitement," Sutton wrote. "From the time you disarm the guard to the time you enter the vault, all of your juices are flowing. And then comes the exhilaration of getting into the vault, the satisfaction of the escape, and a temporary sense of happiness that it has come off exactly as you had planned." Afterward came "a let-down feeling," a sense of disappointment. "Twenty thousand or forty thousand, what was the difference? I always felt that way when it was over. Emotionally drained and physically exhausted."

The previous afternoon, Charlie had gone out to look at motorcycles. He had always wanted one but felt he wasn't mature enough to ride a cycle in a safe and responsible manner. He would ride it too fast, take unnecessary chances. At the local Honda dealer, he saw there were plenty of bikes that could carry Polanski, Bloom and the others across country to the river, then be put on a boat. He considered telling this to Peterson, but hesitated, telling himself he didn't particularly care if the truck was robbed, that he was only concerned with finding the person or persons who had run down Victor. Beyond that he was tired of Peterson's disbelief.

On Sunday and Monday he again went down to Troy to try to find Hensley and talk to Polanski's sister to see if she had the slightest idea about which of Polanski's friends might have a boat. But Hensley had apparently vanished, and Blanche Siegel could tell him nothing except that her brother's friends were disreputable types who could only get him in trouble. Charlie had even driven to several marinas and looked around, but no particular boat caught his eye. Twice he had seen a dark blue Volkswagen but both times he hadn't been able to follow it. The trouble, of course, was there might easily be several hundred dark blue VWs in the Albany area.

In Saratoga, he and Riklin again called motels, hotels, tourist homes, rooming houses, covering an area that extended from Lake George over to Bennington and down to Albany. The only result was that Charlie got a sore ear. Again, driving around Saratoga, he kept noticing a dark blue Volkswagen, and once he even gave chase and dramatically pulled over an elderly man who was not Polanski but a retired high school history teacher who thirty years earlier had given Charlie a D+ because Charlie had refused to play John Wilkes Booth in a pageant about the Civil War. He gave Charlie a sharp look as if to say, "Still cutting up, Bradshaw?"

But Charlie kept searching, even though it seemed random and haphazard. He worried about Polanski, not that he might get hurt or killed or arrested—after all, if you rob armored trucks these are only the usual dangers. No, he was worried about his partnership with Bloom, since it seemed that what Polanski was after and what Bloom was after were quite different.

"Working with others," wrote Sutton, "you are at the mercy of your crime partners, and honor among thieves is a myth. You involve yourself with a very low grade of person when you become a thief. The vast majority is basically unstable and therefore unpredictable."

Charlie closed the book and stood up. He would see Peterson one more time.

It was a warm day in the middle of June, and downtown Saratoga was full of shoppers—tourists for the most part who hoped to authenticate their vacation by buying something with the name "Saratoga" on it. Usually he avoided walking up Broadway so he wouldn't have to pass his ex-wife's boutique and so perhaps run into her. Charlie often thought that Marge had married him just so she could be in the same family with his successful cousins. When he divorced her and quit the police department, she had found it almost unforgivable—not because she cared two hoots for him but because she imagined herself the only one with a grievance. As a result, whenever she saw him, she would make some sign to indicate he had hurt her deeply. Actually, she didn't feel so much hurt as affronted. He had removed her from the one family she admired.

This Tuesday Charlie thought he could get by her store without being noticed, but as he was walking swiftly past, he happened to notice Marge in the window putting the top half of a black string bikini on a mannequin. To see his ex-wife holding this tiny garment while standing next to the naked mannequin was so startling that when she caught his eye, Charlie blushed as if he'd been having dirty thoughts. Marge frowned, then narrowed her eyes. She seemed to know he was having dirty thoughts, that he'd always had dirty thoughts. Charlie lowered his head and hurried up the block toward the police station.

The brief encounter shook him, because there was something about it that seemed to sum up their years of marriage. Marge was a tall severe woman of the sort, Charlie often thought, who wore outfits rather than clothes. Their relationship had never been warm. Constantly, she had urged him to be active in the Rotary, the Lions, the American Legion, and constantly he refused. Charlie hated clubs. But the memory of her complaint made him think of Doris. Hadn't her complaint been the same, that he was a misfit? But certainly she hadn't been urging him to join anything. Her only remark was that he lived on the perimeter of life. But perhaps that was true and perhaps he would have to change that—not by joining the Elks or by moving into Saratoga, but by attaching himself more completely to the community.

It was this uncertainty that led Charlie to stop at Peterson's secretary to ask if he was busy instead of just wandering into his office. As a result, he had to cool his heels for thirty minutes until Peterson was willing to see him. Entering the office at last, he looked around for signs of hard labor but saw nothing but several photographs of Irish setters on his desk along with half a dozen do-it-yourself silver frames in various stages of completion.

"Sorry to keep you waiting, Charlie. Something came up."

Charlie nodded and glanced pointedly at the photographs. "I was wondering," he said, "if you'd learned anything more about Polanski."

Peterson walked around to the front of his desk and leaned against it with his arms folded. "Nothing yet, Charlie. These things can take time. We've sent out bulletins, of course, and every cop under the sun has their descriptions as well as those Massachusetts plates."

"They're not using them anymore," said Charlie. "They've got Connecticut plates now. I don't know the numbers."

"How the hell do you know that?"

"I just do, that's all." Charlie felt displeased and didn't plan to give anything away.

"Well, you know I feel the whole thing's a joke. A seventy-eight-year-old man with cancer robbing a bank or an armored truck? He'll probably turn up dead or in California or just show up at home after a two-week drunk." Peterson spoke with a sort of ironic tone, in the way, Charlie thought, that one might speak to an eccentric distant cousin.

"What about the bullet and the fake license plates? What about the fact that he was at the hotel and that he's with these other guys?"

"I sent Novack over to talk to that guy at the cabins, what's his name, Bellamy. Those cabins are pretty dirty. Like I said, the bullet could of been there for months. And maybe Bellamy's right, maybe they just came up to the races. An old guy, Charlie, how could they get away?"

Charlie started to tell Peterson his theories about boats and motorcycles, then paused. Peterson would only laugh. Yet even as he thought this, he knew he should tell Peterson everything. But why? Hadn't he told Peterson everything and gotten nowhere? Better to deal with it himself.

"Anyway, Charlie, I'm glad you dropped by, because there's something I wanted to discuss with you. You know, your cousin James is a good friend of mine and sometimes we talk about you and we've been concerned with how your life is going."

Charlie tried to imagine what was coming but couldn't. Peterson looked embarrassed and stared down at the carpet.

"The truth is, Charlie, when you gave up your job with the police department, you gave up everything. Not only your paycheck and benefits, but also the respect of many people here in Saratoga. That's not good, Charlie. It's like being cut adrift. What I want to say is that I'd like you to come back to the department."

Charlie looked at Peterson as if he had gone mentally haywire in the way a spinning carnival ride can occasionally go out of control, sending its passengers rushing through space at a hundred times the regulation speed.

"I left the department," said Charlie, "because I'd had enough of it."

Peterson poked at something in his ear, then pulled down the corners of his blue vest. He avoided looking at Charlie, and after a moment he took out a white handkerchief and blew his nose. "I know you left the department by your own choice, and certainly we've had our differences. But what I'm saying is I'm prepared to let you have your job back as sergeant in the Community and Youth Relations Bureau. Not only that but you'd have a chance of making lieutenant."

It struck Charlie that if he rejoined the police department and put himself under Peterson's supervision, it would mean no more detective agency, no more going off on his own. He'd have to accept Peterson's interference in all aspects of his life and probably even have to move in from the lake. On the other hand, he would be a participating member of the community and he'd be working with kids, which he liked. There was even a chance he'd again be able to coach Little League baseball, maybe be assistant coach. Beyond that, he would have a salary he could count on and no longer have to endure the worry and criticism of his family. The hard part, however, would be putting up with Peterson. And Charlie also knew that Peterson wasn't offering him the job because he wanted to help him but only because he was afraid of being shown up by him. Peterson wanted him in a place where he could be controlled. But on the other hand again, it would mean no longer living on the periphery.

"I don't know, chief. I'll think about it."

Peterson pursed his lips and looked stern. "There're a lot of people in the department who'd be dead set against this, Charlie."

"I realize that."

"I can't just go on offering. You have to tell me when you might make up your mind."

Charlie thought a moment. The idea was so peculiar that it wasn't real to him. "By the end of the week. I'll let you know by Saturday at the latest." He started to tell Peterson about Polanski and the boat, then hesitated again. No, he thought, I'll keep that to myself.

After leaving Peterson's office, Charlie walked up Broadway to Victor's apartment. He thought how much he liked Saratoga in the summer and how comfortable it might feel to be a policeman again. As he walked, he nodded to several people he knew, then waved when a friend honked from a passing car. Would this be better as a policeman, even a police lieutenant?

Charlie was greeted at Victor's door by the cat, Moshe, which was one of those cats that must have been separated too early from his mother because he had an insatiable hunger for companionship and affection. Charlie cleaned Moshe's cat box, then gave him fresh food and water, sneezing and blowing his nose as the cat rubbed against his ankles and purred. The cat was lonely. Charlie recognized the feeling; he was often lonely himself. When he had finished, he sat on the couch for ten minutes, holding Moshe and scratching him behind the ears and rubbing his thumb along the line of his jaw, even though his eyes were running so badly he could hardly see. Every time Charlie sneezed, Moshe jumped off the couch, only to scramble back seconds later. At last Charlie could take no more and fled.

Immediately on leaving the Algonquin, Charlie ran into his cousin Jack, who grabbed his hand and began shaking it. He didn't shake hands up and down, like most people, but forward and back like the rod connecting the driving wheel of a steam locomotive. It always took Charlie a second to adjust to this idiosyncrasy and it made him feel faintly apologetic.

"Charlie, that's great news about the police department," said Jack, "really great."

"What do you mean?" Charlie had no wish to surrender the tiniest fragment of information.

"Haven't you seen Peterson?"

"I just left his office a little while ago."

"Didn't he tell you about the job?"

"What job?"

"Didn't he tell you about letting you have your old job back?"

"Oh, that. Yes he did." Charlie glanced up at his cousin and wondered how he always managed to look so healthy.

"Well, you accepted it, didn't you?" asked Jack with a slight note of apprehension.

"I told him I'd let him know this weekend."

"For Pete's sake, Charlie, this is the chance of a lifetime. I thought you'd snap it up for sure."

Jack seemed suddenly depressed. It had always irritated Charlie that his cousins and many others seemed to feel he had left the department under a cloud and not by his own choice. "I appreciate your concern, Jack, but you must see that I might not want to be a policeman anymore. I have another kind of life. I told Peterson I'd think about it, and I will. He'll know by this weekend."

"Charlie, please promise me you'll give it your serious consideration."

"Sure, Jack," said Charlie, backing away. Next, he thought, his cousins would try to get him hitched up again with his ex-wife. "I'll think long and hard, you know me."

Half an hour later, Charlie was sitting in Victor's room at the hospital. He had just told Victor that he could leave the hospital the following week and come and stay at the hotel. Now he was waiting to see how Victor would take the idea.

"You mean your mother wouldn't mind?"

"It was her idea," Charlie lied.

"And Raoul?"

"He doesn't like it, of course, but so what? In a way you were hurt in the line of duty, and so it's the hotel's obligation to take care of you."

"Do I get room service, too?" Victor began to raise his voice as he recovered some of his brashness. He had not been expecting to stay at the hotel, and his feelings were touched in a way that he often tried to guard himself against.

"Maybe. I mean, you'll get fed, but go easy on the lobster and champagne." The fourth set of initials within the lipstick heart drawn on the cast covering Victor's shoulder had been crossed out and replaced with a question mark: V.P. + ?

Charlie looked back at his friend, who appeared to be studying the shape and design of his thumb. He wondered if many people had such trouble dealing with their emotions and if he, in fact, was one of them. "I also wanted to tell you," continued Charlie, "that Peterson has offered me my old job back."

"You're kidding." Victor tried to straighten up but only

managed to swing slightly from the wires holding him in traction.

"I'm dead serious. He said I might even make lieutenant."

"A leash, Charlie, he wants to put you on a fuckin' leash. You make any little move he doesn't like and he'll yank you back. A leash and a muzzle, a doghouse and a Cyclone fence, that's what he wants for you." Victor kept trying to sit up, struggling with his casts and raising his head off the pillows.

"You think so? It would solve a lot of problems."

"Yeah, so would death. He'd take your balls and put 'em in a little jar on his desk. You'd have to ask his permission even to take a leak. I hope you told him to kiss your ass."

"I said I'd think about it." Charlie stuck his legs out in front of him and looked at his disreputable penny loafers. He knew Raoul hated them, which was partly why he wore them.

"Jesus, Charlie, this thing with Doris must of made you wacko. You couldn't do anything anymore. Peterson wants you in a box. Workin' as a cop, it'd be worse than being in jail."

"My cousins want me to do it."

"Sure, they'd be happy to see you as a cop or in a straitjacket or as a paraplegic, it's all the same to them. Charlie, this would kill you."

"Well, I said I'd think about it and I will. I mean, we're not making any money, Victor."

"Vic."

"Okay, okay, but we're broke."

"But we're having fun, you got to say that." Victor raised and lowered his eyebrows several times like Groucho Marx.

"Look at you, half your bones busted and you can say you're having fun?" It almost made Charlie laugh, but he was too depressed to laugh.

"Hey, it'd be worth it if it kept you from working for Peterson. You were an asshole when you were a cop. You couldn't help it, I mean, that's what cops are. It's what they call an occupational hazard. Now forget it, will you? Let's hear no more of this crazy talk." He was silent a moment, then reached over for his glass of water and sipped a little through a bent straw. The bandage around his head was coming loose and was tilted at a rakish angle.

"So tell me about this Polanski," said Victor. "Why haven't you caught the bozo?"

"Because he's hiding. The only chance I have of getting him is when he tries to rob that truck."

"Then what will you do?"

"Then I'll find out if he was the one who ran you down."

"That doesn't matter much anymore," said Victor. "I mean, I'm still pissed, but it's like being hit by lightning or having a cliff fall on you—one of those things the universe doles out as random punishment."

"I'm getting him for my pleasure, not yours. The trouble is, if it wasn't Polanski or his crew, then it must have been the guy with the ring. In which case I'm stuck. Or maybe it was someone outside the picture altogether. Then I'm really stuck."

"And you've found no trace of them?"

"Nothing. They came into the hotel, reserved a table for dinner, then went into the bar for a drink. You took their picture and they left, not staying for dinner. Maybe they were staying nearby, maybe they were just driving through. In any case, I haven't been able to find them."

"What about Polanski? When d'you think he'll make his move?"

"Very soon. You know, that's the kind of thing I can do best: asking questions, devising a plan, carrying it out. You just crank up the process and it's like being on a railway track. Eventually you get where you want to go. But the man with the ring and the woman, the one who's crying, that's the real mystery. Why was she scared? What was wrong?"

That night around eleven-thirty Charlie again parked on Union Avenue by the corner of Nelson. There was no moon but the night was clear and he could see stars, even the Big Dipper. For the past two weeks it had been mostly sunny, but that was supposed to change and rain was expected by midmorning. Although Charlie was looking up Nelson Avenue, he wasn't thinking of the Burns truck; he was thinking of the crying woman. Artemis had said that she and the man had loved each other, and Charlie was wondering just how and why such a love might lead them to run down Victor, steal his camera and search for the roll of film.

Then he saw the Burns truck rushing toward him down Nelson with the patrol car right behind it. He thought how they repeated this rush each day so it was habit, so it would be hard to think anything might go wrong. The patrol car had its lights and siren going. Even though the truck took the corner on two wheels, the driver was steering with one hand. In the patrol car, one of the policemen was grinning, while in the backseat Emmett Van Brunt no longer looked anxious; he looked bored.

About a minute later, Joe Riklin came by on his Vespa and waved. Charlie followed him into town. If the truck had not gone by within the five or so minutes that it was expected, Charlie would have driven back along Nelson to see if anything was wrong. Parking across the street by the drugstore, Charlie watched the unloading of the money.

Two patrolmen stood nearby with shotguns. Several more were scattered between the bank and the corner.

Joe had pulled his Vespa alongside the Renault. "No sign of anything. How long do we keep this up?"

"It's going to rain tomorrow," said Charlie, "and there's supposed to be fog. Also, it's Jacket Day at the track, which means a good-sized crowd."

"Won't the rain keep people away?" As he straddled the Vespa, Riklin kept revving the motor, making little burps of noise.

"No, everything can be seen from inside. Also, the mud makes it more exciting. Just make sure you've got plenty of gas in your scooter."

14

It was raining but not hard—one of those soft summer rains which seems half fog and makes all the lights shimmer. Joe Riklin was sitting on his Vespa in the parking lot of the Saratoga Raceway about fifty yards from the exit. He was waiting for the Burns truck. It was eleven forty-five p.m. and water was dripping down his neck. He wore jeans, a jeans jacket and a blue Red Sox cap and was pretty much wet through. But instead of being cold and miserable, he felt excited, and when he saw the truck accelerating across the parking lot, he kick-started his Vespa and by the fourth try he heard its comforting little roar. It was a rust-colored Vespa that had once been purple and had a rather scratched and cracked plastic windshield. It was so devoid of charm that he liked to think of it as punk, a punk Vespa.

He waited for the truck and patrol car to pass through the gate and then followed them, doing a slight wheelie as he accelerated up Nelson Avenue. The parking lot was nearly empty and there were no other cars out on the street. The shock absorbers on the Vespa had disintegrated to the point that as Riklin bounced along, his teeth kept clicking together and the world became an animated jiggle. Looking ahead through his blurry windshield, he saw the truck and patrol car pass Crescent. Then, to his surprise, he saw a man run into the street carrying two road-repair barriers with flashing yellow lights as well as a detour sign pointing left.

"Road closed!" a man shouted at him. He was a young man in a blue windbreaker and a black cap. Farther up the road, Riklin saw a utility truck pointed toward him with its brights on and yellow lights flashing.

Riklin turned left, then pulled right into the driveway of the dilapidated Victorian rooming house on the corner, bounced across its backyard and around the far side of the garage. His back wheel spun in the wet grass. He proceeded along a row of bushes skirting the house until he reached the sidewalk by Nelson Avenue. Then he flicked off his lights and turned left, while urging as much speed as possible out of the Vespa. Looking over his shoulder, he saw the man standing in the middle of the road facing him.

"Hey!" shouted the man.

Riklin saw him running to a red motorcycle that was parked in the high grass by the fence to the flat track. It had the high front fender and swayback seat of a dirt bike but had a headlight. Then Riklin turned away as he focused on what was going on farther up Nelson Avenue.

As the Burns truck and patrol car reached the flashing yellow lights and high beams of the utility truck, both seemed to fly into the air. The utility truck was parked right in the middle of the street, and the Burns truck had to brake violently and pull to the right. The patrol car was only a few feet behind it.

Swerving to the right, the Burns truck suddenly shot upward and tilted over on its two right wheels. It careened past the utility truck, then veered to the left, still balancing at a forty-five-degree angle, then it veered right again with its tires making one long screeching noise. For a moment the truck looked almost graceful, like a skater or dancer defying gravity in an effortless swoop, but after several seconds it crashed over on its right side and rolled onto its roof. As it slid upside-down along the pavement, there was the loud scraping noise of metal against stone, almost like a bellow of pain. The patrol car was also up on two wheels, rushing along at that absurd angle, but then it bounced down to all four tires, only to smash into the rear end of the upside-down Burns truck, flip over on its side and crash into the chain-link fence separating the road from the flat track.

Riklin nearly fell off his Vespa as he peered over his windshield to see what was going on. He swung into the lawn on his left, sliding on the grass, then skidded to a halt. Jumping from the scooter, he ran toward the upside-down Burns truck, trying to keep bent over behind a row of shrubs that bordered the sidewalk. He was aware of many things happening at once and he tried to absorb it all, knowing he would have to describe it to Charlie. Thirty feet from the truck, he threw himself down on the wet grass and crawled half under a bush in order to watch.

Both the Burns truck and the patrol car had hardly come to a stop when four men appeared from behind the flashing yellow lights of the utility truck, which Riklin now saw wasn't a real utility truck but an Econoline van with magnetic signs and lights attached to the top. All four men were wearing gas masks. One of them ran to the patrol car and threw something through the window. Immediately, there was a dull explosion followed by a column of smoke. Riklin thought they had blown it up or set it on fire until he smelled the tear gas. Another man had run to the back door of the Burns truck, attached something to the lock, then dashed away and flung himself on the ground. There was a small explosion and the doors were thrown open. Someone threw a canister into the back of the truck, and there was a loud poofing noise, then more tear gas poured through the wrecked doors. Two men jumped into the back. There was a gunshot, then a shout. With its tires pointing at the sky, the truck looked like a great dead animal—an elephant or hippo. One of the men began carrying out canvas bank bags, holding two in each hand.

Riklin crawled a little farther under the bush. The man on the red motorcycle slid to a stop nearby. "Some kid got through on a scooter," he shouted. The motorcycle was a Honda dual-purpose dirt bike. Maybe a 350, Riklin thought.

"We haven't seen anyone," said the man carrying the bank bags. "Get the motorcycles!"

The man ran to the back of the utility truck, opened the door and began wheeling another dirt bike down a ramp onto Nelson Avenue. Then he went back for a second. He kick-started both and let them idle. The bikes were Yamahas and had yellow gas tanks and fenders and knobbly tires. Farther up Nelson Avenue, Riklin could see more barriers blocking the road at Wright, the next street, and a man running back toward them. Oddest of all, he thought later, was the old man who stood in the midst of this chaos counting in a loud voice while two of the men carried the money bags to the motorcycles and another stood with a gun near the police car and another dragged the bags out of the truck and the sixth, the one who had come up from Wright Street, stood with a gun near the cab of the Burns truck.

"Ninety-eight, ninety-nine, one hundred, one hundred and one!" He was a thin old man in a black raincoat. He wore no hat and his gray hair shone with drops of water.

Creeping forward a little more, Riklin noticed a metal ramp, made, it seemed, from a large Erector set, just on the other side of the utility truck. Riklin guessed it was about eight feet long and four feet high. Rushing into the flashing lights, the driver of the Burns truck probably hadn't even seen it. Riklin wondered what he had thought when his truck went shooting into the air. As for the cop car, it had been only a few feet behind the truck and the driver hadn't had time to brake or turn before he shot up the ramp as well.

One of the men in the Burns truck had dragged out the driver and two guards and left them on the pavement. They were handcuffed and kept gagging and coughing. Then he went to get the policemen. Opening the back door of the patrol car, he dragged out Emmett Van Brunt by his shirt. The rain became heavier and beat down on the exposed underside of the truck. Van Brunt seemed unconscious and lay on his belly in the street as the man handcuffed his arms behind him. Then he dragged out the other two policemen, handcuffed them and dumped them on top of Emmett. There was a lot of coughing and shouting, punctuated by the counting of the old man.

"One hundred and ten, one hundred and eleven!"

There must have been thirty bags of money. One of the men was linking them together with rubber tie-downs, then dividing them between the three bikes so that five bags hung down on each side. Riklin found himself worrying that the money might get wet.

"One hundred and eighteen, one hundred and nineteen, one hundred and twenty! Let's go!"

The men ran to the bikes. One of the Burns guards struggled to his feet and stood with his arms handcuffed behind him, swaying as if drunk as he coughed and tried to throw up. Then all six of the thieves were mounted and the bikes roared off, not up Nelson Avenue or down one of the side streets but through the open gate into the grounds of Saratoga Race Track.

Riklin ran back across the yard for his Vespa, lifted it and kicked down the starter. It caught on the sixth try, and he slid roaring across the yard onto Nelson. To his left, he could see two of the policemen trying to sit up. They looked wet and disheveled. Farther up Nelson he saw flashing lights and heard sirens. Then he lost sight of them as he passed through the gate to the track. A quarter of a mile ahead, he saw the three dirt bikes on the road around the outside of the track approaching the deserted stables in the backstretch. Although their lights were on, they were fairly quiet, and Riklin guessed some work had been done on their mufflers. The back of the Vespa slid sideways in the mud, and Riklin roughly jerked the handlebars to the left, then right as he tried to straighten out the scooter. When he looked up again, the dirt bikes had passed around the far left-hand side of the stables and disappeared.

Riklin skidded and bounced along the muddy road, and when he also rounded the stables, he saw the bikes passing through another gate into a dark wooded area. His headlight was off and he could hardly see where he was going. He kept bumping across ruts and brushing up against the fence on his left. Behind him, he saw a patrol car coming through the gate at Nelson Avenue, making a lot of noise and flashing its lights. Then came a second patrol car and a third.

The second gate led into the grounds of Yaddo, an artists' colony between the track and the Northway, situated on property that used to be the old Trask estate. Most of it was wooded, and the road through the gate was overgrown as if it hadn't been used in fifty years. Riklin had once visited the Rose Gardens and walked around the huge stone mansion. He'd seen people sitting by a swimming pool and painting outside and heard the constant clack of typewriters, but then a man had stopped him and politely explained that this area was only for the guests. He imagined the same man trying to stop the three dirt bikes. At the end of this road, which was hardly more than a muddy path, was a better road surrounding several small lakes where Riklin had fished several times as a kid. This other road then led around to the main gate, which exited onto Union Avenue.

Wet branches kept slapping across the plastic windshield of the Vespa as Riklin made his way forward. He could see almost nothing, although far ahead were the taillights of the dirt bikes. One of them seemed to have stopped for a moment. Then there was a gunshot. Riklin was afraid they had heard him, and he crouched down on the seat. There were several more shots, and a bullet struck the front of the Vespa. Riklin veered to the right and plunged down a hill. He leaped backward off the scooter into the darkness, then heard the Vespa crashing ahead for several yards until it came to a stop and there was silence—comparative silence, at any rate, because the rain was beating heavily through the leaves and from somewhere behind him on the overgrown path came the frustrated roar of a car stuck in the mud.

Riklin scrambled to his feet. His Red Sox cap had fallen off, and he patted the ground around him but couldn't find it. Hurrying back up the hill, he found one of the patrol cars sunk to its axles in the mud while a second car had come to a stop behind it and was honking its horn. A third car sat behind the second. Car doors opened and closed and men shouted angrily.

Riklin stayed out of sight.

"To hell with your fuckin' liquor stores," he heard someone shouting.

"Get Tidings on the radio and tell him to block the main gate!"

"It's too late. They must be through it already."

Now a fourth patrol car came bouncing down the overgrown lane. It stopped and began honking.

"Back up, back up!"

There was a clunk as the car went into reverse gear, then a whirring of tires. Riklin watched the fourth car dig itself into the mud. Farther along he saw a fifth patrol car, but he didn't stay to watch it get stuck. Turning right, he began to make his way along the lane to the lake. There was mud up to his ankles and his clothes were sodden. His right knee was bruised where he had fallen, but he hurried forward as best he could with a half skip and hop.

Reaching the lane that bordered the lake, he turned left toward the main gate and tried to run. On a hillside near where two of the lakes almost joined was a small stone tower with lights in the windows. Riklin saw a man's face pressed to the glass. Somebody writing something, he thought, or painting something or composing something. Then the tower was behind him. There were some streetlamps farther ahead and he could see their lights reflected in the water. Once out onto Union Avenue, he'd catch a ride back downtown and find Charlie. By now, he guessed, the dirt bikes were five miles away.

Riklin jogged along in a sort of limping run as the rain beat down on his bare head. To his right he heard the long hiss of water falling against water as the rain hit the surface of the lake. Reaching the main driveway, he turned left toward Union Avenue. There were more lights now and he could see the stone mansion rising behind him in the fog. As he passed between the stone pillars at the entrance, he saw a car parked just off the road. It was Charlie.

Seeing Riklin limping toward him, Charlie jumped out of the Renault. "I thought you'd have to come through here," he said. "Are you all right? Where's your Vespa?"

"Cracked it up. Someone shot at me, but I'm fine, just twisted my leg, that's all." He climbed into the Renault as Charlie got in the other side and started the motor.

"We'll pick up the Vespa tomorrow," said Charlie. "I've got some old clothes in the back, if you want to change." Riklin, Charlie thought, looked like he'd been rolling around in the mud. "Here's my towel from swimming. I'm afraid it's still a little damp."

Riklin took the towel and began drying his face and hair. "There're about half a dozen cop cars stuck back there in the woods."

"Serves them right," said Charlie. "Were there three motorcycles or four?"

"Three. Those dual-purpose dirt bikes with two men on each. I figure they got about thirty bags of money." He began to tell Charlie how the Burns truck had rushed up onto the ramp and flipped over.

As Charlie listened, he drove out Union Avenue toward the lake, then turned off toward Schuylerville.

"They never even saw the ramp," said Riklin. "They just shot right up and turned over like some kind of daredevil trick." Riklin had taken the clothes from the back and was pulling them on—a pair of blue coveralls spotted with paint and an old blue flannel shirt. "So what do we do now?" he asked.

"We're going over to the river," said Charlie. "Then maybe we'll rent a boat."

15

Charlie was standing in the forward part of the boat gripping the bow rail as he stared ahead into the darkness. Joe Riklin stood next to him with one foot up on the forward locker. Along with the roar of the 235-horsepower Chrysler engine there was a slapping noise as the boat—something called an Atlantic City Skiff—seemed to leap across the ridges of water. They were running at full speed without lights, which Louie Sardo found funny. Anytime he broke the law and was still stone sober he found it hilarious. At the bottom of the small windshield on the console was a bumper sticker which read, "Easy Does It."

Ever since rousing Sardo from watching Johnny Carson fifteen minutes earlier, Charlie had worried he might be making a mistake. What if Polanski had a plane somewhere? They could even have taken off from the lake—a small plane with pontoons on Lake Saratoga, what could be easier? If he had told Peterson what he had learned, then maybe the police chief wouldn't have wound up with five patrol cars stuck in the mud up to their axles in the Yaddo woods. It was wrong to take it all on himself, especially if he really wanted to rejoin the department.

Now, because he had kept silent, Polanski was probably getting away.

Next to him, Joe Riklin had crawled onto the locker and was leaning forward over the gunwales in a way that reminded Charlie of a dog with its head thrust from the window of a speeding car. The rain had become just a drizzle, but the drops stung Charlie's face and he kept wiping his eyes with his handkerchief. All three men wore yellow slickers. They were going straight down the middle of the Hudson, and both shores were lost in fog. They could have been anyplace. Charlie imagined hitting a barge or even a floating log. In the faint light from the control panel, he could just make out Sardo's face, his wide grin and the shimmering drops of water caught in his black beard. He was a man who liked risks, and for a moment Charlie wondered if this was his boat or if he had conveniently borrowed it. In his left hand, Sardo held a can of Diet Pepsi, and he swigged from it as he stood behind the center console. Charlie guessed they were going between thirty and forty miles per hour.

"There's something up there," said Riklin.

Charlie signaled to Sardo to cut the speed, and the high drone of the motor slowly descended in pitch.

"What did you see?" asked Charlie.

"I don't know, some kind of light."

"What is it?" Sardo called.

Charlie made his way back along the port side. "Joe saw a light on the river."

Sardo cut the engine entirely, and they all listened. From somewhere ahead in the darkness, Charlie heard the departing roar of another motor.

"A pair of Volvo Pentas," said Sardo, restarting the engine. "Must be a good-sized boat."

As Sardo increased his speed, the sound of the other

boat disappeared. Charlie felt the bow rise up, and he got a better grip on the side of the console. His eyes ached from trying to stare into the dark.

"Can you drive this thing?" shouted Sardo over the sound of the motor. He was about six inches taller than Charlie and loomed above him.

"Don't know anything about it." Charlie felt a twinge of terror and tried to push it from him.

"It's easy. Shove this lever forward for speed, back to slow down. The steering wheel works like a car more or less. This is the tach and this is the engine stop, never mind the rest. Take the wheel and let it rip. I'll go forward and see what's there. But watch me—we may have to stop fast."

"Are there brakes?"

"Not unless you want to drag your feet in the water."

"What if I hit something?" said Charlie, taking Sardo's place. It all seemed unfamiliar and confusing.

"Then you'll have bought yourself a boat. Let's go."

Charlie slowly pushed the throttle forward and felt the bow continue to rise as their speed increased. The light from the tachometer and several other gauges kept him from seeing much beyond the console itself. Even though he held the wheel straight, he imagined a sudden bend in the river which would send them plummeting onto dry land and into some farmer's cow barn. He tried to remember if the river made any turns. It seemed pretty straight all the way to New York, but surely there were islands and bridges and sand bars, all sort of obstacles with which to collide. The wind tugged at his yellow rain hat. He wondered if the other boat was really Polanski and Bloom. Then he eased the throttle forward another half inch.

"Pull it a couple of degrees to starboard," called Sardo.

Charlie turned the wheel slightly to the left.

"Starboard, starboard," shouted Sardo, "and faster—what's the point of creeping along?"

Charlie turned the wheel to the right and pushed the throttle forward several more notches. The loud whine of the engine climbed a few notes, and he watched the needle on the tachometer creep to the edge of the red. Even though he was an excellent swimmer, Charlie hated to swim where there were no lines on the bottom and where the water wasn't that pale chlorinated green. He eased the throttle forward a bit more. The small windshield gave him a little protection from the rain, but when he peered around it, staring into the darkness, he could see nothing. He winced. It was like running at full speed with your eyes shut. He had known boys to do that in high school as a dare and it had always turned out badly.

"Cut the speed!" shouted Sardo.

Charlie yanked back the throttle, and the engine died to a purr and coughed several times. Both Riklin and Sardo were leaning over the bow rail. Charlie could just make out their shadowy yellow forms. After a moment, Sardo came back and took the wheel.

"We're getting too close to them."

"Is it who we want?"

"I guess so. Who else are you going to find running without lights at one in the morning? Also, it's a big enough boat so you could load on some motorcycles."

"You think they heard us?"

"Nah, they're too noisy. What do you want to do now?"

"Just follow them, but don't let them see you. They've got guns." Realizing he'd been right about Polanski was an immense relief to Charlie.

"I got a shotgun under the seat," said Sardo. "Don't you have a gun?"

"There must be at least seven of them. We can't just attack." Charlie's .38 was stuck in his belt but he hoped he wouldn't have to use it.

"Take them by surprise and sink their boat," said Sardo. "Easiest thing in the world. Or I could just blow off their rudder. Things like this, you gotta be decisive."

Charlie could see Sardo grinning in the light from the gauges. His beard made him look like a pirate. "I think it'd be better to wait and see what happens."

"You know," said Sardo, "if they came over from Saratoga on dirt bikes, then I bet they cut through the battlefield. The boat was probably tied up somewhere around Bemis Heights." The Saratoga battlefield was where the rebels had defeated Gentleman Johnny Burgoyne in 1777. It was now a national park, extending several miles along the river.

Sardo eased the throttle forward, increasing their speed. Charlie worked his way along the port side until he was squatting on the forward locker next to Riklin. In another moment of doubt, he imagined the other boat full of blue-haired ladies on an expedition, something about birds or fish or PCBs. But no, he knew Polanski was up there. Presumably the boat would dock around Albany, and Polanski and the others would go rushing off. At that point Charlie could do little but call the police. Wouldn't it be better to contact the police right now, tell them the boat was coming downriver? Sardo's boat had no radio, so they would have to stop, most likely in Mechanicsville. Still, Charlie hesitated. He wanted to get to Polanski without police interference. He wanted the chance to talk to him.

As it was, they passed through Mechanicsville as far behind the other boat as possible without entirely losing sight of it. Because of the fog, the lights of the town, the red and green of the traffic lights, the colored lights from gas stations and neon signs—all seemed to paint the air rather than create specific shapes. The yellow slicker and rain hat offered some protection, but Charlie's clothes were wet underneath and he was freezing. Riklin seemed not to notice the cold but continued to lean over the gunwales, occasionally signaling Sardo to speed up or slow down or watch out for something or that they were approaching a bridge.

Sometimes Charlie caught a glimpse of the other boat through the drizzle before Sardo backed off. He could see the bridge and after bulkhead, the white of the transom and the silver of the ladder. It seemed about thirty feet long, maybe less. Charlie wondered how much space would be needed to fit three dirt bikes in its cockpit. Both boats were going about thirty miles per hour. Even so it would take another half hour to reach Albany. Thinking of Peterson and his roadblocks, Charlie found himself smiling, then he chided himself for being smug.

"We should just ram them like Sardo says," said Riklin. "Make it a surprise attack."

"Too dangerous."

"Yeah, but it'd sure be warmer than going all the way to Albany. Shit, for all we know, they're going down to New York City." He spat over his shoulder and into the black water.

But as it turned out, their ride was nearly over. The boat didn't even go as far as Albany but stopped about eight miles north, at Waterford on the western shore. Suddenly they seemed almost upon it, and Sardo had to cut the motor and swerve off to the port side so that Charlie stumbled and fell against the bow rail.

"They're docking," said Riklin.

Sardo drifted downstream as they stared through the fog toward the bulky shape of the other boat.

"Looks like a Bertram," said Sardo in a loud whisper. "Not new but still not a bad little boat. What's the plan, chief?"

Charlie came back to the console. He took out his .38 and glanced at it. The gun seemed absurdly small. "Work your way over there," he said. "And you might dig out that shotgun as well."

The shotgun was in the locker beneath Sardo's seat, a sixteen-gauge over-and-under. Sardo removed it, broke it open, loaded it, then put the rest of the box of shells by the throttle. "So you're figuring on a fight after all?"

Charlie didn't say anything. Then across the water came the sound of one of the motorcycles, then another.

"Get over there," said Charlie. "Cover their deck with the shotgun. I'll cover the bridge." He hurried forward and crouched down behind the bow, keeping his gun pointed at the large white boat.

"Anything I can do?" asked Riklin.

"Just don't get shot."

Even as he spoke there was a gunshot. This was followed by more shooting by two or more guns—five shots altogether. Charlie ducked but couldn't see anyone, so he held his fire. They were about fifty feet from the other boat. A third motor started, not a motorcycle but a car. It sounded like a Volkswagen. All three motors grew louder, then diminished as they drove away.

"Let's go!" shouted Charlie.

The engine roared as Sardo shoved the throttle forward. Charlie stood up on the locker, preparing to jump onto the foredeck of the Bertram. He felt vaguely piratical. As Sardo pulled alongside, Charlie pushed himself up on the gunwale and jumped across the two or three feet of water to the other boat, grabbing onto its bow rail, then swinging his way along the side deck toward the cockpit. There was no sound, and he imagined someone up on the bridge putting a bullet through the top of his head. As he held onto the handrail, he saw Sardo covering the cockpit with his over-and-under.

Charlie made his way along the gunwale and prepared to jump into the cockpit, then stopped. Someone was sitting in the fighting chair, slouched down.

"Watch out for that guy, Charlie," called Sardo.

Looking over the man's shoulder, Charlie saw he was holding a gun in his lap. "Drop the gun!" Charlie shouted as he jumped into the cockpit. On the other side of the chair was a red Honda dirt bike. The transom tuna door was open and a thick plank led from it to the pier.

The man in the chair let go of the gun, and it slid off his lap and fell to the deck. Then he slowly swung the chair around toward Charlie. It was Tommy Polanski. He'd been shot, and his black raincoat was dark with blood. A large arc light stood at the end of the pier, and it made Polanski's face look yellow. When he saw Charlie, he grinned.

"You're Charlie Bradshaw," he said. "I beat you, didn't I? I got away with it." His voice was a rough whisper. Charlie thought he looked a hundred years old.

As Sardo tied his boat to the pier, Riklin jumped across to the bigger boat and pulled himself up the ladder to the bridge. "Hey," he shouted, "Frank Hensley's up here. He's been shot. I think he's dead."

Polanski tried to sit up in the chair but couldn't manage it. "Bloom got him." He coughed and again tried to sit up, putting his hands on the arms of the chair and pushing. "Never had much hope for him, but I didn't think he'd kill us."

"Are you hurt badly?" asked Charlie, leaning over him and pulling aside the raincoat to see where he was shot.

It never occurred to him that it might be Hensley who owned the boat.

Polanski waved Charlie away, then slid farther down in the chair. "Let's put it like this," he said. "The cancer won't get me."

Charlie turned back to Sardo. "Can you work the radio? We need an ambulance and you'll have to call the police." He pushed aside Polanski's hand and again opened his coat. Polanski had been shot once in the right lung, then again in the abdomen. Charlie thought of the expanding bullet that had been found at the Forget-Me-Not. "Can I get you anything?" he asked. "Some water?"

"There's whiskey in the cabin." Although he must have been in pain, Polanski seemed perfectly relaxed, almost happy.

"I'll get it," said Riklin.

Charlie was uncomfortable with the way Polanski kept grinning at him, as if they'd known each other a long time. He had a thin face and his gray hair was tangled. Damp strands were plastered down across his forehead. His thin lips and wide mouth made his grin look like something on a scarecrow. Riklin gave him a tumbler full of whiskey. Polanski took a mouthful, then started coughing. When he had sufficiently recovered, he looked up at Charlie and grinned again.

"Aren't you going to congratulate me?"

"For what?" Charlie knew for what, but he didn't mean to say.

"For knocking over that truck. For getting four hundred thousand dollars and not having to shoot anyone. For leaving all those cops stuck in the mud. For beatin' you even though you were looking for me. For pullin' off the impossible caper." Polanski's voice was as raspy as static on a radio.

"But you got shot," said Charlie.

Polanski waved a hand at him as if it were a trivial concern. "You know what that asshole means to do with the money? All those guys, they're headed down to Florida and they're going to make a killing in cocaine. Get a plane or a boat and bring it up from some island. I mean, where's the fun in it? It's like being a businessman, all fuckin' seriousness and ambition. I laughed at them. They thought I was a crazy old fart and I just laughed at them. They want to be millionaires. Big fuckin' deal."

"They're going down to Florida right away?" asked Charlie. Up on the bridge, he heard Sardo shouting into the radio.

"Nah, Bloom's got a place south of Albany. That's where we been after you chased us outta Saratoga. I told Bloom we should forget about you, but I knew better. You had the whole thing figured out. You're stubborn, like your old man."

"What do you mean?" Somehow it seemed perfectly logical to Charlie that Polanski should have known his father.

"I met your old man a few times. He was a smart fellow, but a loser. I'm not being insulting, you understand, but you'd get him into a game and he wouldn't know when to quit. Had a bullish quality about him, and he'd keep going and going no matter how much he lost. He was stubborn, like one of the most stubborn people I ever met. That's pretty dumb in a gambler but not bad for a cop. Don't think I bear a grudge. I mean, I do smart things and I do dumb things and the really dumb thing was to go into that hotel." Polanski began to cough again, and he drank more whiskey. His hand shook and some of the whiskey spilled down his chin.

"Why'd you do it?" asked Charlie. Riklin was sitting

on the red Honda staring at Polanski, as if unable to believed how relaxed he seemed.

"I really liked Saratoga," said Polanski. "Not now, of course, now it's just a developer's paradise, but way back before they caught me and stuck me in prison." He struggled again to sit up. Charlie leaned forward to help him, lifting him up in the seat and surprised at how light he was.

"I remember when they repealed the old Agnew–Hart Law," Polanski continued, "and all the bookies came back to the betting ring at the track. That was probably in '34. A great bunch of people—Blue Jaw Magoon, Jenny the Factory, the Dancer, Irish John Cavanagh. Then at night you could go over to the Chicago Club or one of them other places. It's all gone now, but that one hotel, you know, the Bentley, I mean it's not really the way things were but it looks a little like it. We were staying at those cabins on the road to Glens Falls and I convinced Bloom to go to the Bentley with me. Freddie Hollander came too. They kept laughing at me, like I was a kind of joke. You know what kinda places they think are classy? Atlantic City and Vegas, maybe Palm Beach. So we had a couple of drinks. The moment I saw that funny-looking guy with the camera I knew I'd made a mistake. Sure enough, he shot it off right in our faces. Somebody had just gotten married. I thought fuckin' Bloom was going to break my jaw, he was so mad."

Charlie had the picture rolled up in his inside pocket. He took it out and held it in front of Polanski, turning the chair so the light from the arc light shone on the picture.

"That's us, all right. Didn't I say he was pissed? He looks pissed and I look nervous. Later on Bloom went back and searched this guy's office at the hotel, also some other place. I guess he was a private dick or something."

"A car ran him down on the street the next day," said Charlie. "Did Bloom do that?"

"If he did, he didn't tell me. Nah, he didn't do it. Bloom's the quiet type. He might cut his throat in a dark alley, but he wouldn't run him down in broad daylight. There was a couple rolls of film in that office, so Bloom thought he'd fixed it. Then you turned up and we knew we were wrong. Frank Hensley said how you'd showed him a picture. I can't tell you how angry I was I ever went to that hotel. In the old days I'd of never been so stupid. Bloom wanted to kill you. He found out you had a place on the lake. He and a coupla guys were going to go and finish you off. But I figured you'd never guess the kind of job we were planning, and if you did, the cops'd never believe you. Besides that, I sort of liked your old man. I don't know, Bloom said I was soft. Maybe he's right."

"It was a pretty good robbery," said Riklin. "I watched it."

"They were slow blowing the back of the truck, but otherwise they did all right. We practiced it over and over out in the country." Polanski grinned. Charlie thought he was like a coach after a winning game. Then he began coughing again, doubling up in the chair and spilling his whiskey.

"An ambulance is on the way," called Sardo from the bridge, "and the cops as well."

"Look at the picture again," said Charlie, kneeling down beside Polanski. "You remember anything about that woman who's crying?"

Polanski drank some more whiskey and tried to focus on the picture. "I was behind her. But I remember her coming in. Good-looking but nervous. Never could stand nervous broads. They always got problems."

"What about the man she was with?"

"I don't recall him, except I think he was bald, yeah, he was bald. Right after that guy snapped the pictures we got out of there. Then Bloom went back early the next day and searched those offices. He's a pretty cold-blooded fellow, I gotta say that for him. He'd of made a good safecracker."

"Where's his place south of Albany?"

"You're going to get him, aren't you? Stubborn, just like I said. I remember I was still in town when your old man shot himself. Me and some other guys sent flowers. What I liked about him, no matter how much he dropped, you'd never see him wince. Some guys really start to whine. What the fuck they play for, they can't take it? Your old man, he'd always have a joke, always have a little something to tip the dealer. I can see him strolling upstairs with a smile to the wife and kid, then putting a bullet in his head. A class act."

"Where's Bloom's house?" Charlie repeated.

But Polanski wasn't ready to tell. He drank some whiskey and rolled it around in his mouth. "You know, Bloom never had any sense of himself as a thief," Polanski continued. "He thinks he's a kind of aristocrat. He talks a lot about Vietnam and stuff. He's a cynic, you understand me? Like he thinks he deserves this money and deserves to make even more selling cocaine and then he's going to have a lot of nice things and nice broads and belong to a country club and drive a Mercedes and shit like that. I told him, I'm just a crook. That's good enough for me, that's good enough for my friends. I mean, I rob stuff that nobody else can get away with. Bloom just wants the money. What the fuck do I want money for? I got cancer."

"Where's his house?" said Charlie again.

"You really want to get it outta me, don't you?"

"He killed Hensley and shot you."

"I don't care so much about me, but he shouldn't of shot Frank. Poor Frank was just doing me a favor. A fuckin' paper hanger, strictly small-time. This was his first real job." Polanski drank the rest of the whiskey and casually tossed the glass over the side of the boat. "Go down to Coxsackie, then west through Norton Hill toward Medusa. Two miles out you take a left turn on an old paved road. There's a little mom-and-pop store on the corner, you can't miss it. Go another two miles and there's a white farmhouse. It's pretty run-down. The barn burned sometime back and the silo's standing up by itself. I guess Bloom shouldn't have shot me either. He thought it'd be easier that way, just shoot me and Frank. That's plain laziness. He probably knew right from the start that he'd shoot me. He kept asking what I planned to do with my share of the money. Shit, I got cancer. What chance would I have to spend it? He probably knew I didn't care about getting away. Better to get shot than be eaten up by that shit. But still, you know, I'd like to live long enough to see the papers."

"How come you robbed the liquor stores?" asked Charlie.

Polanski stared at him for a moment, then grinned. "I had to keep those guys tough, had to keep them occupied, had to keep them from becoming afraid. Also it confused the cops."

Charlie heard sirens. "Did you ever know Willie Sutton in Attica?"

"Not well. He always had his nose in a book, trying to be a big jailhouse lawyer, figuring how to get his ass out. I mean, he always had a good word for a guy, but he was, you know, preoccupied. Not that I didn't have a lotta respect for him. He was a star." Polanski began coughing again.

"Can you start that cycle?" Charlie asked Riklin.

"There's no key. I'll have to hotwire it."

"Get it onto the dock. I want to be gone before the cops arrive."

"What're we going to do?"

"I think we'll pay Bloom a visit."

"He'll kill you," said Polanski. "He's got no blood in him."

Riklin wheeled the bike across the plank onto the dock, fiddled with some wires, then started it up.

"Sardo," called Charlie, "you stay with Polanski. When the police get here, tell them to call Peterson in Saratoga."

"Will do," said Sardo, climbing down from the bridge. "You want my shotgun?"

"That's okay, I'm just going to look around."

It had stopped raining. Charlie climbed over the transom to the dock, where Riklin was sitting on the bike gently revving the motor.

"Hey, Bradshaw," called Polanski in a hoarse whisper, "you'd of never learned anything if I hadn't gone to that hotel, you gotta admit that. But I had to see it again. All those people, they're dead now. They were my friends. What's money good for but to throw away—that's what your old man used to tell me."

"Let's go," said Charlie, climbing on the back of the motorcycle. He felt depressed by Polanski and his dying and wanted to get away from him. All these people were acting out some dumb fantasy, and they didn't care who they hurt so long as they could make it pay off.

"You think Bloom ran down Victor?" asked Riklin.

"No, but we've started something, so we might as well

finish it. Also, he shouldn't have shot those two old guys."

The cycle rolled forward off the dock, then accelerated. Right away they passed the ambulance. Then came the first of three patrol cars. Charlie waved to each of them—the sort of wave that appeared friendly but wasn't. Maybe I'm getting cynical, he thought.

16

It seemed to Charlie that if you put an ant on a Frisbee, then flung the Frisbee just about as hard as you could fling it, that ant would feel as Charlie himself now felt balanced precariously on the small seat of the Honda 350 rushing down the New York Thruway at two-thirty in the morning. Still, it was invigorating, and as Charlie hung on to Joe Riklin he wondered if at long last he was mature enough to own a motorcycle and perhaps should go out and buy one soon.

It was probably the motorcycle that gave Charlie the idea of capturing Bloom and the four others single-handed. Being a dramatic piece of machinery, it led Charlie to think in dramatic terms. Riklin encouraged him in this.

"You got a gun," he shouted back over his shoulder. "They're probably sleeping. It'd be easy."

So as they continued south, Charlie remembered how Sheriff Pat Garrett had surprised Billy the Kid at the old Maxwell Ranch, how FBI man Melvin Purvis had waited for Dillinger outside Chicago's Biograph Theater. The motorcycle was certainly something like a horse, and Charlie thought of Wyatt Earp hunting down his brother's murderers, at last killing Johnny Ringo in a close gun duel in the Whetstone Mountains. The rain had stopped and the

road was empty except for a few trucks. The Honda made
a high whine that reminded Charlie of a dentist's drill.
They were still wearing Sardo's yellow slickers. Riklin was
slippery to hang on to, and Charlie wondered what would
happen if he slid off the back. Then he tried to stop thinking about it. Negative thoughts, he was cursed with negative thoughts. He wondered what Doris would think if
she saw him now. Maybe he was destined to be a loner,
the solitary righter of wrongs. Then he caught himself
again, wondering why he was thinking such foolishness.
He would settle this matter with Bloom, take them into
custody, then go back to the Saratoga police department
with an extra feather in his cap. This would be his last
extracurricular fling before returning to the fold.

He was full of hope. There seemed nothing foolhardy
about trying to capture five armed bandits who did calisthenics each morning and had just cold-bloodedly shot
down two men. Once or twice Charlie worried that they
should have brought Sardo's shotgun, but they probably
wouldn't need it. Even the towns they drove through seemed
to conspire to build Charlie's confidence. Getting off the
turnpike at Exit 21B, they passed the villages of Climax
and Surprise on their way to Norton Hill. It was a winding
road through overgrown farmland, and Riklin enjoyed
taking the curves at high speed, telling Charlie to bend
his body with his and not get nervous. It began to rain
again, and the drops stung their faces.

Stopping for the light in Greenville, Charlie saw a telephone in front of the red brick Pioneer Insurance Building.
Should he call Peterson? There seemed no need. The light
changed and Riklin accelerated out of town and up the
long hill toward Norton Hill. Birch and pine trees bordered the road. On the other side of Norton Hill, they
took the right-hand fork onto a rough narrow road that

ran past dairy farms. It became much hillier. Riklin slowed a little, and they began to look for the mom-and-pop store that Polanski had told them about.

"You think that old guy will die?" asked Riklin over his shoulder.

"I don't know. He was pretty badly shot up."

"Think of knocking over that Burns truck—I hope I can do something like that when I'm seventy-eight."

The mom-and-pop store had a big red Coca-Cola sign under the name Maggie's. It was a small brown building with two Mobil gas pumps. Near a light on the front of the building was another telephone. Charlie looked at it for a moment, then turned away.

"There's the road," he said. "Go slow and keep it quiet. And measure off a mile, okay? We'll go that far, then walk."

Riklin turned left. The road was bumpy and Charlie bounced up and down on the back of the cycle. His .38 was tucked into his belt, and with every bounce he could feel it cut into his flesh. The road was lined with trees, but at the top of a hill they passed a dairy farm with a white house and a satellite dish to pull in TV channels from all over the world. Then they were back in the woods again. After several minutes, Riklin pulled over to the side and cut the light. Charlie got off the back.

"Better push the bike off the road," he said.

He waited as Riklin leaned the Honda up against a tree. It was very dark but he could just barely see the shine of Riklin's yellow slicker. He decided they would have to take the slickers off before they got close to the house. Then Riklin joined him and they hurried up the road at a slow trot. Charlie took out his revolver and held it in his right hand, pointing it down at the ground. He thought of how Texas Ranger Frank Hamer and his posse had

fired 187 bullets into Bonnie and Clyde in an ambush near
Gibland, Louisiana. Then he stopped thinking. Ahead he
saw a silo sticking up like a cautioning finger. Near it was
a small white farmhouse with a light on in the back and
a dark van and a VW Beetle parked in the driveway.

Charlie and Joe Riklin stopped at the edge of the road
and looked at the farmhouse.

"I hope they don't have a dog," said Riklin. "Dogs can
really fuck things up."

They moved forward along the shoulder. A row of
sprawling oaks separated the road from the pasture. Charlie could feel the old acorns under his feet. He kept his
eye on the house while trying not to stumble. They reached
the corner of the yard and crouched down next to a wall
made of flat stones.

"Better take off our slickers," said Charlie. They took
off their raincoats and shoved them under some bushes.
Charlie felt chilled and hoped he wasn't getting a cold.
Drops of water, whether rain or just drops from the trees,
fell on Charlie's head and down his neck.

"There's someone on the porch," whispered Riklin.

Peering into the dark, Charlie could barely see the glow
of a cigarette on the front porch of the house. He waited
a moment, uncertain what to do. Then he saw the cigarette
fly in a high arc. The door opened and a beam of light
shot out into the yard in a long wedge. Then the door
slammed shut.

"Let's get over by the van," said Charlie.

Ducking down, they ran across the yard. The van was
about thirty feet from the lit window at the back of the
house. Charlie knelt down by the front tire on the pas-
senger's side. The lit window seemed to be the kitchen.
Now and then someone walked in front of it. He wondered

why either of them had ever thought they would all be asleep.

"Stay here," said Charlie. "I'm going to circle around." He hurried across the backyard to a shed directly behind the house. Not only was the kitchen light on but an upstairs light as well. There was a small back porch, and light shone through the window of the kitchen door. The house had a tin roof and a center chimney that was missing some bricks. Charlie guessed it had two rooms upstairs and four down—an old dairy farm that some family had gone broke running until they got smart and moved west. Charlie ducked down again and ran past the far side of the house to where the barn had once been. When he reached the silo, he heard the fluttering of pigeons somewhere in the dark. Beyond the silo were pastures. Charlie ran along the edge of the yard until he reached the road. Pausing about a hundred feet from the house, he tried to see any sign of movement. The upstairs light blinked out. Charlie crossed the road, where there were more sheds, then worked his way back along the shoulder to the driveway. It was raining again, and Charlie began to shiver. He started to sneeze, then rammed one finger under his nose and held his breath. He crossed the road and hurried back across the lawn to the van.

"What'd you see?" asked Riklin. He spoke with an eagerness that made Charlie think he had no sense of their danger.

"Nothing, except they all seem to be awake."

"It'll be light in about an hour."

"I'm going to take a look through that window," said Charlie.

Riklin had hunkered down against the van, trying to find a dry place. "Don't get shot," he said.

Charlie crouched down and ran toward the house. The grass was wet and slippery, and once he lost his balance and stumbled, fell forward onto his knees. Then he jumped up again and ran to the window, ducked down with his back to the clapboards. He could hear voices but couldn't pick out the words. The rain on the metal roof made a constant rattling noise. Charlie turned and raised his head. The window was about two feet above him. He took a step back, then peered over the sill.

Three men were seated at a yellow Formica kitchen table. Two had their backs to Charlie and the third, Bloom, was half facing him. The center of the table was piled with stacks of money, while scattered around it in a sort of motif of violence were several revolvers. Bloom appeared to be arguing, but Charlie couldn't hear what he said, just an angry muttering. He was hard-faced and thin-lipped, with an attentive look as if he would be impossible to surprise. There was no sign of the other two men. A trickle of steam was rising from a blue metal coffeepot on the stove. Directly over Bloom's shoulder was the window in the kitchen door.

Charlie ducked back down. He could work his way around to the back porch, sneak up to the door and put a rock through the window, then cover the three men seated at the table. Riklin could be at the other window and Charlie would order one of the thieves to toss the guns to him. But where were the other two men? What if they rushed in when they heard the noise or, even worse, ran outside? And then maybe he wouldn't be able to get the drop on them. The kitchen door was fairly thin. They could easily shoot through it before Charlie could say "Hands up" or "It's all over, boys." Crouched beneath the window, Charlie began to ask himself just what he thought he was doing. He felt no fear, but that too was dangerous, since it could make him foolhardy. Even if he didn't worry for himself, he should worry about Riklin. Not only was he unarmed but he was just a kid. If anything went wrong, the men would certainly kill him. Did Charlie really imagine he could capture five armed men? And why would he want to, why would he take that chance?

Kneeling in the mud and with rain dripping down his neck, Charlie decided he was as bad as Tommy Polanski, that he was living in some old cops-and-robbers fantasy—the shining hero who would bring in the bad boys strapped to the backs of their horses. And how much was he doing this to humiliate Peterson, to get even for Peterson's refusal to believe him about Polanski, for making fun of him? Surely by this point Peterson was kicking himself. The moment his cars had become jammed up in the Yaddo woods he must have realized the error of his ways, and although he would never tell Charlie that he, Chief Peterson, had made a mistake, they both knew he'd been pretty stupid.

But was Charlie any less stupid? Even if he successfully captured the five men, he was still putting himself above the law, the outsider who settled the problems of the world on his own terms. It was dangerous to get embroiled in fantasy, not just because one might get killed but because one lost a sense of what was true and what wasn't.

Charlie ran back to the van. Riklin was still crouched by the front tire.

"We going in?" he asked. There was a happy quality to his eagerness, as if he was about to pull off a complicated prank.

"Go back to that store and call Peterson," said Charlie. "Here's some change. Tell him we've located the other five men who robbed the truck. Then have him meet you at the store. He'll have to call the state and local cops, but tell him to move fast. It'll be light soon and these guys might be leaving."

Riklin didn't speak but remained crouched by the side of the van. Then he said, "Are you scared?"

"Joe, it's a stupid thing to do. There're five armed men in there. I'm not Wyatt Earp or Wild Bill Hickok, I'm just someone with too many foolish ideas."

"You are scared, aren't you?"

"Do as I ask. These guys just shot two old men. I don't want them to get away. Make sure you tell Peterson not to make any noise. He'll have to take them by surprise."

Without speaking or even looking at him again, Riklin turned and ran back across the grass to the bushes where they had hidden their yellow slickers. Charlie barely caught a glimpse of color as Riklin put his on. Peering into the cab of the van, Charlie tried to see if the keys were in the ignition. They weren't. He imagined standing in the rain for the next hour. Then, after a moment, he ran across the yard to the shed behind the house. The door was missing from its hinges. Charlie ducked inside and settled down to wait.

He found himself thinking of the girl with the weak blood vessels in her brain, Lynn Schorr, whose death had sent him looking for Riklin. She had come to Saratoga hoping to escape her weakness, and it had killed her. Even so, she had had a short time to love and be loved. Maybe it was worth it. Riklin still grieved for her, but at least he was young and in the summer Saratoga was full of pretty girls. Charlie wondered if she wasn't one of the lucky ones: to have loved and escaped without disappointment.

Then there were Charlie and Doris. He had courted her for four years. They had gone out, had some good times, they'd made love, but always Charlie had known that her feelings were not as strong as his. And now he was cut off. Like a balloon whose cord has been snipped, he was drifting away. He wanted to clear his mind of her, get back to his life, meet other women, but she remained lodged in his head. He knew he wouldn't talk to her again or at least wouldn't try to convince her of his romantic worth. If only he could stop thinking of her. She would float through his mind at the worst times, while he was trying to be brave or intelligent or mature, and all would be swept away.

Then he began to think of the crying woman in the photograph. According to Artemis, she and the man with the yellow ring had been in love. Yet why was she crying and why had she looked so fearfully at the camera? Charlie could think of no other way to trace her than what he had already done, no way to find the man with the yellow ring. He had even shown the picture to jewelers, hoping the ring was some rare object, but they had smiled and again Charlie had realized he was living in a romantic story. He tried to imagine the crying woman at that very moment sleeping somewhere, probably next to some man. Would it be the man with the yellow ring or someone else? And was she still sad?

It was getting light, a dull gray light, but now Charlie could make out the trees through the rain and see the van and VW in the driveway. The light in the kitchen was still on. Charlie checked his revolver, spun the chamber and made sure everything was dry. As the light increased, he glanced behind him into the shed and saw the two yellow Yamahas, mud-spattered and resting on their kickstands. Through the door out the back was a cow pasture, and beyond that Charlie could just make out the first of the Catskills looming against the gray sky. Riklin had been gone for an hour. Charlie imagined Peterson refusing to believe him, or perhaps Riklin hadn't reached him or perhaps he hadn't tried.

A screen door slammed. Charlie looked up to see a man carrying two battered suitcases toward the van. Then the door slammed again and Bloom emerged with two more suitcases.

"Put them all the way in the back," Bloom called, "then someone can sit on them."

Charlie knelt down on the floor of the shed. He felt very much on his own. Reaching into his jacket pocket, he found half a dozen more shells for his .38. He lined them up on the floor in a neat row. Then he lay down on his belly facing the house. He had never been a good shot, never even enjoyed practicing. He watched both men return to the house. Perhaps they'll stay there, he thought.

But then another man emerged and carried a suitcase and several brown paper bags to the van. All the men were in their late twenties or early thirties. They looked fast and decisive. A fourth came out carrying more bags.

"Is that it?" called the third man.

"Just a few more."

Charlie watched them put the bags and suitcase in the VW and return to the house. He looked at his watch. It was nearly five a.m. Riklin had been gone an hour and ten minutes.

The door opened again. Two men came out, then Bloom and the other man in the picture, whom Polanski had called Freddie Hollander, then a fifth man. Several were carrying backpacks and rolled-up sleeping bags.

"Should I lock it?" called Hollander. All wore jeans, short jackets, and sneakers or cowboy boots. One had a Detroit Tigers cap. They stood paused in a ragged line between the house and the driveway.

. "Why bother?" said Bloom. "There's nothing to steal."

Charlie watched them start to walk across the yard. It was still drizzling but the men seemed not to notice. They looked like men for whom the world didn't much matter. Charlie thought of them shooting Polanski and Frank Hensley. Riklin had been gone nearly an hour and fifteen minutes.

When the first man had gone half the distance to the driveway, Charlie took hold of the revolver with both hands, pointed it at the van and slowly squeezed the trigger. The gun exploded and the windshield of the van became criss-crossed with thousands of little cracks.

"Raise your arms," shouted Charlie, "or I'll kill you where you stand!"

He hadn't expected to be believed and he wasn't. Mostly he was impressed that he'd managed to hit the van. The men dropped their bags and began reaching for guns. Charlie pointed at their legs and fired again and missed, then fired a third time. By now they were shooting back, and their bullets snicked and smacked against the wood above him. Charlie fired two shots in quick succession and one of the men went down. Freddie Hollander grabbed the fallen man and began dragging him back to the house. Since Charlie was still firing at knee level, he didn't think the man was badly injured.

"Give up," shouted Charlie. "You'll only get hurt!" Or worse, he thought. A bullet whanged into one of the dirt bikes behind him and ricocheted away. Charlie fired again and was out of bullets. As he reloaded, he saw one of the men sprinting toward the van. Charlie fired twice and the man dove to the ground, then began crawling back toward the house. He had four bullets left.

There was a moment of stillness interrupted by distant sirens. Instead of being relieved, Charlie felt irritated. So

much for stealth, he thought. The kitchen window smashed
open and a hand poked a gun through it and fired twice.
Again, one of the bullets ricocheted off a motorcycle. Now
more of them were shooting from the house, smashing
the windows and poking their guns from them just like in
the movies. Charlie fired two more times just so they
would know he was healthy. The sirens were getting louder.

"Give up," shouted Charlie. "This is your last chance."
He fired again and realized he had only one bullet left.
But then the orange-and-blue state police cars started
to arrive: sliding, bumping, screaming along the road,
screeching to a halt as state troopers and police in a variety
of uniforms tumbled out, drawing their guns or hefting
rifles or shotguns, running along through the trees bordering the pasture, ducking down on the other side of the
van and VW, sending into the small house a barrage of
bullets as officers issued commands through bullhorns.
Several shots were fired back at the police, but then they
stopped as more and more police began firing. Charlie
saw Peterson off on the far side of the yard, pointing in
one direction, then in another. He stuck his gun back in
his back pocket. He didn't feel like shooting anymore.

There appeared to be policemen everywhere, on at least
three sides of the house, and Charlie saw several more
over by the silo. The rain had gotten heavier and the fifty
or so policemen were getting drenched. But they didn't
seem unhappy. They looked like they were doing what
they were born to do, firing their guns as fast as possible
into a little house with nobody firing back. Charlie guessed
that a bullet from a .44 magnum would cut through the
entire house like a toothpick through a wet tissue. He
crawled a few feet back into the shed. He had no doubt
that the police would shoot him as quick as anyone. On

both sides of the house, troopers with tear-gas guns shot canisters through one window after another.

For almost fifteen minutes, they continued their barrage, splintering windows and doors, running along the border of the yard through the rain, shouting directions, calling to one another. Charlie saw one fat policeman fall and thought he might be shot, but no, he had only slipped on the wet grass. What a good time they seem to be having, thought Charlie. In his memory it seemed that a policeman's strongest emotion was indignation, and after the robbery of the Burns truck and getting five patrol cars stuck in the mud, Charlie imagined there were about a thousand indignant peace officers between Kingston and Montreal. He kept his eye on Peterson over by the bushes where Charlie had hidden his yellow slicker. There was a state police captain with him and several men who Charlie guessed were FBI. More cars were arriving all the time.

At last the state police captain lifted a microphone connected to a pair of outside speakers on one of the cars. "Stop your firing," he called out. "Stop firing."

Slowly the shooting came to a halt until there was only one plainclothesman with a rifle down behind the van who fired again and again into the kitchen.

"Hold your fire!" shouted the captain.

With the guns silent, the only noise was the rain hammering on the metal roof as if trying to echo the gunfire. No sound came from the house.

"Come out with your hands up!" called the police captain. He was a tall man named Hibbard. Several times when Hibbard had been a lieutenant, Charlie had gone fishing with him up on Lake George. He wasn't a bad sort once you got him in regular clothes. A minute went by, then another.

"Come out with your hands up," Hibbard repeated.

Charlie wondered if the police got their lines from the movies or if it was the other way around. When the FBI had trapped the last of the Barker gang in a house in Oklawaha, Florida, in January 1935, and spent forty-five minutes turning the house into a fragment of Swiss cheese, they had finally ordered the black handyman, Willie Woodbury, to go in and see if anyone was left alive. Nobody was.

Charlie saw Hibbard signal with his arm, and about a dozen troopers with rifles, gas masks and bulletproof vests began moving across the front yard toward the house. When they had almost reached the front of the house, Charlie saw a movement on the back porch. Someone was lying there. Suddenly a man jumped to his feet and came sprinting across the wet grass toward the shed where Charlie was hiding. It was Freddie Hollander. He got about ten feet before anyone noticed. Several policemen started to shout. Then someone fired, then another and another. Hollander was a couple of yards from Charlie. He looked terrified. At last he leapt through the air, landed on his belly in the grass and slid half through the entrance to the shed.

When Hollander saw Charlie, he froze. They were lying about five feet from each other. Charlie started to reach for his revolver, then saw that Hollander was unarmed.

"Get out of here," said Charlie. "Hurry up!"

Hollander jumped to his feet and ran to one of the yellow Yamahas, leaping onto it and kick-starting it at the same time. There was a loud roar like the noise of a chainsaw and the bike shot through the back of the shed and out into the field. There were more gunshots. Then Charlie saw Hollander disappear among the trees. A patrol car bumped across the yard toward the field. It will only get stuck, thought Charlie. He wondered why he had let the man go. He was sick of the shooting and wanted to go home.

Suddenly half a dozen troopers came barreling through the front of the shed. They grabbed Charlie, yanked him to his feet, threw him up against the wall and ripped the gun from his back pocket, shoved their magnums against his head and handcuffed him. Then they threw him out onto the grass.

Charlie landed on his stomach and rolled over, squinting as the rain beat down on his face. "You dumb sons of bitches!" he shouted. "I got you here! I'm Charlie Bradshaw!"

"Where'd the other one go?" shouted an officer.

"You murderous bastards," answered Charlie. "You awful, murderous bastards."

"Let him go," said someone off to Charlie's left.

Charlie twisted around and saw Hibbard approaching with Chief Peterson. Two of the troopers pulled Charlie to his feet. They didn't look apologetic.

"Jesus, Charlie, why didn't you stop that guy?" said Peterson. "Isn't your gun working?"

Charlie rubbed his wrists, then took his revolver from one of the troopers. "I'm not a cop," he said. "It wasn't any of my business."

Inside the house were four dead men. All had been hit five or six times. The money was in the truck. Charlie hoped that Hollander had been able to take a little, but it didn't matter much. He doubted he would get far. Charlie sat in one of the police cars with the heater turned up full-blast and kept blowing his nose. Riklin sat beside him. He hadn't said any more about Charlie being scared. Actually, he seemed in a state of shock. Charlie watched the troopers and local police rushing around, looking officious. An ambulance came to take away the bodies. None of the police had been shot, but one had fallen and twisted his ankle. Charlie decided that he liked his fantasies better than their fantasies. At least in his no one got killed.

Around six-thirty, Peterson came over to the patrol car. He looked at Charlie with an expression that Charlie could only think was dislike, although mixed with it was a little distrust.

"What happened to Polanski?" asked Charlie.

"He's in the hospital. They don't expect him to live."

"Why couldn't you have asked those guys to surrender first?" asked Charlie. "You didn't have to kill them all."

Peterson looked toward the farmhouse as if seeing it for the first time. It had stopped raining and there were traces of blue sky. To the south the Catskills looked green and lovely.

"Hey, Charlie," said Peterson, "at least we got the guy who ran down your buddy."

"No," said Charlie. He wanted to call Peterson names. He wanted to shout at him, but all he said was: "None of those men did anything to Victor."

17

As a private detective, Charlie saw himself as having good cases and bad ones, successes and failures, and this particular case, which involved the crying woman and the person who had run down Victor, he always saw as one of his failures.

For weeks after the robbery of the Burns truck, he had tried to trace this woman. He had contacted personally all the motels, hotels, tourist homes, etc. He checked the car rental agencies. He talked to everyone in the Bentley and at all the restaurants up and down Broadway. No one remembered her or recalled a balding man with glasses wearing a ring with a yellow stone on the little finger of his left hand. People grew irritated with his questions, and when they saw him coming they rolled their eyes or pretended they didn't see him.

He even contacted the honeymoon couple, Peter and Patricia Irving, in Utica. Did they remember a crying woman and a man who wore a ring with a yellow stone on his little finger? But no, they had been preoccupied and didn't remember anyone in the bar.

"By the way," said Irving, "where are my pictures? I ordered fifty."

"I'll see about it," said Charlie.

But Victor was no longer interested in pictures. He didn't have a camera and didn't want to buy another. They only got him in trouble. As for Irving, Victor would send him the pictures when he got around to it.

Several days after the robbery, Polanski died in an Albany hospital, and several days after that Charlie drove down to Troy to the funeral, where he and Polanski's sister and a couple of newspaper reporters were the only mourners. The priest described how Polanski had been a good man who suffered long and bitterly, but who was always kind to those around him. One of the reporters went to sleep. His head fell back and he made snorting noises until the other reporter poked him.

Freddie Hollander, the robber who had escaped on the motorcycle, was not found. Police said he was a dangerous customer who used to sell marijuana and a variety of pills to students at Cornell. Peterson continued to be disturbed that Charlie had let Hollander get away and did not repeat his offer of taking Charlie back into the department. Charlie was sorry about this, because he had worked up a little speech on why he would never work for any police department ever again.

The summer passed too quickly. Fortunes were won and lost at the track, mostly lost. The Chamber of Commerce described the summer as "triumphant," meaning that much money was spent in the gift shops. Charlie managed to get through July and August without coming to blows with Raoul, and in September he handed in his resignation, which nobody seemed to mind. There was no farewell party and nobody told him he would be missed except the bartender, Eddie Gillespie. The Bentley had been a huge success and already Charlie's mother was talking about expansion and continued renovations. It was rumored that she would be elected businesswoman of the year.

Riklin stayed on as assistant manager, but in September he quit to try his luck in New York City. After the robbery his relationship with Charlie remained cool due to the fact that he thought Charlie had been afraid to capture Bloom by himself. Charlie put it down to Riklin's being eighteen. He didn't worry whether he was a coward. Although Charlie was a man with various insecurities, he never wondered if he was brave or not brave. He couldn't see the point of it.

Doris got engaged to her science teacher, and Charlie stopped going to the Backstretch. He had dinner with Artemis a couple of times and once she even convinced him to stand up on the back of her horse, Phillip, but Artemis was too regal in Charlie's eyes and their relationship remained platonic. Once Charlie went out with a fifty-year-old nymphomaniac recommended by Victor and the woman ripped his shirt. He didn't take her out again. Victor healed and returned to work at the hotel and detective agency. When at last it became necessary to buy another camera, he bought a cheap Polaroid jobby, and although he snapped a lot of quick shots, he only took pictures of people he knew: Charlie tying his shoes, Charlie inspecting his face in the mirror, Charlie cutting his fingernails.

All in all it was a pretty good summer, but running through it, like a bass note just above the surface of perception, was this question about the woman in the photograph. And so of Charlie's many cases, this was the big failure, the one that no amount of detecting could solve. He saw it as a failure even though he finally discovered who she was. But he felt he couldn't take credit for it.

The discovery was purely accidental, and if someone had told him that he only found her because he was always looking, he would have waved the suggestion aside. Yes, he found her, he knew who she was, but it was a fluke, something dropped from the sky, and it didn't alter the fact that he had basically failed.

Charlie found the woman in late October. He had been driving back from Buffalo, where he'd interviewed for the job of process server. He could have had the job if he wanted, but at the last minute he turned it down. It would mean leaving Saratoga, and as he had sat in a dingy office answering questions about his personal habits and if he drank or had ever had a nervous breakdown, he found himself thinking that Saratoga was his home and he didn't want to leave, no matter how pleased Peterson and his cousins might have been.

For the entire month of October Charlie had been fooling around with a useless diet where he stuffed himself on grapefruit and was constantly hungry. That morning he had had no breakfast, and by the time he had driven forty miles, he finally admitted he could stand it no longer and he stopped in Batavia at the Howard Johnson's for an oversized cheeseburger, French fries and a chocolate milkshake. And because he was still thinking in terms of carbohydrates and calories, he paid an extra couple of bucks and got the limitless salad bar as well.

As he ate, he glanced through the local paper, and when he reached the third page he stopped so abruptly that the waitress gave him a quick look to make sure he wasn't choking on his food. In the first column at the top of the page was a picture of the crying woman, although here she wasn't crying and even seemed about five years younger—a pretty, almost fragile-looking dark-haired woman smiling at the camera with a mixture of nervous-

ness and embarrassment. Under the picture was the head-
line "Harriet Rehnquist Killed in Accident."

She had been driving on Route 5 late at night and apparently had fallen asleep at the wheel. Her Buick had
struck a tree, killing her instantly. She was alone in the
car. There were no witnesses. A truck driver had come
upon the scene at three a.m. and called the police on his
CB. She had no traffic record and had never had a previous
accident. No explanation was given as to why she had
been out driving so late by herself.

Her husband was the well-known lawyer Michael Rehnquist, former mayor of Batavia, former this and that,
current president of the Rotary Club—his list of accom-
plishments and memberships was like those of Charlie's
three cousins combined. Harriet Rehnquist had been active in a dozen different organizations, chairman of the
library board, the women's group at a local church. She
had two daughters away at college. Her age was listed as
forty-one. The funeral would be held the next morning at
ten a.m. in the Episcopal church.

Although it meant nothing, Charlie was struck by the
fact that Batavia was hardly more than ten miles from
Attica prison, where Tommy Polanski had spent so much
of his life and where he had met Bloom. Batavia was also
the home of Batavia Downs, a harness track, and Charlie
wondered if Polanski had ever seen it or had regularly
read the racing results while in prison and if that had led
him to think of the robbery.

Charlie finished his cheeseburger and drove the rest of
the way into Batavia. There seemed no question as to
what he should do. After driving around for five minutes,
he stopped at a large white house on the main street with
a sign in front which read "Rooms." It was run by a
middle-aged woman by the name of Mrs. Chappit. Charlie

told her he wanted a room for one night, preferably not on the street. She led him to a comfortable room on the second floor with a white chenille bedspread, a yellow wicker chair and a small black-and-white TV. He would have to share the bathroom but she wasn't expecting anyone else. He was the first guest in a week. Did he have business in town? Yes, said Charlie, you could say that. On the wall above the bed was a large picture of a half-dozen dogs in caps and bowler hats drinking, playing cards and smoking dark cigars. One dog had an eyepatch, another was playing the harmonica.

Charlie still had the local paper, and somewhat clumsily he managed to turn the subject away from Mrs. Chappit's lack of paying guests to the death of Mrs. Rehnquist and what a pity it was that she had died so young.

"She was a true lady," said Mrs. Chappit. "I'd see her at the library and she always had a good word for everyone."

"I wonder what she was doing out so late," said Charlie.

Mrs. Chappit shook her head. She was a stout woman whose round red face was surrounded by a mass of white curls. "My friend Duchess and myself, we've been asking the same thing. I'm surprised her husband let her go out at that hour of the night. She'll be sorely missed. Each summer she'd hold the church picnic in her own yard. There'd be a big yellow-and-white-striped tent and all the chicken you could eat for five dollars. I've never known a woman to spend so much time with her flower garden. She'd take flowers to the church and hospital and nursing home, practically every week. I don't know what we'll do without her."

When he was alone, Charlie began asking himself what he was doing, then stopped. Once again he was going to a funeral, it was as simple as that. In the phone book, he looked up Michael Rehnquist's address, and a few minutes later he drove over to look at the house—a great rambling white Victorian mansion with a cupola. A young man was raking leaves. From the branch of an oak in the front yard hung a rope swing. A border of dwarf marigolds was still in bloom along the sidewalk, but the other flower beds, which appeared to surround the house, had already been plowed and mulched. Charlie drove back to the rooming house, then walked around town for an hour or so. At a local men's store, he bought a white shirt and a dark blue necktie. Then he stopped at a lunch counter for a cherry Coke and to buy a Louis L'Amour novel, which he spent the rest of the afternoon and evening reading. It dealt with cattle wars in Montana and a young woman who loved two young men equally, a good one and a bad one, and couldn't decide between them.

The next morning Charlie got up at eight, showered, then happily accepted the coffee and two jelly doughnuts offered by Mrs. Chappit. He found it almost impossible to stay on his diet away from Saratoga. Shortly before ten he drove over to the Episcopal church. Along with his new shirt and tie, he wore a brown sport coat and tan slacks. There was a great crowd at the church, and had he arrived any later, he wouldn't have found a seat. As it was, he was crammed in the corner of a rear pew next to a young woman who cried quietly for the entire service.

The coffin stood at the front of the church surrounded by flowers, and their scent was everywhere. The minister spoke at length about Harriet Rehnquist's virtues and contributions to the community. At one point Charlie wondered if he hadn't made a mistake. But he knew he hadn't made a mistake, and constantly he stared around the church, looking for a somewhat overweight balding man in his mid-forties. There appeared to be a dozen possibilities, but Charlie had no opportunity to get close to them. The service lasted about forty-five minutes and at the end Charlie waited as the coffin was carried from the church and the immediate family filed out to the cars that would take them to the cemetery. He was struck by the extent of the grief, how much people appeared to care for the dead woman. Once outside Charlie continued to look for balding men, managing to eliminate several possibilities but then having to add one or two more. As the procession of cars drove off to the cemetery, Charlie hurried to his Renault and drove after it, at last taking his place at the very end of the line.

It was a warm fall day and absolutely cloudless. In the cemetery, Charlie kept catching the whiff of burning leaves. Robins were preparing to fly south and squirrels busily gathered acorns. Charlie followed the crowd across the cemetery, which was on a large piece of rolling ground at the edge of Batavia. There were many stone angels and crypts with weeping dryads. Whenever he saw someone who was overweight and balding, Charlie would work his way toward him through the mass of people until he was close enough to take a look at his hand. By the time he reached the gravesite, he had eliminated five more men.

A tall distinguished-looking man with thick white hair who Charlie thought must be Michael Rehnquist stood talking to the minister under a blue canopy. With him were two young women, his daughters. Both were beautiful, looked like the woman in the photograph, and both were crying. The dirt from the grave was covered with a green rug of Astroturf. There was no stone—that would come later, something large and imposing. Charlie wondered again how she had happened to have the accident, if she really had fallen asleep while driving. Near the coffin, he saw another man a few years younger than himself, almost bald and with a face so tight and withheld that he seemed in physical pain. Maybe he was about twenty pounds overweight. Charlie began working his way toward him.

The minister said a prayer and began speaking again about the dead woman. Charlie was hardly listening. He had approached to within ten feet of the balding man, watched him wipe his eyes with a white handkerchief, and saw that on the little finger of his left hand was a ring with a large yellow stone. The man wore glasses with heavy black frames and a dark blue suit. His remaining hair was light brown and very fine, almost like a baby's hair. He had high cheekbones and his cheeks had a sunken quality, like the cupped palm of a hand. Charlie stayed about ten feet to his left and a little behind. He looked like a kind man and was certainly grieving. Charlie tried to imagine him running down Victor, then trying to back over him.

Charlie waited for the service to end. He didn't know when it was, but at some point the other man noticed him and seemed to recognize him. When Charlie glanced at him again, he saw the other man was edging away through the crowd. Charlie began to move as well, trying not to step on people's feet and saying "Excuse me" and "Pardon me" over and over again. Nobody paid him any attention except the balding man, and then he apparently disappeared, or at least Charlie lost sight of him. Then Charlie saw him again. He had gotten through the crowd and was on the far side of the graveyard, running while his dark blue suit coat flapped open behind him. Charlie pushed his way free of the people and began to run as well. He heard angry voices, but he didn't care. Whoever the man was, Charlie meant to catch him.

A low chain-link fence separated the graveyard from the woods. Charlie climbed it by the spot where the other man had disappeared. From somewhere ahead he heard the rustling of leaves and underbrush. Charlie ran into the woods, keeping one hand held up in front of him to push away the branches. He caught a glimpse of the other man's blue coat, heard the constant crackle of dead leaves. Charlie ran faster. Branches seemed to reach and grab at him. Ahead he could see the other man, running wildly with arms outstretched. They were both running uphill, and Charlie's heart pounded against his ribs. As he ran, he loosened his tie, pulling free the top button of his shirt. His revolver was back in Saratoga. Had he had it with him, he would have fired. He felt furious with the other man, as if all the frustration of the last four or five months had come together to be focused on one person. A branch struck him across the face, then his foot got caught up on a root and he fell forward onto his shoulder in the leaves. When he got to his feet, he heard nothing. The woods were silent.

Charlie ran forward again, trying to listen at the same time. He heard a noise like a moan and stopped. Silence. He hurried forward again, broke through some bushes, then lost his footing. He was on the edge of a small ravine. He slipped backward, fell on his butt, then slid about ten feet on a bed of leaves, scraping himself and bumping his elbow on a rock. At the bottom of the ravine was the other man. He had crammed his handkerchief in his mouth and was trying to make no sound. His left leg was twisted around in a way that legs don't normally bend. He had apparently run through the bushes and fallen. The leg was clearly broken. Charlie got to his feet and stood over him, straddling his knees. The man looked terrified, as if he expected Charlie to kick him or beat him or tear his heart from his body. Charlie knelt down by the man's leg. There was no blood. Grasping it firmly, he twisted it back until it was straight. The man screamed, a high noise like metal tearing. Charlie ignored it and continued to manipulate the leg until he thought the bone was more or less in place. He didn't care if he hurt him; he wished he could hurt him more.

"Undo your belt and give me your tie," said Charlie.

As the man unhooked his belt and pulled it free, Charlie found several branches about an inch in diameter and two or three feet long. The man's leg was broken between his knee and his ankle. Charlie put a stick on either side of the leg and wrapped the belt and tie around it. The tie was maroon with a pattern of little silver Model T Fords.

When Charlie finished, he stood up again. The man continued to look terrified. Charlie had a sudden desire to kick him. "You tried to kill my friend Victor with an automobile," said Charlie after a moment. "I want to know why."

The man didn't speak. The handkerchief was still between his teeth and he was biting into it. There were tears in his eyes and he refused to look at Charlie.

Reaching down, Charlie grabbed the edge of the handkerchief and yanked it out of the man's mouth so that he grunted and fell back. "Okay, let me tell you why," said Charlie. "You were having a drink with Harriet Rehnquist in the bar of the Bentley when Victor accidentally took your picture. She was frightened that her precious reputation would be ruined and you decided to get the film. First you ran down Victor and took his camera. When you found the camera was empty, you searched his apartment. Now, either you tell me the rest or I'll drag you up this hill by your broken leg. Once we get into town, I'll make quite a scene. It's up to you—what d'you want?"

The man lay on his back looking at Charlie. He had torn the left shoulder of his dark blue suit and some sort of white material was poking through. His expression was a mixture of fear and pain. Slowly it changed to pain and surrender. "She didn't know anything about it," he said. "Didn't know I did it. I mean, not until the next day when she read the paper. Then she guessed what happened. I could never hide anything from her. She always knew everything and now she's dead."

His name was Fletcher Murdock and he worked at a bank. He was married with three children, but his wife cared nothing for him and the feeling was mutual. He had met Harriet Rehnquist three years before, although of course he had known who she was. He had been in New York on business, and happening to have a free afternoon he had gone to the Museum of Modern Art. There he had seen Harriet. It was strange in a way. He had seen her many times in Batavia and they had never spoken, but there in New York, 350 miles from home, they had been quite cordial. She had recently taken an adult education class on Impressionism and talked about Monet, how he had gone blind and painted all those water lilies in the midst of war. Almost on a dare, Murdock had tried to pick her up. They had coffee, then later went out to dinner. She had come down to New York for a couple of days by herself just as a treat.

When Murdock found himself in bed with her nobody could have been more astonished than he was. But afterward she had begun to cry and he sat with her most of the evening trying to console her. She had never been with a man other then her husband. What must he think of her? She was terrified that someone they knew might have seen them together. Really, all he wanted was to calm her down and return to his hotel room. But when he finally got away and was comfortable in his own bed, he couldn't get her out of his mind. All night he thought of her—how fragile she was, how delicate. In the morning he called her, meaning to invite her to breakfast, but she had already checked out and returned to Batavia.

"I went home the next day," said Murdock. "I kept thinking about her. I'd remember how she looked and smelled and the touch of her skin. I'd never loved my wife and with Harriet I realized I'd never loved any woman ever before, maybe no other human being. When I got back, I went to her house. They had an account at our bank and I pretended there was some small difficulty. She was terrified. Luckily her husband wasn't at home. I made her promise to meet me, just talk to me for a few minutes. She was certain I'd give her away. She had a small office in the library and I met her there that afternoon. It was right off the stacks and I slipped in without anyone seeing. Even though she was terrified, she said she couldn't stop thinking about me. When she said that, I thought nothing of our difficulties or the trouble we were making for ourselves. Everything seemed perfect, as if we had suddenly been released from our lives. We made love right there in that little office, right there on the floor."

What followed was months, then years of secret meetings, lying, suspicion, tears and recrimination and the constant threat of scandal. Harriet was terrified they would be discovered, that they would go someplace and meet someone she knew, that her husband would find out, that her reputation would be ruined and her daughters humiliated. Yet always they took more chances, greater and greater risks. Once Murdock had secretly gotten into her house. They had made love in her husband's study. Once she had come to his office in the bank. And the very recklessness, even foolhardiness of their meetings seemed to drive them on until finally they decided to spend a weekend in Saratoga.

"I had wanted to show her some fancy place. We had

this idea of what Saratoga used to be like, you know, the glamour. This hotel had just opened up, the Bentley, it would have been too dangerous to stay there, but I convinced her to come for a drink and maybe a late dinner. She was dead set against it, but I pushed her, I made fun of her for being frightened. So she gave in. We were sitting in the bar. You can't imagine how nervous she was. Then this couple came in and we knew them. Not them, really, but I knew the man's brother. He's the publisher of the newspaper here in Batavia and owns a lot of real estate. Harriet knew the man too, at least had met him, and of course she knew the brother. His name was Irving, Peter Irving, and the brother's name was Larry. Irving and this woman had just been married. They didn't notice us. They were too busy with each other and most likely wouldn't have recognized us. We were going to leave, get out behind them through the dining room.

"You see, I was supposed to be in Buffalo. Harriet had told her husband she was visiting an old friend in New York City. The friend, of course, had been warned. If we were spotted in Saratoga there'd be no explaining it, especially if we were seen together. Harriet couldn't forgive herself and kept saying she'd been such a fool. We were just about to leave when this man came in and started taking pictures. There we were right smack in the photograph. This Peter Irving and his wife were all excited. We heard him ordering dozens of copies, you know, for friends and family. It was a nightmare. Even if Peter didn't recognize us, it seemed certain his brother would see the picture, his brother or any of a hundred people in Batavia, and of course there we would be, together in a hotel in Saratoga. Can you imagine the questions?"

For the three years they were together, Harriet had often been on the edge of hysterics, on the edge, Murdock thought, of having a breakdown. Many times she had threatened suicide. The night after Victor had taken their picture she was immensely upset, shouting and cursing Murdock for ruining her life. He stayed with her. She hit him and scratched his face. She seemed full of hatred and wouldn't consider leaving her husband, or becoming a subject of gossip. The thought of other people talking about her, mocking her and laughing at her, drove her crazy. At last he gave her some tranquilizers and around five she fell asleep.

He had gone out to the hotel where he asked someone who the photographer was. Then he found his address in the phone book. He drove over to Victor's apartment house and waited. He had no plan, didn't know what he could do. When Victor finally came out, Murdock watched him. How cheerful and uncaring he seemed. The camera was over his shoulder and Murdock assumed it had the film. He grew furious at the thought of how their lives could be wrecked by this man. He meant just to grab the camera, to push Victor aside and steal the film. Then Victor stepped into the street. Murdock couldn't explain the anger that swept over him, as if Victor were the center of all that had gone wrong. He wanted to break him, to destroy him. And so Murdock had run him down, then tried to back over him. He missed but at least he got the camera. When he discovered it was empty, he had actually wept.

Murdock had then searched Victor's apartment, looking everywhere for the film. Unable to find it, he returned to the motel. Harriet was gone. He was frantic. He thought she was dead. She was always saying how she would do something to herself. Murdock drove back to Batavia that night, staying off the turnpike because of the damage to his car from where he had hit Victor. Later, when he discovered that Harriet had taken a bus to New York and then flown back to Batavia, he called her, but she refused to speak to him. Already she knew that a man had been run down in Saratoga and that his camera had been stolen. The car had been described.

"For days I tried to get her to see me, but she refused. I'd hang around outside her house. The neighbors noticed me and there was bound to be talk. I didn't care. I didn't see why we couldn't just go away together, start another life. She was so concerned about what people thought—not that, actually, but that she would be the subject of gossip.

"After two weeks she agreed to see me. I had thought she'd stopped caring for me, stopped loving me. But I was wrong. Even this short separation was worse on her than on me. She couldn't sleep, hardly ate. But she was still frightened. We were certain the photograph would suddenly appear, that I'd be arrested and she'd be dragged into court. I couldn't make her stop crying. I tried to kiss her and she pulled away, started screaming at me. Then she started hitting herself and scratching her own face. She said she wanted to erase herself. I had to wrestle with her. Believe me, I was frightened for her. I didn't know what to do. I would have agreed to anything. She said we couldn't meet, that we had to end it once and for all."

They stopped seeing each other but couldn't stop thinking of each other. For Murdock it meant constant tension and sleeplessness. Not only was he sick with desire for Harriet Rehnquist but he was certain he would be arrested for trying to kill Victor. He had his car repaired. He even sold it and bought another. It seemed impossible he hadn't been seen, that the car hadn't been traced. And then there was the picture. Each time he saw Larry Irving, he was sure that Irving would speak to him, ask what he'd been doing in Saratoga with Harriet Rehnquist. Each time he happened to see Harriet she looked ill—on the street or in the supermarket. At last she sent him a note that she had to see him. Two months had gone by. It was the very end of August. They met in her small office at the library.

"She meant to tell me I had to leave town, that she wouldn't be able to get me out of her mind until I was gone. She wanted to be stern, wanted to make me hate her. I slipped through the door. She was standing by her desk. She looked angry, then her whole face changed. We couldn't help ourselves. We made love right there. The door wasn't even locked, anyone could have walked in. Afterward, she wouldn't stop crying. I tried to talk to her. I was afraid someone would hear her. Then I just left, I crept away.

"The whole month of September was awful. It was like living with a gun to your head. We would agree not to meet and then meet. We would agree never to speak and then speak. You see, we loved each other. I felt like such a fool, you know, like I was sixteen. I constantly worried about her. She looked sick. I tried to tell her that she should go away. She had a sister in San Francisco. I don't know if her husband worried or not. He never seemed to notice her, and her daughters were away at school. She threw herself into more and more work—school board committees, fund-raising drives. Nothing helped. We saw each other again at the end of the month. She had gone for a walk out here in the woods. I happened to see her and followed her. I was always trying to follow her. Again we made love. It was something we had no control over."

Then unaccountably, ten days ago, she seemed to get better. She was cheerful, seemed relaxed. He would see her out to dinner with her husband and she'd be laughing—a beautiful woman without a care in the world. Late one night he saw her in her car. It was past midnight. He'd been playing cards with some friends. He couldn't imagine what she was doing out so late. He even felt jealous, as if she had found herself a new lover. He demanded to see her, and they met again in her office at the library. She seemed very calm. She'd been out driving, she said, just driving around. She hadn't been able to sleep. He was amazed at how calm she was. She touched his cheek. "I feel so sorry for you," she said. He wanted to make love but she pushed him away. It was the first time she had been without desire. She stroked his hand and again urged him to leave Batavia. He said how he was still worried about the photographs, and she actually laughed. When he started to leave, she called him back just as he was at the door. She stood close to him, touching his face, running both hands lightly over his cheeks and forehead, touching his eyes, as if she were blind and were making her body remember him. "I have no regrets," she told him.

"The next morning I heard she was dead," said Murdock. "I was in my office at the bank and I heard the secretaries talking about how some woman had had an accident, that her car had gone off the road and struck a tree in the middle of the night. They didn't mention her name but I knew who it was. I walked out of the bank. I drove out to where she had died. The car wasn't there, of course, but there was broken glass. It was a straight part of the road. I wanted to do the same thing. I wanted to drive at that tree at a hundred miles per hour, but I couldn't make myself do it. I wanted to shoot myself, I wanted to die in some easy way, but I couldn't make myself do it. I couldn't even cry. My throat was like sandpaper. I got out of the car and stood by the tree. I bent down and picked up pieces of glass. I rubbed them between my hands until they were red and bleeding. She had no regrets. I had lots of regrets. I was left behind."

Charlie was sitting on a log several yards away from Murdock, who lay with Charlie's coat under his head. Charlie disliked the man, although he wasn't sure why. The story had touched him and he felt pity, but it didn't affect his dislike. There seemed something not self-indulgent exactly, but a refusal to struggle against unfortunate circumstance—as if Murdock felt himself forced to accept life and the world as they unfolded without protest or struggle, as if he was a certain way and life was a certain way and there was nothing to be done about it. Given a choice between Tommy Polanski and Fletcher Murdock, Charlie would come down hard on the side of Polanski.

And even though Murdock was revealed to have had a reason for running down Victor, it wasn't a good one. In fact, there was no good reason. It made Charlie feel glad that Murdock had broken his leg. But maybe he also felt envious of Murdock, of the love he had experienced, of that passion, as if he had known the fire, while Charlie knew only something smaller—the heating pad or electric blanket. But that was no justification for anything, especially not for trying to kill Charlie's best friend. Yet how dreadful to be left, to feel that love for another human being and have that person die, be dead, exist no longer on the face of the earth.

"Let's go," said Charlie, pushing himself to his feet.

Murdock began to look scared again. "What are you going to do?"

"Help you back to town." Charlie bent over Murdock's shoulders and slowly lifted him so he was balancing on one leg. His face was as pale as cloud and Charlie hoped he wouldn't pass out. "Where are your glasses?" he asked, looking around.

"Gone, I don't know, they fell off. What are you going to do?" Murdock repeated.

"Get you to a doctor." Charlie took Murdock's left arm over his shoulder, then put his other arm around Murdock's waist. He took a step forward. Murdock hopped forward on one leg. He grunted as he dragged the broken leg after him.

"Are you going to report me to the police?"

"No."

"Why not?"

"Because I'm not a policeman."

"But why'd you come here, how'd you find me?"

Charlie didn't care to say that he had accidentally seen Harriet Rehnquist's picture in the paper. "Because I wanted to know what happened. You nearly killed my best friend. He's a good man, he's got his faults but he's still a good man. But even if he were an awful man, it wouldn't give you the right to run him down." Charlie got angry just thinking about it.

Murdock didn't say anything. With difficulty, Charlie got him to the top of the ravine. Several times Murdock moaned and even cried out. Both men were sweating. Charlie was perhaps a bit rougher than he should have been but he didn't care.

As they were making their way back through the woods, a question occurred to Charlie. "How'd you recognize me at the funeral?" he asked. "How'd you know me?"

Murdock slipped and tightened his grip on Charlie's shoulder, pinching him with his fingers. "I'd talked to you before. You're the one I asked about the photographer. You told me his name."

"I did?" Charlie was astonished.

"I came back to the hotel a little before six. I guess you were just getting off work. I asked you the name of the photographer, said I wanted to order some pictures. You said his name was Victor Plotz."

"But how'd you know about me? I mean, why did you run?" He felt overwhelmed by the realization that he had led Murdock to Victor.

"You were wearing a name tag, Charles Bradshaw, night manager. Then in the paper it said the photographer had also been a private detective and that he worked for the Charles F. Bradshaw Detective Agency. When I saw you at the cemetery, I knew you'd come looking for me."

Charlie didn't say anything. He tried to remember seeing Murdock that morning in the hotel, but his mind was a blank. He remembered taking a nap in Victor's office, then getting up at five and finishing some paperwork before leaving the hotel. People were always asking him questions. He'd probably answered without paying much attention.

"What about the photograph?" asked Murdock.

"It was never sent to Irving. Victor was laid up for about two months, then later he wasn't interested. Irving's called the hotel several times. I'll send him the pictures and make sure that Harriet Rehnquist is cropped out of them." He decided not to tell Murdock that the camera had missed him altogether, that he had found him only through the ring with the yellow stone. Even if the picture had been sent to Irving, it seemed doubtful anyone would have known that the man with Harriet Rehnquist was Fletcher Murdock, assistant bank manager and failed murderer.

"Just one more question," asked Charlie. "Where'd you get that ring?"

"This?" said Murdock, raising his left hand. "Harriet gave it to me as an anniversary present. Our first anniversary. Is something wrong with it?"

"No," said Charlie, "just curious, that's all."

Charlie got Murdock back across the cemetery and into his car. Then he took him to the hospital. He didn't talk anymore or ask any more questions. He wanted to get away from Batavia as fast as possible. His dislike for Murdock continued, and he partly regretted not turning him over to the police.

On the way back to Saratoga, Charlie continued to wrack his mind for any memory of talking to Murdock that morning at the beginning of June. Maybe he'd been groggy with sleep. Maybe he'd been thinking too hard about Doris Bailes.

Near Utica the engine of the Renault began to make a peculiar rattling noise which quickly rose in volume to a banging beneath the hood. The temperature gauge shot into the red, and Charlie pulled over to the side. After an hour's wait, a tow truck pulled him into the next rest area. He had blown a rod; the whole engine was shot. He would have to take a bus the rest of the way. He called Victor, who said he'd pick him up at the Spa City Diner when his bus got in late that afternoon.

18

It was raining when the bus pulled into Saratoga and almost dark. Even so Charlie saw Victor standing under the awning in a somewhat rumpled and dirty tan raincoat and a Red Sox cap. His arms were folded across his chest and he was grinning. Then he tipped his cap to a pretty woman who got off the bus. Seeing Victor as his old self, Charlie felt a great wave of comfort and relief.

"Fuckin' freezin' my ass off, Charlie," said Victor, shaking his hand. "Let's grab a cup of coffee and some blueberry pie."

Charlie followed Victor into the diner, which was in fact a rather elaborate Greek restaurant. On top of the main entrance was a statue of a small brown horse.

"I've told you for years to dump that hunka junk," said Victor over his shoulder. "Whatever made you think the Frogs could make cars in the first place?"

"It was comfortable," said Charlie, wondering where he'd get the money for a new car. "I liked it."

Once they were settled at a table and had ordered their pie and coffee, Charlie asked, "Have you seen my mother?" Although he had been gone only three days, it seemed longer.

"Saw her this morning. What a great old broad. She's

thinking of closing the hotel for the winter and going to Paris."

"Paris?" He couldn't imagine his mother in Paris.

"That's right. She said she wanted to pick up some culture before it all cranks up again next June. Her plan is to spend a couple of months in some bank or maybe it was on some bank, I don't remember."

"The left bank?"

"You got it. Anyway, Raoul's got a job for the winter in Key West and Suzanne's already gone. I told your mother she should leave the place open. Not the whole place, of course, just the downstairs and maybe the second floor, keep the bar open and open the restaurant on weekends. Have about a dozen rooms. Shit, you could keep it running with just the parents of Skiddies or maybe the Skiddies themselves. College girls like amorous adventures, let me tell you."

"What did she say?" The thought of Raoul moving to Key West filled Charlie with quiet pleasure.

"She said she'd give it her serious consideration. And you know who'd be running the place? Yours truly. I'd be the winter Raoul. I bet I could even stick a few broads into those rooms and have a fine old time. The point is, you can work too. You don't have to go to Buffalo or anyplace like that."

The waitress brought their coffee and pie. Charlie took a tentative sip and burned his tongue. "Thanks for the offer, but I think I'll stay out of the hotel business. It doesn't suit me. Of course, if you need advice or anything like that, I'll be glad to help, but I don't want to work there."

"So you're going to Buffalo after all?" Victor began to look depressed. He wore a gray sweatshirt that exactly matched his gray hair. Spilling a bit of pie right over his heart, he tried to wipe it off but only made a mess of it.

"No, I'll stay in Saratoga. I guess I'll put most of my time into the detective office. There's more insurance work we can do."

"I don't know," said Victor. "I've sort of lost my faith in you as a private detective."

"What do you mean?" Charlie tried sipping his coffee again. It was still hot.

"Well, what was your biggest case, I mean the most important case of your whole career, can you tell me that?"

"You mean getting back those paintings that were stolen or that girl who ran away or . . ."

Victor reached across the table and tapped Charlie on the wrist with his sticky fork. "Charlie, you hurt me. What was your most important case? I am. Me. Old Vic Plotz. Did you ever find the guy that ran me down? Nope. He's still strolling around free and happy. That hurts me, Charlie. I have little pains. Sometimes I limp. I have bad memories. And I think, where's my revenge, how can I get my hands on the guy that tried to squash me? I trusted you, Charlie. You're the big detective. You can solve anything. Why, the fuckin' cops are terrified of you. But can you find the fellow that tried to crush your old pal like someone might crush an ant? No way. And now you tell me you're going to crank up the detective agency again. I can see I'm going to have to give you a lotta free meals. Come work at the hotel. I'll let you take care of the bar."

Charlie thought of Fletcher Murdock lying at the bottom of the small ravine with his dark blue suit and broken leg, and of how pathetic he had seemed. Charlie took a bite of blueberry pie and wiped his mouth. "I'm sorry about that, Victor—"

"Vic."

"Okay, okay, but maybe Peterson was right. There're

probably five hundred people out there with a motive, five hundred jilted lovers or jealous boyfriends or people who couldn't take a friendly joke. Any one of them could have run you down. I looked and looked but instead of eliminating suspects, I only found more. The whole thing was a failure from start to finish."

Victor looked at him skeptically. "You don't seem to be worrying much about it."

"There's nothing more I can do. I did my best. For me the case is over. I failed."

"You sure you're telling the truth?" asked Victor. "You got a funny way about you when you lie. Your voice gets a little squeaky. Maybe you really know who did it. Maybe you caught him and are just not saying. You caught the fucker and let him go. My killer, the guy whose heart I should eat on a plate. Is that right, is that what happened?"

Charlie glanced around the diner and counted about a dozen people he knew—the barber who cut his hair, a woman he used to have a crush on twenty-five years ago when she was thin and a strawberry blond, a man who had beaten him up when they were both in fourth grade. He looked back at Victor, thought about his droopy eyes and red oversized nose. He thought how he probably liked this person better than anyone else in the world. "Jesus, Victor, what can I say? You're my best friend. Would I lie to you?"